I0712820

MANIAC
The Kensington Killers
(Book Three)

MIRA GIBSON

Copyright © 2024 Mira Gibson

Cover Design: Book Cover Zone

Mystery Royalty

mysteryroyalty.com

All rights reserved.

ISBN: 979-8-9901812-5-0

This is a work of fiction. Names, characters, places, and incidents either are the product of the author's imagination or are used fictitiously. Any resemblance to actual persons, living or dead, events, or locales is entirely coincidental.

Prologue

"MY DAUGHTER tried to kill me."

Nora's frail hand fluttered from her lap to her throat where bruises had formed.

As she touched eyes with the detectives seated across from her, she added, "I found out that my daughter killed her infant son. That's why she tried to kill me. Because I found out."

Nora looked on anxiously as the detectives exchanged a glance. She couldn't get a read on them. Shouldn't they be shocked? They weren't leaning across the table. They were hardly on the edge of their seats.

The older detective had introduced himself as Detective Crouse, and the younger one was Toliver.

Nora wondered if they knew Danny.

The older detective, Crouse, scratched his jowls and frowned like a bulldog.

"Who did you say your daughter is?" he asked, as he finally picked up the pen that had been resting on a legal-sized notepad.

"Danny Foster," she repeated for the second time, tempering the exasperation in her voice. "She's Detective Danielle Foster. She works at this precinct as a Special Victims Unit investigator."

Though Crouse pressed the tip of his pen to the notepad, he didn't write the name down. Nora took that as a good sign, though. He obviously knew Danny. Both of them did.

The interview room felt airless.

Nora couldn't breathe, but maybe that was because her own flesh and blood had tried to crush her larynx only a few hours ago.

"She was on maternity leave," she went on, sensing that the detectives needed an explanation. "And once the baby was born, Danny couldn't handle being a mother. It was too much for her, psychologically. The next thing I knew, baby Gregory was dead. Danny killed that innocent boy."

Overcome with emotion, Nora burst out in tears, not for the loss of her grandson, but rather for the fact that she was here. She had lost Danny.

Her daughter *had* tried to kill her. That was true, and it broke Nora's heart.

The younger detective, Toliver, spoke up, "We were under the impression that Foster's infant died of S.I.D.S."

Collecting herself, Nora swallowed the lump in her throat and found the strength to go on.

"We all did," she allowed. "But I found out that baby Gregory was smothered to death. There was an autopsy. You can check with the Kings County Medical Examiner's Office."

"How did you find this out?" Toliver asked.

His eyes were bright—*he believed her!*—yet his discerning expression told Nora that he needed information from her. Information that could be verified.

She didn't have any.

So, swapping Danny for herself in the story, she reconstructed the chain of events for Detectives Crouse and Toliver, all the while she stroked her tender neck.

"I learned of all this from the baby's father, a man named Thomas O'Toole. He goes by Tommy and owns the bar O'Toole's on Caton Avenue."

Detective Toliver's mouth curled. He was fond of O'Toole's. Most of the cops in Kensington favored the place over the trendier bars that had cropped up throughout Brooklyn over the years.

"Danny and Tommy had been on the rocks," she went on. 'They were an 'on again, off again' type of couple. They were 'off again' when Danny had the baby, *and* when she *killed* the baby. Weeks later, when they got back together, Tommy learned that Gregory had died of S.I.D.S. He must have suspected foul play. I guess he ordered an autopsy, discovered that the baby had been asphyxiated, and he told me."

"He told you what?" Crouse questioned.

"What do you mean?" Nora didn't get it.

Toliver clarified, "What exactly did Tommy tell you?"

"That Gregory had been killed," she supplied, as if that was all the information the detectives would need.

"Who jumped to the conclusion that Danny was responsible?" Crouse asked.

"What are you talking about?" Nora replied, upset. "She's the mother. The baby was found dead. Danny killed the baby."

Detective Toliver calmed Nora down when he said, "We'll look into this, of course."

"Look into it?! You'll arrest Danielle Foster! She tried to strangle me to death in my apartment earlier today! Look at my neck!"

Nora couldn't see straight, she was so mad.

If Homicide didn't arrest Danny for the murder

of Gregory O'Toole, then Nora feared that her daughter would have *her* arrested. Nora's back was to a brick wall. The only saving grace was the fact that Danny *had* tried to kill Nora, and the marks on Nora's throat proved it.

"Do you think my daughter would try to choke me to death for no reason?" she raged on.

Detectives Crouse and Toliver leaned back in their chairs to claim some space.

"I found out she killed her son, and she tried to kill me to keep me quiet!" Nora yelled so loudly that she began coughing.

"Take it easy," Crouse suggested, as he made a few notes.

"Would you like a glass of water?" Toliver offered.

"I would like you to arrest my daughter."

"Here's what we're going to do," said Toliver. "You were attacked. We can see that. We're going to get you to the hospital for medical attention. We'll get you there. The police will take photos of your neck—"

Nora interrupted, "And get the DNA! I had to claw my way out of Danny's grasp. I'm sure her skin is under my fingernails."

"Absolutely," Toliver agreed.

"She killed Gregory," Nora insisted.

Detectives Toliver and Crouse touched eyes for the tenth time.

Then Detective Crouse asked, "The night Gregory died, as far as you know Danny was alone with the baby?"

Nora's mouth pressed into a hard line.

She didn't want to have to correct him.

"Mrs. Foster?"

"No," she admitted.

"Danny wasn't alone that night?" asked Toliver, curious.

Nora didn't say a word.

Detective Crouse asked her, "Who else was there?"

She folded her arms, hardened to stone, and insisted:

"My daughter has scratches all over her face. She tried to kill me. I clawed my way out. I want her arrested for attempted murder, *now*."

Chapter One

THE SCRATCHES still stung.

As Detective Danielle Foster walked along Church Avenue in the humid heat of May, she resisted the temptation to touch the worst scratch. Red, raised, and stinging, the scratch ran from her cheekbone to the corner of her mouth on the left side of her face.

She had disinfected it with rubbing alcohol and had tried to cover it with concealer and foundation makeup, neither of which had worked.

The other two scratches were superficial. One cut across her chin and the other ran down the side of her neck.

She hadn't even felt her mother digging her nails in.

All she felt now was guilt.

She had lived her entire life never knowing that deep down inside of her lurked evil. It had been more than an emotion. The darkness inside of her that had risen up had been the power that had strangled her mother within an inch of Nora's life. As if that dark force had its own *will*... a life of its own. Separate from Danny. Maybe even at odds with her.

Danny didn't trust herself.

The only thing keeping full-blown terror at bay was the fact that she *had* regained control of herself. She had walked away. She would have never been able to live with herself if she had killed her mother. But since she hadn't gone through with it, she had a chance at recovering from this.

She told herself that she was in no danger of going to prison. Nora would never report the attack. She couldn't. Nora knew that if she did, Danny would then expose the infanticide and have Nora arrested for having smothered Gregory in his crib...

Nora couldn't send Danny to prison without sending herself there as well.

Danny reminded herself of this, as she came to the corner of Westminster Road and Church Avenue.

She glanced around to get her bearings.

North of Church Avenue was Prospect Park. The southern corner of the block was dominated by St. Christopher's Cathedral, Parish Hall, Rectory, and the associated private school, St. Christopher's Catholic School. The elegant stone buildings of the parish seemed to establish an entire world that clashed with the gritty, Kensington neighborhood—stone statues and green ivy juxtaposed with bodegas, barber shops, and delicatessens.

The church was the landmark, however. When the 66th Precinct had called her cell this morning about the murder at the Brooklyn Ballet Studios, the dispatch officer had told her the ballet studio address, mentioned the location would be hard to find, and gave her St. Christopher's as a landmark.

An even better landmark was the behemoth African-American detective who was standing on the opposite side of the street.

Detective Carter Dobbs spotted her, and Danny waved. He was wearing a suit, as usual. His police-issued Glock was holstered under his arm, as usual. And, as usual, he looked angered, which meant that either Danny was late, or someone at the crime scene wasn't cooperating.

She glanced up and down the avenue, waited for a gap in the traffic, then she started walking briskly towards Carter, as a warm breeze cut across the avenue.

April showers had certainly brought late-May flowers, blue skies, and warm winds, but Danny could already feel the hot, humid grime of Brooklyn clinging to her skin.

"What the hell happened to you?" Carter asked, noticing the long, raised scratch across her cheek the moment she reached him.

"Good morning to you, too," she said.

"Seriously—"

"I don't want to talk about it."

"You get a cat or something?"

"I said, I don't want to talk about it."

He teased, "Was the cat trying to get out of the bag?"

"Something like that," she grumbled.

"Danny, seriously, what happened to your face?"

Danny stared him down.

"Alright," he agreed, dropping it.

Carter pulled the glass entrance door open for Danny to step inside a shallow entryway that immediately led to a set of stairs.

The glass door only had the address number, 1128, but no other indications that the location belonged to the Brooklyn Ballet Studios.

"The studios are upstairs," Carter told her.

As they started up the narrow staircase, the sounds of city life pounded through the walls and poured in from the street.

Carter said, "It looks like a staged suicide."

"What makes you think it's a staged suicide?" she asked her partner quietly.

When they reached the landing, he shot Danny a funny look.

"I only had a glance around," he told her. "But my impression is that everything was staged."

"Well, I figured it couldn't be a real suicide," she agreed, since the Special Victims Unit had been called.

There was another glass door on the other side of the landing. 'Brooklyn Ballet Studios' was written across the glass in bold, red letters.

Carter pulled the door open for Danny and quietly asked her, "Are you sure you're okay?"

What was she supposed to tell him? That she had completely lost control over herself? That Nora had pushed her too far? Was she supposed to linger on the landing and tell her police partner of barely two months that she had tried to kill her own mother? She had been overcome with rage. Rage that Nora had murdered her baby, and rage at herself for not doing anything about it. How could she tell Carter that her mom had admitted murdering Gregory to Gregory's father, not as a means to unburden her soul, but for the purposes of intentionally destroying Danny's relationship with the man?

"Leave it alone, Carter," she warned, as she yanked the glass door open. "I already have a feeling about this one."

"You and me, both," he agreed.

On the other side of the glass door was a proper anteroom with a front desk, though no one was seated behind it. The walls were covered with huge, black and white photographs of ballet dancers twirling, leaping, and contorting their lean, muscular bodies into shapes that defied human flexibility.

Danny noticed the place smelled of leather and hairspray.

The Chief Medical Examiner, Jill Andover, stood with forensic investigators on the far side of the anteroom. They had set up a table with their equipment, but experience told Danny that Jill hadn't gone into the crime scene yet. She wouldn't until Danny and Carter had gone in first, gained their impressions, and invited her team in.

Jill looked bright eyed and focused, though she was still recovering, both physically and emotionally, for having fallen in love with a homicidal psychopath earlier in the month. The word around the precinct was that Jill had declared she was taking a long break from dating. Carter didn't believe it.

Carter and Danny stopped at the forensics table, grabbed plastic gloves, and pulled them on, all the while they greeted Jill and the rest of the team.

"Let us know when we can get in there," Jill reminded Danny.

"Of course," she said, and Jill pushed her shoulders back, pleased.

That's what Danny loved about Jill. The woman was passionate about her work.

Jill stepped in close and discreetly asked her, "What happened to your face?"

"New cat," she lied.

Too smart for her own good, Jill disagreed. "That scratch is too wide to match a cat's claw."

Carter told Jill, "Leave it alone," on Danny's

behalf.

"We're ready when you're ready for us," Jill reiterated, accepting that if the detectives didn't want her to know something, she wasn't going to know it, especially if it was personal.

Carter walked Danny through the anteroom towards the crime scene, as he explained, "Brooklyn Ballet Studios has three studios and two communal dressing rooms. One for men and the other for women. In-between the two dressing rooms is a single dressing room."

"Handicapped?" she guessed.

He shook his head. "You ever meet a handicapped *professional* ballet dancer?"

"Right."

"The single dressing room is generally not used, I'm told, unless the ballet company is doing a run-through in their costumes, in which case the principal female ballet dancer would get the room."

"Okay," she said, digesting the specifics that he had learned, as they came to the single dressing room in question.

"I mention this because the victim was found dead in the single dressing room this morning."

"The victim is male," Danny pointed out. It was one of the few details she had learned from dispatch.

"And the company wasn't planning a dress rehearsal today," he added.

"Which makes the location of the crime peculiar."

"You ain't seen nothing yet."

Carter used a gloved hand to open the dressing room door.

Danny stepped inside the windowless dressing room, which was much larger than she had expected. A rectangular room twice the size of her bedroom. Brick walls. Pre-war architecture and floors. There was a long counter at the back of the room with a wall of mirrors behind it, stools lined the length of the counter.

At first, she saw the victim's reflection in the mirror.

He had been hanged.

The sight stopped Danny dead in her tracks.

Carter closed the door behind them, as Danny turned on her heel to face the hanging dead man.

"He's a 'special victim' because he's naked?" she asked Carter, but he didn't seem to know.

As she absorbed the full magnitude of the scene, Carter took a slow lap around the dressing room and said, "My gut tells me that this case should've landed in Homicide, but maybe the family name was a deciding factor."

The victim had the toned physique of an athlete, though his musculature was lean. Danny guessed the man was 5'10" or 5'11", but it was hard to say with him hanging from a rope. Dark brown hair, Caucasian but distinctly Italian.

His hands were tied behind his back, which would've been impossible during a suicide.

The rope he had been hung with was wrapped around one of the iron beams on the unfinished ceiling. These pre-war buildings around Kensington often had exposed brick, lofty ceilings, and exposed load-bearing support beams, all of which offered a uniquely 'Brooklyn' aesthetic. Clearly, the Brooklyn Ballet Studios enjoyed the aesthetic, too.

Not only was the rope wrapped around one of the support beams, it was also anchored to a masonry hook. The masonry hook, another architectural relic of pre-war buildings, was fixed into the brick wall about five inches off the floor.

Danny crouched and had a close look at the knot used to tether the rope to the masonry hook. She was no sailing expert, but the knot looked professional.

She stood and asked Carter, "What were you saying about 'a family name'?"

"I think this is a case for Homicide," he began explaining. "The guy's naked, sure, but my gut tells me that Homicide should've been called, and then their department could've determined if the naked factor crossed the Special Victims Unit line. We got the call straight off the bat, and I think that's because the Vic is a 'Campopiano'."

"Campopiano?"

She locked eyes with Carter.

He nodded. "Bobby Campopiano."

"Of the Campopiano crime family?" she asked, thrown.

When Carter confirmed with a nod, she breathed, "Damn."

"If this is a mob hit, then Homicide should've been called."

"To say the least," she agreed.

"So, why were we called?" Carter wondered.

Danny knew Carter well enough to know that her partner already felt toyed with, as if the killer had Carter in mind when he had orchestrated this complex crime scene.

She also knew the answer to his question.

"The captain must want this investigation to stay quiet. The press rarely bothers S.V.U. unlike Homicide. Plus, you know Homicide would treat the Vic like a pawn in a mob war. We won't."

"I think the Vic *is* a pawn in a mob war," he grumbled, as he picked up a sheet of paper that had been left on the long counter. "Care to read the fake suicide note?"

She shot him a crooked smile, took the paper from him, and said, "Don't mind if I do."

Carter complained, "Mob hits are clean. One bullet to the back of the head—"

"You've watched too many mafia movies—"

"This scene doesn't look like someone who personally knew the Vic killed him. It looks like someone staged the crime to look like a suicide. It's a neat mess, if that makes sense. It looks like a bunch of crime bosses dreamed up the most convincing way to kill a guy so that it would appear that someone personal to the Vic had killed him, and then staged the homicide to look like a suicide."

She glared at him. "You gonna let me read this?"

"Do you know what I'm saying?"

"This is a ballet dancer," she reminded him. "Let's not jump to conclusions."

Danny concentrated on the weirdly typed 'suicide' note. She skimmed it, then read it closely.

"Well, at least we know why S.V.U. was called," she concluded as she set the so-called suicide note down.

"That thing reads like a badly—"

"I get it," she agreed. She read the highlights out loud. "*'I can't live with the memories of sexual abuse any longer... I want to end it all... If I don't take my own life,*

16

then I know I'll kill him... Everyone in my family loves Father Silva and they never would have believed me... Attending St. Christopher's Catholic School ruined my life...'"

Sarcastically, Carter told her, "The suicide note should've been signed 'Red Herring'."

"It's not *that* unconvincing."

He screwed his face up at her.

"If this Father Silva priest is still working at St. Christopher's, if he's still alive, let's talk to him," she suggested.

"That's just what the killer wants."

"Maybe Father Silva is the killer?" she said, but Carter didn't like it.

Danny folded her arms and got down to business.

"Who called it in?"

"A couple of dancers," he said, as he opened the door.

"Let's get Jill in here, talk to the dancers, and see if anyone had it in for Bobby Campopiano."

Danny exited the dressing room and Carter followed after her, but left the door open for the forensics team.

"Jill," she said. "The place is all yours."

"Great," she replied, as she gathered her laptop computer and portable equipment.

One of the police officers, a young Irish-American guy named Sean Quinlan, stepped into the anteroom from one of the ballet studios where he had been holding the two dancers who had called 911.

Officer Quinlan was quick to grab the largest of Jill's equipment satchels when he saw her struggling.

His helpful nature and boyish good looks were lost on Jill. She frowned, didn't thank him, and rushed into the dressing room.

Quinlan followed after her, but paused in front of Danny and Carter to let the detectives know, "The dancers have been practicing in there."

"Practicing?" Danny asked, surprised.

Quinlan nodded. "Stretching, warming up, and doing their routine," he elaborated. The fact of the matter obviously didn't sit right with him.

It didn't sit right with Carter, either.

"Not crying or trying to make sense of the unfathomable?" Carter pointed out.

"The show must go on, I guess," Quinlan figured with a shrug.

Jill filled the doorway of the dressing room, irritated that her most important equipment had been delayed.

"Officer Quinlan," she barked. "Are you helping? Or are you *helping*?"

Turning on her heel, she huffed back into the crime scene, as Quinlan's cheeks turned pink.

He started off, and Danny told him, "Once Jill is set up, I want you to stay outside the door, on the landing. Don't let anyone into the anteroom. Ballet classes are canceled until further notice."

"Roger that."

"Oh, and Quinlan?"

"Detective?"

"She's not ready to date."

The police officer's cheeks turned pink for the second time, but he straightened his spine, which gave Danny the impression that Quinlan begged to differ.

As he continued into the dressing room, Danny asked, "Aren't you going to 'roger that' Quinlan?"

Carter chuckled.

"What's so funny?"

"Jill's ready to date," he quietly explained. "But guys that are *into her* aren't her type."

"Oh, please."

"I know women."

"I bet."

Danny and Carter started through the anteroom and crossed a long hallway. There were three ballet studios, all on the right, and all with their doors open. The last studio on the right was where the detectives found the ballet dancers who had discovered Bobby Campopiano's dead body hanging from rope this morning.

Officer Quinlan had been correct.

The ballet dancers were in the concentrated throes of practicing when Danny and Carter entered the studio.

A male ballet dancer and a female one. Both wore traditional ballet slippers.

The woman wore a black leotard and pale pink tights. Her dark hair was pulled back into a very tight bun that sat on the top of her head. She looked like she had been surviving on a diet of cigarettes and determination for the entirety of her twenty-eight years.

She trotted, hopped, and then leapt into her partner's arms. Her long legs shot into the air, as the male ballet dancer held her over his head.

Turning and twirling, they hardly noticed the detectives that had stomped across the marley floor to get their attention.

"Excuse me," Danny spoke up. "I'm Detective Foster and this is Detective Dobbs."

Out of breath and pleased with themselves, the dancers released one another and padded over to the detectives.

"Sorry to keep you waiting," Danny went on. "We have a number of questions for you. Can we start with your names?"

"I'm Tracy Jones," said the female dancer. Her hands were planted on her hips, as she fought to fully catch her breath. Her skin was slick with sweat. "I'm with de Corps de Ballet tier," she mentioned, using impressive French pronunciation. "This is Eric."

"Eric MacDermott," said the other dancer, as he shook Danny's hand then Carter's. "Soloist."

Danny wondered if the titles were supposed to mean something, and the same curiosity must have crossed Carter's mind.

"Meaning, you dance all by yourself?"

Eric smiled, having caught his breath. He pushed his light brown hair off his forehead.

"Yes, I'm a 'soloist' by contract, which means I'm generally cast to perform solos in our ballets."

"He's Bobby's understudy," Tracy clarified, and by the looks of it, Eric didn't appreciate the distinction. "That's why he's here today. Bobby and I have a pas de deux in Romeo and Juliet. We agreed to all meet this morning so that Eric can practice Bobby's role."

"Understudies are always guaranteed at least one performance per production," explained Eric.

Danny made sure that she understood. "So, Bobby was cast to play…?"

"Friar Lawrence," Tracy supplied. "And I'm the Nurse."

"Minor characters," Eric humbly added.

Carter understood and asked Eric, "You're not the understudy anymore, are you?"

"No," he said as a breezy grin came over him. "Now I'll dance as Friar Lawrence in all the ballet performances."

It piqued Danny's interest, but she didn't probe.

Instead, she asked them, "Can you walk us through what happened when you got to the ballet studios this morning?"

Carter added, "No detail is insignificant. Tell us everything you can."

Eric's mood shifted. "I'm sorry, didn't Bobby hang himself?"

Carter told them, "Detective Foster and I are detectives with the Special Victims Unit. No, we don't believe Bobby took his own life, though it may turn out that he did. At the moment, we're proceeding as though this is a homicide."

Tracy's dainty eyebrows knit together and her big brown eyes widened.

Eric asked, "What does Special Victims Unit mean? Like the TV show?"

"How was Bobby a 'special victim'?" Tracy cut in before Carter could answer.

Carter leveled with them. "We don't exactly know what made Bobby a 'special victim,' except that if this was a homicide, the perpetrator intended it look like a suicide. Generally, Detective Foster and I investigate sex crimes. The fact that Bobby was hanged without any clothes on probably caused the precinct we work for to assign the case to us."

Tracy found her voice and remarked, "Who would kill him *like that?*"

Danny assured her, "That's what we're here to find out."

Carter got the interview back on track. "Please, if you could tell us what happened, starting with when you showed up this morning."

Tracy and Eric looked at each other, trying to decide who should begin. The dancers obviously had a close, personal relationship. Eric stood a few inches taller than Tracy, but he was relatively short for a man. He was maybe 5'8" but his lean build made him look taller.

In Danny's observation, Eric and Tracy had veiled chemistry. She suspected they might be dating, but then again, considering that Eric was a ballet dancer, it crossed Danny's mind that he could be gay.

Tracy took the floor.

"Well, we didn't just 'show up.' I reserved the studio a few days ago. We have an online system, so I booked the ballet studio through that. All of the company dancers have keys."

Danny and Carter touched eyes, and Carter asked, "So, anyone can get in here at any time?"

Eric confirmed, "The company dancers can, for sure."

Danny was sick of the terminology already. "What do you mean, 'company' dancers?"

Tracy explained, "This location, Brooklyn Ballet Studios, is a rental business. We, meaning Eric, myself, and about thirty-two other dancers are professional ballet dancers contracted with the Brooklyn Ballet. Brooklyn Ballet pays Brooklyn

Ballet Studios, I think monthly?"

Eric confirmed, "Yeah, I think a monthly flat rate."

"So, any of the company dancers can book rehearsal time here. We all have keys to get in. We can practice whenever we want."

"But the online calendar has blackout dates and times," Eric added.

"Because this studio also hosts non-professional adult ballet classes, children's ballet classes, and all that," said Tracy.

Carter asked, "Do you know of any surveillance cameras here?"

"There aren't any," said Tracy. "Except maybe outside on the street?"

Danny realized, "If the Brooklyn Ballet Studios gave keys to thirty-two, or thirty-four professional dancers, they may have supplied keys to any of the other programs, teachers, and students—"

"Probably," Tracy agreed.

Carter angled away from the dancers and spoke quietly in Danny's ear.

"Jill will have a time of death for us. I doubt we'll have to go through dozens of potential suspects who have keys. I'll get Quinlan on the street to talk to businesses that have surveillance cameras covering the sidewalk."

"Would you?" Danny replied to get the ball rolling right away.

Carter excused himself to do just that, and left the room, as Danny returned her attention to the dancers.

"Okay, Tracy, you booked the studio. You both have keys. Who arrived first and how did you discover Bobby?"

As Tracy went on, Danny sized up the petite ballerina. She looked strong, wiry in fact. Danny doubted that Tracy could've overpowered Bobby on her own. But Tracy and Eric might have been able to… It was an avenue to consider, though if the dancers were telling the truth about their minor roles, and Bobby's minor role, Danny hardly thought they would have killed Bobby just to steal a bit part.

"We arrived at the same time," she went on. "Met downstairs on the street and keyed in together. We had coffee, which we bought across the street. So, of course I had to use the ladies' bathroom the second we got here."

"I went straight into the studio," Eric interjected. "There was no need to change, because I came with everything on and just took off my sweatpants."

"When I got out of the bathroom, I was walking by the anteroom and that's when I noticed that the single dressing room door was open."

"It was *open*?"

"Yeah, which was weird, because that door is usually closed. All the dressing room doors are generally kept closed. But whatever, it wasn't *that* weird. As I walked by, though, I could see the dressing room mirror. It caught my eye because the mirror was reflecting Bobby, but I didn't really know what I was seeing at first."

"Then I heard you scream," said Eric.

"Right, because I crept into the dressing room, and as I pushed the door inward, opening it more, I saw Bobby in the mirror. He was basically hanging behind the open door, because of how the dressing room is set up..."

"I noticed that, yes," she allowed.

"I screamed." Tracy went on. "Eric ran in."

"I saw he was dead, pulled Tracy out of the room, and I called the police."

"We stayed in the anteroom until Officer Quinlan arrived."

"The cops were here in less than five minutes, honestly," said Eric.

Danny jotted the bullet points down on her hand-sized notepad then asked for their contact information, trusting that Officer Quinlan had already taken their statements formally.

As she tucked her notepad into the back pocket of her jeans, she asked them, "Can you think of anyone who would've wanted Bobby dead?"

Tracy fell silent, but to Danny it looked as though the young woman's mind had latched onto a response that she wasn't about to let herself admit.

Eric focused on Tracy. He wasn't so much racking his brain as warning Tracy to keep quiet.

Danny found it odd.

"If you can think of anyone, or if anything comes to mind,' she said as she found her business cards in her wallet. She handed each of them a card. "Give me a call on my cell or at the precinct. Both numbers are listed, as well as my email address."

Eric asked, "Can we stay and practice?"

Danny stared at him for a moment. "No, I'm afraid you'll have to leave until we're finished investigating."

Finally, Tracy said, "Bobby was trying to cut ties with his family. He wanted to change his last name.

He thought being a 'Campopiano' was dangerous."

Eric looked like he was about to boil over.

Danny told her, "We're aware, and we're planning on looking into it."

Eric shook his head. "Bobby wouldn't have made it into the ballet company if he wasn't a Campopiano. The name made him famous."

"That's not true," Tracy disagreed. "He hated being a Campopiano."

"Doesn't matter if he hated it," Eric shot back. "I'm telling you, he wouldn't have gotten into the company if he didn't belong to that family."

"Why?" Danny asked.

"It's obvious," he told her. But that wasn't enough, so he insisted, "The Campopianos are loaded. The artistic director and board probably thought Bobby's family would fund us. If you ever saw Bobby perform ballet, you would agree it wasn't his skills as a dancer that got him into the Brooklyn Ballet, for Christ's sake."

"Eric!" Tracy balked.

"I'm just saying what *everyone* thought!"

As the dancers began quibbling, Carter returned, entering the ballet studio.

"Danny?"

"Yeah?" she asked, as she turned.

He looked thrown.

"What?" she asked.

"A word?"

She crossed the gray marley floor and stepped out of the studio. Carter walked with her into the anteroom and turned on his heel. She followed and again asked him:

"What?"

Confused by the situation himself, Carter told her, "Homicide wants to speak with you."

"What?"

"Detectives Crouse and Toliver are outside."

Chapter Two

SITTING ON THE suspect's side of a two-way mirror was the last place Danny wanted to be. But she had seen this coming. The moment Detective Crouse had urged her into the back of his unmarked police car, she had a strong guess as to where she was going and why.

But she couldn't believe it.

Alone in Interview Room Three on the first floor of the 66th Precinct, Danny caught sight of her reflection in the mirror, knowing full well that two homicide detectives were observing her from the other side of the glass.

She did not look good.

The scratches her mother had left on her face told their own story.

She wondered if her lieutenant knew she was in here. The captain obviously did since he oversaw all the investigations at the 66th. Had the district attorney, Sarah Hovey, been looped in?

Danny could only imagine what Nora had told the police. Danny hadn't wanted her mother to go to prison. Clearly, the sentiment wasn't mutual.

Mutually assured destruction was how Nora had chosen to proceed, but Danny already knew she didn't have it in her to destroy her mother.

She was not looking forward to this.

The door swung open. Detective Crouse entered, holding a manila filing folder in his hand. His partner, Detective Toliver, followed and closed the door.

They sat on the interrogation side of the small

table. Tension rose between the homicide detectives and the S.V.U. investigator who had solved more cases in the past year than both men combined over the course of their entire careers.

Danny knew how to play this, not that she wanted anything to do with the game.

"We're going to cut to the chase, Foster," said Detective Crouse. He was smart enough to know who he was dealing with. "You're not arrested. We just want to talk."

Detective Toliver added, "If you had done something worthy of investigation, Internal Affairs would be handling it. I think we all know that?"

Toliver glanced at Crouse amicably then turned his attention to Danny, offering her the same phony attitude of camaraderie.

Danny folded her arms. "Why am I here?"

Crouse opened the manila filing folder and asked, "Your mother is Nora Foster?"

"That's right," she confirmed.

Crouse picked up a color photograph of Nora from the folder and slid it across the table, turning the image right-side up for Danny.

The image of Nora was harrowing. She looked old, pale, and forlorn—heartbroken. Her chin was tipped up, exposing the dark bruises on her throat. There were puncture marks deep in her neck where Danny's fingernails had broken the skin.

Tears stung her eyes but she blinked them away, clenched her jaw, and swallowed down the emotions that were threatening to spill out of her.

"That's your mother?" Crouse asked.

"You know that's my mother," she snapped.

Crouse and Toliver exchanged a look, but

Danny kept her attention fixed on the sad image of her mother. Nora the victim. Nora the baby killer.

Danny felt like her mind was splitting in two.

Detective Crouse leveled with her. "Your mother came into the station a few mornings ago to report this. She claims you attacked her with the intent to take her life. The accusation is attempted murder—"

"I know what the accusation is," she shot back.

"Did you do this?" asked Toliver as he pressed his index finger against the glossy print where purple bruises had formed on Nora's throat.

Danny locked eyes with him, but said nothing.

Toliver nodded. He understood. If he were in Danny's position, he wouldn't talk, either.

He had to lay the facts on the table, though.

"Your mom also claimed that you killed your infant son."

"She said that?" Danny blurted out.

She knew that saying anything would only harm her, but she lost control and a volatile reaction tumbled out of her.

"*Who* was there that night alone with the baby? *Who* ordered the autopsy? Who—"

In a delayed reaction, she regained control and shut her mouth.

Detective Toliver asked, "Are you saying you weren't there when your baby died?"

"Your *mother* was?" Crouse added for clarification.

She said nothing.

Crouse informed her, "As far as Nora understands, the baby's father, Thomas O'Toole, ordered the autopsy."

Nora actually had the audacity to tell the police that?!

It took every shred of self restraint that Danny possessed to keep her mouth shut.

"Then Thomas, horrified that *you* had killed your son, told Nora," Crouse went on.

He was obviously trying to provoke her.

Perhaps playing the 'good cop,' Toliver assured her, "It'll be easy enough for us to find out who ordered the autopsy. Jill Andover would've handled it at Kings County Hospital. We've put a call into her office."

Jill had conducted the autopsy as a favor. Danny doubted there would be any paper record of it. However, Greenwood Cemetery would have records of exhuming Gregory's coffin. Danny wasn't about to mention that, though.

She didn't see the harm in asking them, "Did you talk to Tommy?"

After a moment's hesitation, Toliver admitted, "No."

"Let's address the elephant in the room, shall we?" Crouse suggested. "You look like hell, Foster. Your mother said she had to claw her way out, and frankly, you look like someone who got clawed."

She remained stoic and didn't respond.

Detective Toliver said, "You know we have to ask to take photos of you and collect the material under your fingernails even though you probably showered. You know we have to go through the motions."

"No, you don't," she informed them. "If you arrest me, you can do what you like." She stood from the table. "Until then, you haven't got a legal right to do anything, and you know it."

As she turned for the door, Detective Crouse

warned her, "If you don't cooperate, we're going to proceed in our usual fashion, and you know how we operate."

She cut her eyes at them over her shoulder and promised, "If I cooperate, my mother will end up in prison. I'll die before I let that happen."

She threw the door open, but as she left the cramped interview room, Crouse called out after her:

"You could end up in prison, too, Foster!"

She didn't take the bait, but kept walking.

When she reached the bullpen, coming into the Special Victims Unit department, Carter was seated at his desk. His attention locked onto her, as she crossed through.

"I have to talk to the lieutenant," she told him without slowing down.

"What did Homicide want?" he asked. "Danny?"

"Give me a minute," she told him over her shoulder.

"Is Homicide trying to steal our case again?"

Ignoring her partner in favor of trying to put out the fire that Nora had started, she knocked on the lieutenant's door even though it was ajar.

"Yeah?" said Franco from inside the office.

She poked her head in. "I need to speak with you privately."

"Come in," he said, waving her in, though he was absorbed in one of the reports on his desk.

She closed the door behind her and sat on one of the chairs in front of his desk.

Lieutenant Martin Franco had a hard edge. He rarely went soft on his detectives. Over the years, Danny had earned his respect as one of his smartest investigators. She knew she could ask for favors. But she also knew that Franco wasn't her friend or father. And right now, if he was aware of Nora's allegations and if he had authorized the interview that had just blindsided her, then Franco very well could be her enemy.

Franco tore his attention away from whatever had consumed him.

"What's going on?" he asked, though he was still mentally preoccupied.

In fact, he looked like he was about to boil over, but she didn't take it personally.

"I may have a problem with Homicide," she stated. "Do you know about this?"

"What problem?" he said, genuinely unsure of what she was referring to. "The Campopiano case is yours, period. If Homicide steps as much as one toe onto your territory, I'll have the captain bring the hammer down so hard on them that their grandchildren will be born brain damaged."

Franco *was* mad.

But not about the infanticide and attempted murder suspicions that were now looming over Danny's head.

His hands balled into fists on his desk, as he said, "This is my chance; *our* chance, as a department. The Campopiano murder opened a door that I've been trying to unlock for years."

Before she could ask, he barked, "Where's your partner?"

Franco obviously hadn't heard about Nora and Homicide. If she brought the issue to the table now, she might have to deal with it. She would definitely have to deal with telling Carter what was going on.

The situation was a ticking time bomb, fair enough, but Danny wasn't about to detonate the explosion before the appointed time.

"I'll get him," she told Franco, as she hopped up from her seat.

She opened the door and yelled, "Dobbs! Franco's office!"

Carter wasted no time, left his suit jacket on the back of his chair, and joined Danny in the lieutenant's office.

"Have a seat," Franco said.

Franco conquered whatever had been boiling his blood. He was filled with pure, unbridled determination now. His dark eyes brightened, as the taste of victory filled his mouth.

"I fought Homicide for the Campopiano case," he began explaining. "Thank God the guy was naked. I've wanted an 'in' with the Campopianos for ages."

Danny and Carter touched eyes.

Franco opened a folder on his desk that was thicker than a telephone book.

"This is between the three of us," he warned. "The matter goes beyond S.V.U. in fact, but I haven't been able to pursue it as an S.V.U. lieutenant. It's been a 'pet project,' you could say."

He patted the thick folder.

Proud of his instincts, Carter asked, "You think Campopiano was a mob hit?"

"I'm not saying that, no," Franco countered. "I've been keeping my eye on a dirty judge."

Danny felt her eyebrows shoot up to her hairline.

"But I haven't been able to catch the guy. He's

been too clean. I haven't obtained hard proof against him that can be used to nail his ass to the wall. But he has overruled jury verdicts and sent criminals walking. Some of those criminals have been the perps that S.V.U. has taken off the street. That's what first got my attention years ago. More than anything, this dirty judge has let certain members of the Campopiano family walk."

"Who's the judge?" Danny asked, and Carter was highly interested, as well.

"Harlan Ellsworth."

It took Danny a moment, but she knew the name and remembered the judge. She had sat in Judge Ellsworth's courtroom a handful of times over the years when the district attorney, Sarah Hovey, had asked Danny to testify in various criminal court cases.

Carter hadn't been with the 66th Precinct long enough to know the judge.

Franco went on, "Full disclosure, I suspect Ellsworth is in the habit of taking bribes. I don't know the specifics of it, though. What I do know is that the Campopianos have never seen the inside of a prison. Within this file, I have arrest records for a number of the Campopianos. If you look at the evidence, the arrest, and the charges, there's no way these guys shouldn't have at least gone to trial. Ellsworth has dismissed cases outright...."

"I could go on, but I won't. You get the idea. Someone murdered Bobby Campopiano, and you're going to find out who. And in the process, you're going to talk to the Campopianos, get your thumb on the pulse of how they operate, and see what you can find out."

"Lieutenant," Danny objected. "We aren't exactly undercover cops."

"Carter was," he argued. "And you're adorable. Mirabelle Bauer wouldn't have taken a liking to you if you weren't."

Danny begged to differ that she was *adorable*, but she couldn't deny that Carter was one hell of an undercover investigator when he needed to be.

Franco planted another seed in his detectives' minds.

"Someone hanged Bobby Campopiano. Harlan Ellsworth is dirty. The second you two show up asking questions, it's going to trigger the same pattern I've been tracking." Again, he tapped the thick file. "If the murder was at all mob related, whether committed by the Campopianos or by another crime family, then the killer is going to try to bribe Harlan Ellsworth to make the whole thing go away. That's what my gut is telling me.

"I've never had an 'in' like this before, like I said. We have a real chance to nail this dirty judge to the wall. Whatever you need from me, and I mean *whatever* you need, just let me know and I'll get it for you."

Carter glanced at Danny and suggested, "Time to inform the family."

"Sounds like it," she agreed.

As they stood, Franco told her, "Get yourself cleaned up, Danny. You look like you got whipped in the face."

"Thanks," she said dryly.

As the detectives made their way to their desks, Carter mentioned, "I started a suspect list on a shared file and emailed you the link. And I researched the Campopianos, compiled cursory information on the family members, including where each of them work."

Danny pulled out her chair and sat, as Carter added, "Get this, they all live in the same house."

That got her attention. She screwed her face up, as he sat down across from her at his own desk.

"What do you mean?"

"There are three generations of Campopianos all living in the same house on Argyle Road. Only one of the kids is 'single,' so you have a house full of married couples and in-laws and babies."

"That's as Italian as it gets," she remarked.

"That's what I call a zoo," he countered. "As far as I could tell, the only Campopiano that wasn't living there was Bobby."

"So, Tracy and Eric were correct. Bobby had cut ties with his family."

"Maybe," said Carter, unsure.

"Alright, partner. If we're going to inform the family, where should we start? At the house on Argyle?"

"We could give it a shot. Bobby wasn't married. His parents, Maria and Guido Campopiano, both work. Guido owns Rocco's Italian Restaurant, and Maria works for the Brooklyn Museum. I say we start at the house, and head to Rocco's if need be."

Danny stood and gathered her things. It was getting warm out, but she threw on her black blazer, adjusted the holstered gun on her hip, and was ready to go. Despite the humidity, Carter put on his suit jacket, and after making sure he had the keys to their unmarked, police-issued, Ford Crown Victoria, they headed out of the 66th Precinct.

Warm winds breezed across the avenue, as Danny and Carter made their way to the parked sedan. It was almost painfully bright, so the moment she sat in the passenger seat, she found her sunglasses in the glove box. The dark aviators were huge, but did the trick.

Carter settled behind the wheel, turned the engine, and as they drove off, he said what they both were thinking.

"Franco expects us to conduct two investigations."

"Yup," she agreed.

He stared at her then traffic demanded his attention.

"How often does this happen?" he asked her.

"Never."

He let out a laugh that sounded like pure frustration.

"Did you see the look on his face?" he asked her. Of course, she had. "That's what a shark looks like when there's blood in the water."

"Carter, you looked at that dead body for less than a second and determined it was a mob hit," she reminded him. "Franco's just asking us to look at the case from that angle. Weren't you going to do that anyway?"

"You can't deny Franco seemed hairbrained."

"What do you care?"

Taken aback, he said, "What's with you?"

"What do you mean?"

"What's with your face?"

"Back off, Carter."

"Why did Homicide want to talk to you?"

"You want to do this?" she challenged, pissed.

"Not really," he shot back. "But I'm not going to let you keep secrets."

"Yes, you are," she hotly returned, and there was nothing he could do about it.

"Fine," he grumbled. "Yes, I think it's a mafia hit. And frankly, that would've been daunting enough. You think I want to end up whacked? Investigating the mob comes with serious risks. Investigating a dirty judge comes with… I don't know what the hell it comes with, but it has to be worse."

"I'm not going to disagree."

"Plus, look at me."

"And risk falling in love?" she teased.

"I mean, I can go undercover in the Kensington Projects. I can go undercover in the red light district, interface with pimps and drug dealers. Hell, I'm a pro, I practically wrote the book on how to close a case at Vice. There's no way in hell I can go undercover with the Italian mafia."

"No one's asking you to."

"Franco literally asked me to."

"He's dreaming," she assured him. "Whoa, slow down. That's Argyle."

Carter squeezed the brakes and eased a hard left onto Argyle Road.

Getting her directional bearings, she remarked, "We're a block from St. Christopher's, and Brooklyn Ballet Studios is only a few blocks northwest."

"You know what I think?" Carter said, as they crawled down Argyle, looking for the Campopiano house.

"Yeah, I do," she said, happy to be a smartass. "You think it was a mob hit."

"I think the killer is in the mob, yes. But that crime scene…"

When he didn't finish his point, Danny asked, "You think it's personal? Ballet related?"

There was a vacancy along the curb, so Carter pulled the Crown Vic over and parked.

He killed the engine, pulled the key, unbuckled, and told her, "If you're in some kind of trouble, you have to tell me. I'm not messing around, Danny. Homicide talked to you. Your face is all scratched up. You're going to tell me why, or I'm going to find out."

He let that hang for a moment so that the seriousness could land on her conscience. But he didn't force her to talk.

Instead, he climbed out of the car, stepping into the late morning sunshine, while Danny sucked in a deep breath and gathered her faculties.

Would she tell Carter what was going on with her? Of course. Eventually.

Eventually, Crouse and Toliver would formalize their investigation. Eventually, Franco would be informed. Eventually, what Nora started would end in a bitter mess of rage and handcuffs and prison sentences. And eventually, *inevitably*, Carter would find out the whole story.

But *eventually* wasn't 'now.'

She flipped the passenger sun visor down and looked at herself in the mirror. The dark aviator sunglasses only covered a portion of the worst scratch on her face, but it would have to do.

She popped the passenger door open and climbed out into the sunshine.

"We undershot the address," Carter told her, as

she approached "It's half a block up."

As they walked north along Argyle Road, Danny noticed how quiet the block was. The sidewalk was immaculate. The block was entirely residential, and the pedestrians seemed in no hurry. Some were walking their dogs. Others pushed baby strollers. A jogger passed them, heading north towards Prospect Park.

The townhouses that lined the block soon gave way to a grassy front yard, and there stood the Campopiano residence.

Danny pulled her aviators down her nose and remarked, "That's not a *house*. That's a mansion."

"Market value, 30-million," he informed her.

The mansion could've passed for an annex of the Brooklyn Museum. A white-stone structure of neo-Jacobean design, the mansion was three stories. There were two giant, stone lion statues out front, flanking the foot of the stone steps that led to the huge entrance door.

"Thirty million, huh?" she questioned. "That's a pretty price tag for a restaurant owner."

"Let's see who's home."

They neared the stone lions and headed up the lofty stoop. Having failed to find a doorbell, Carter grabbed the large, iron knocker that was fixed to the massive oak door. He pounded the knocker and took a step back.

A mourning dove cooed from the bushes that spanned the width of the stone mansion.

Danny heard footfall on the other side of the door then it popped open, revealing an Italian-American man dressed in a three-piece suit. Danny pegged him for being in his thirties, but the rugged olive-tone complexion and slicked back hair could be deceiving her.

Carter made introductions.

"This is Detective Danielle Foster, and I'm Detective Carter Dobbs."

"Oh?" the man replied, feigning concern.

"We're with the 66th Precinct in Kensington," Carter said, smartly omitting the particular department they worked for.

Carter turned to Danny and she went on, "We need to speak with the Campopianos, preferably Guido and Maria."

Furrowing his brow, the man asked, "What's this about?"

"It's about their son, Bobby," she told him.

"I'm Bobby's older brother, Jimmy Campopiano," he said easily, as he offered to shake Danny's hand.

He gave her a respectful handshake then shook Carter's hand.

"What about Bobby?" asked Jimmy. When the detectives hesitated, he mentioned, "Neither of my parents are home, and Eva's at school. I had a late morning with my wife, but I was about to head out. This is serious? Something serious happened?"

Danny nodded.

"Come in, come in," said Jimmy, as he pulled the door wide open and stepped aside.

Danny followed in after Carter, coming into a grand foyer with arched ceilings and an elegant marble statue of the Blessed Virgin Mary.

As Jimmy led them around the statue of Mary and into a traditional Italian sitting room, Danny noticed the overwhelming Catholic decor of the home.

Somewhere upstairs a baby cried.

The sitting room was furnished with classic Italian luxury furniture. The sofas and settees were a unique pearl color. The floors were covered with huge Bisterne area rugs, and there was a massive chandelier overhead. Gold trimming wrapped the walls and archways.

"Have a seat, please," Jimmy invited, and the detectives eased onto the pearl sofa that looked like it belonged in the Smithsonian. "Pardon the baby. My wife's upstairs," he mentioned as he found his cell phone in the inside pocket of his expensive suit jacket.

Jimmy placed a call and pressed his cell to his ear as it rang. "My father isn't far," he told them. "I'll call my mother next."

From upstairs, a woman yelled, "Jimmy?"

"Everything's fine, Catherine!" he yelled back, then redirected his attention. "Pop, two detectives are here. Here at the house. Two, yes. From the precinct. They're here about *Bobby*. I'm gonna give Ma a call."

Jimmy was pacing.

"Fine, *you* call her, but come to the house," he barked.

"Jimmy!"

"Catherine, I said, everything's fine!" he yelled at the ceiling. "My wife had a baby," he told them, growing agitated by the second.

Jimmy raked his fingers through his dark hair, slicking back the chunks that had come loose.

He stopped pacing and asked, "What happened to Bobby?"

From upstairs, Catherine yelled, "Jimmy, what's going on down there!"

The baby wailed terribly.

"Ah," he seethed, his world coming undone. "Excuse me, please."

Jimmy turned on his designer, patent leather loafer, and walked briskly out of the sitting room.

As he trailed through the massive house, he called out, "What's with you? You can't watch the baby, eh? I'm dealing with something, Catherine!"

The argument that followed came muffled through the ceiling.

Danny turned to Carter. "Bobby wasn't living here?"

"Not according to the dancers, but we'll find out."

"Who else lives here?"

"That I know of, the parents Maria and Guido. *Guido's* parents, Pasquale and Rosanna. Maria's brother, Tony and Tony's wife, their adult son, Nico, *his* wife, and their kid. Plus, Maria and Guido's teenage daughter, Eva."

"That's a soap opera."

From upstairs, Jimmy yelled, "You're not even dressed!"

"The hell I care!" yelled Catherine, as they stomped across the floor.

The front door opened and a man, who Danny could guess was Guido Campopiano, yelled, "Jimmy?!"

"Cops are in the front room, Pop!" Jimmy yelled, as he shuffled down the stairs.

From where Danny was sitting next to Carter, there was a lot of yelling, stomping, and more yelling in this household, but she hadn't detected any anger. The Campopianos struck her as a loud family full of hot-headed Italians.

Guido and his wife, Maria, rounded into the sitting room.

As Danny and Carter stood, Jimmy spilled into the room, with his own wife in tow.

Catherine was wearing a white, gauzy nightgown, and holding a screaming baby in her arms. Gorgeous with giant blue eyes and chocolate-brown hair, Catherine bounced her baby in her arms.

"What's this about, Bobby, eh?" asked Guido Campopiano as he pulled a wool Fedora from his head and a worried look came over him.

Carter made introductions, shook Guido and Maria's hands, and Danny did likewise, as she explained, "We're with the Kensington Precinct, the 66th, and yes, we're here to speak with you about your son, Bobby—"

The baby shrieked so loudly that Danny feared she would start lactating.

Jimmy yelled, "Catherine, would you get upstairs with the baby!"

"Alright! Alright! I just want to hear what this is about!"

"I'll tell you what it's about when I know!" yelled Jimmy.

Maria swooped in, gingerly cradled Catherine, and began ushering her out of the sitting room.

"There, there," Maria cooed at the baby, who had quite a set of pipes on her.

Jimmy apologized, "Again, pardon her. Let's have a seat."

The sounds of Maria, Catherine, and the baby quieted as they disappeared upstairs.

Everyone sat, and Danny took a deep breath, preparing to deliver the news that no family ever wanted to hear.

"This morning, your son, Bobby Campopiano, was found dead at the Brooklyn Ballet Studios."

She had barely gotten that much out when Guido gasped. Jimmy turned to stone and stared at Danny. His brow furrowed. His thumb found its way to his teeth and he began gnawing.

"At this point," Danny went on, "we're proceeding as though this was a homicide."

Guido shifted and locked eyes with Jimmy.

Jimmy told his dad, "I didn't see this coming."

Dark emotions were brewing just under the surface of Guido Campopiano's weathered face. He returned his attention to Danny, expecting to hear more.

"Detective Dobbs and I are proceeding with extreme caution, so I apologize for not telling you the details of the homicide, but—"

Guido blurted, "At the ballet? This happened at the ballet!" He glared at Jimmy then locked his sights on Danny. "The ballet, you're telling me? Killed there, eh?" Again, he turned to his son and barked, "The family business wasn't good enough for him? Eh? Would he be dead if he worked for me, Jimmy?"

Jimmy couldn't look at him.

"Would he?" he demanded. Enraged, Guido slammed his fist against his knee. "Would Bobby be dead if he stayed in the family, Jimmy?"

"No, Pop!"

"What the hell did he do this to himself for, eh?"

"I don't know!"

After a long moment, the men calmed down.

Jimmy clarified for the detectives' benefit, "The family owns a restaurant, Rocco's. It's the family business."

Guido asked Danny and Carter, "Do you know who did this to my son?"

Danny told him directly, "No. We only have questions."

The Italian man steadied his emotions, regaining control of himself.

"I'll answer your questions," he agreed. "And so will my son. Won't you, Jimmy?"

Jimmy stared dead at his father. "Yeah, that's right."

Carter led the interview.

"When did you last see Bobby?"

Guido responded first, "Christmas. He came to the Mass at St. Christopher's on Christmas Eve. He stopped by the next day, on the holiday, but didn't stay long."

"Five months ago?" Danny questioned.

"It broke my heart."

Maria slipped back into the room, but wasn't able to sit next to Guido.

Guido wasn't having it.

"I don't want you here, Maria—"

"What? Why can't I be here?"

"Get back upstairs, I'll get you after I speak with the police—"

"What happened to Bobby?"

"Get back upstairs, Maria!"

"Ma, go upstairs!" Jimmy yelled.

"Upstairs, Maria!" Guido fumed, and his wife made her way out again.

When the men were certain Maria was beyond earshot, Guido told the detectives, "We'll tell them, but they can't be here. You wouldn't get a single question answered, trust me. When they hear what happened to Bobby..."

Jimmy shrugged, "Women."

Danny pulled the interview back on track by recapping, "Mr. Campopiano, you last saw Bobby on Christmas. What about you, Jimmy?"

Jimmy became guarded, and his father spoke up, remembering his prior point.

"Bobby wanted to do his ballet," Guido explained. "I wanted him to take a position in the family business. But that wasn't what he wanted to do. His mother wouldn't take my side. That hurt me, but, even so, his mother and myself and Jimmy here, and the whole entire family, loved Bobby and wanted him *here*."

"Here?" Danny asked.

"At the house," Jimmy supplied. "Bobby didn't want nothing to do with us. He moved out."

Carter asked, "When was this?"

"Thanksgiving," said Guido.

Jimmy allowed, "It was *around* Thanksgiving time, but he moved out right before the holiday, I think."

"The point being, he's been estranged from the family. He doesn't come around. He doesn't come to the restaurant. He didn't want to be a Campopiano no more."

Danny wanted to talk to the other members of the family, badly. But she had no choice except to work with what she had, so she reiterated her question to Jimmy.

"When did *you* see Bobby last?"

Jimmy did not want to answer.

When he finally did, Danny knew he was lying.

"Christmas," said Jimmy. "Like my dad and the rest of the family, I hadn't seen Bobby since Christmas."

Danny and Carter touched eyes. The detectives had accomplished the goal. They had delivered the news to the family. If they tried to twist this into an interrogation, they weren't likely to get what they wanted.

But Danny had one more question that had to be asked.

"Mr. Campopiano, Detective Dobbs and I have reason to believe that a contributing factor to your son's murder had to do with his relationship with a priest named Father Silva."

Guido hardened, turning darker than a volcano that was about to erupt.

In a low, almost guttural tone of voice, he growled, "What the hell does Father Silva have to do with this?"

Chapter Three

CARTER'S CELL PHONE had vibrated twice during the home visit to the Campopianos.

After delivering the hard news that Bobby had been murdered, Carter and Danny stepped out of the Campopianos' mansion and into the stark light of day.

As they descended the wide stone steps of the lofty stoop, Danny pushed her aviator sunglasses onto her face.

Carter didn't have the luxury. He squinted, pulled his cell phone out of his suit jacket, and discovered that he had one text message and a missed call, both from his wife, Kathy.

When they reached the sidewalk, Danny pointed out, "Guido and Jimmy did not want their wives in the room."

"I noticed that," he said, distracted. His own wife was trying to get into the room, figuratively speaking. "Excuse me for a moment?"

"Sure," she said, as she turned on her heel and stared at the looming mansion.

Carter skimmed the text message. Kathy wanted to remind him about their marriage counseling appointment that evening.

Over the course of three months, the Dobbs had plowed through two therapists and were now on their third, Dr. Frederick Murphy. Both Carter and Kathy trusted their latest therapist, who wasn't overly coddling like Dr. Valdmanis, nor eerily intuitive like Dr. Ling.

Dr. Murphy tended to mainly focus on setting

and maintaining boundaries, which had benefited Carter more than anyone.

He sent the call through to Kathy. She picked up, and he told her, "Hey, I know about the appointment."

"I think we should bring the kids," Kathy pushed.

Kathy was always pushing.

"To our *marriage* counseling session?" he questioned, as quietly as possible.

"Dr. Murphy doesn't mind—"

"You asked him before consulting me?"

"Carter, Matty is *not* okay," she reminded him. "Just because *you* put someone behind bars doesn't mean that the *trauma* is gone."

Carter didn't disagree. He knew that better than anyone. But he didn't appreciate being lectured.

"You think I don't know that?" he hissed. He couldn't deal with this right now. "I'll see you at the house tonight."

"Carter," she warned.

"You want to bring Matty? Dr. Murphy doesn't have a problem with that? Then fine," he agreed, irritated. "I think if we break down the boundary that separates you and me on one side and the kids on the other, then we're going to have *serious* problems in this family."

"Oh, please."

"See you later," he concluded.

He shoved his cell phone back into the inner pocket of his suit jacket, and the moment Danny looked at him, he snapped, "Don't."

"I'm not interested in your secrets," she assured him. "As long as the feeling is mutual."

"You're negotiating with me now?" he challenged.

She didn't budge.

Boundaries.

Fine.

"Understood," he agreed, and they started down the sidewalk towards their parked Crown Vic.

Carter knew that his youngest son, Matty, had been through a lot. The psychopath who had starred in S.V.U.'s most recent case had kidnapped Matty. Carter had ended up in a cage right beside his son. He wasn't blind to the long-term psychological effects that were guaranteed to result from a trauma like that.

But he also knew that kids were tough. Matty hadn't been drugged or sexually assaulted that night. His son hadn't experienced even a taste of the hell that Carter had been raised in, as a boy.

Recalling Danny's earlier point, Carter asked, "You think Guido and Jimmy were protecting their wives?"

"I think they were being truthful in part," she allowed. "I think that Maria and Catherine would've had such big emotional reactions to the news that we wouldn't have been able to get our questions answered. But I also think that the men kept them out of the room because they feared they wouldn't be able to control what Maria and Catherine might tell us."

"That crossed my mind, as well."

"I'm not sure how we'll be able to talk to Catherine," Danny said, thinking out loud. "With a new baby, she's not going to leave the house. But Maria is a different story. We might be able to catch her where she works."

"At the Brooklyn Museum," he added.

"But when is she going to return to work?"

"That's definitely a question mark," he agreed. After a moment of consideration, he pointed out, "Eva Campopiano wasn't there."

"She's their teenager?"

"The only daughter of Guido and Maria. Bobby's younger sister."

Danny, thinking out loud, said, "We might have to give the family a few days. If you ask me, the Campopianos are as Catholic as they come. They're going to have a funeral Mass for Bobby in a day or two. I doubt they'll leave each other's side until then."

"Do you believe that they haven't seen Bobby since Christmas?"

"No," she told him bluntly. "I think Jimmy was lying through his teeth. They're each individuals, and I think they each continued their own relationships with Bobby. We need to talk to each of them individually, if you ask me."

When they reached the parked Crown Vic, Carter had a thought.

"Let's talk to Silva, the priest, and circle back to the ballet dancers. If Bobby walked away from his life as a Campopiano, he may have walked into a fatal drama with his ballet company."

"Divide and conquer?" she asked him.

"I'll take Silva and you'll...?"

"Talk to the Brooklyn Ballet, the other ballet dancers, the artistic director, the janitor, whoever."

"We also need to check in with Jill and see what she's got for us," he added, as he threw the driver's side door open.

They climbed in, and as soon as Danny shut her door, Carter angled the Crown Vic into the street, heading north on Argyle.

When they reached Church Avenue, he turned right. After a few blocks, he pulled over in front of the Brooklyn Ballet Studios.

Officer Quinlan was standing on the sidewalk out front, which told them that Jill and her forensics team were likely still collecting evidence inside. The body hadn't yet been moved to the County Medical Examiner's Office at the Kings County Hospital.

"Call if you get something," he told her.

"Likewise," said Danny as she popped the passenger side door open and climbed out. "Oh, and Carter?"

"Yeah?"

"Thanks."

A smile came over him, and he said, "As long as I know where the line is, I won't cross it."

Again, she said, "Likewise."

Danny closed the car door and gave Officer Quinlan a nod on her way inside the building.

Carter checked his side view mirror and eased into traffic the first chance he got.

He was starting to feel warm, too warm. The Crown Vic held heat like a damn asteroid. As he drove, he blasted the air conditioner and adjusted the vents.

By the time he reached Westminster Road, having driven along Church Avenue, he felt no cooler.

St. Christopher's had a sprawling presence that dominated the corner of Church and Westminster.

The towering cathedral, which Church Avenue had been named after, occupied the middle of the block. Behind the cathedral were the parish building, rectory building, and a little chapel that was open 24-hours, each spanning Westminster. And finally, there was St. Christopher's Catholic School, which was perhaps even more massive than the church's collective properties.

Crawling south along Westminster, Carter hunted for a parking spot on the street, then saw a sign for St. Christopher's private parking.

"Hallelujah," he breathed, as he turned into a sizable parking lot that separated the religious buildings from the Catholic school.

According to the phony suicide note, Bobby had been molested by Father Silva. Had young Bobby encountered the priest at the church or at the school? Carter would have to find out.

He blotted his forehead with the back of his tie, stepped out into the afternoon heat, and shut the car door.

The humidity had risen along with the afternoon temperature. Brooklyn was known for being hot and sticky in the summer, but this was too much, too soon.

Carter wasn't Catholic. He didn't know the difference between a parish, rectory, or pastoral hall, but the St. Christopher's Rectory Center was the closest to the parking lot, so he reasoned to start there.

The rectory building was a two-story stone structure. Green ivy clung to the stones, creeping around the huge, wooden entrance door. The door was unlocked. Carter noticed there seemed to be no security system in place—no cameras, no checkpoints, no locked doors.

Anyone could breeze in from off the street, throw the main entrance door open, and easily pass into the next anteroom, pulling the door open and stepping through, as Carter was doing now.

There was a middle-age woman seated behind a traditional, executive office desk, though this was clearly the receptionist's front desk. There were chairs along the perimeter of the carpeted room. Carter felt like he was in the admissions office of an ivy league university.

There were a few people seated on chairs. A young couple, probably engaged, were holding hands affectionately. On the other side of the room, a young woman sat alone, as she read a pamphlet.

The receptionist, who was on the phone, appeared mild-mannered and dressed modestly in a high-neck sweater. She wore pearls and smelled faintly of perfume.

Carter pulled his detective badge from his hip, as he neared the receptionist, though she was wrapping up the phone call.

"Yes, Father," she said, as she scrutinized something on her computer monitor. "Yes, I've changed the appointment time. Of course," she said softly, as she nodded in response to the priest on the other end of the line.

She glanced up at Carter and offered him a little smile.

"Will, do, Father," she said, concluding the phone call. As she gently returned the phone to its cradle on the desk, she asked Carter, "Can I help you?"

Carter presented his badge clearly. "I would like to speak with Father Silva. I'm Detective Dobbs with the 66th Precinct."

Her eyes widened. "Father Silva?"

"That's right."

"Of course, Detective, yes, of course," she said softly.

Though clearly overwhelmed, she gathered herself enough to find the right number to call. She reminded herself, mumbling, "Detective Dobbs," and her hands started trembling.

"Dobbs…" She exhaled as if trying to calm her nerves.

She offered Carter a nervous smile, as she brought the desk phone to her ear.

"He isn't expecting you?" she presumed correctly.

Carter could tell she was doing her best to remain poised and polite despite being terrified.

"No," he confirmed.

"Okay," she breathed.

She forced herself to suck in oxygen, an attempt to slow her racing heart.

"Father Silva? Yes, hello, it's the rectory office. So sorry to disturb you. I have a police detective here who would like to speak with you. Detective Dobbs."

She listened intently, pressed her pink lips together, and began nodding.

"Yes, Father,' she agreed, nodding even more. "Will do, Father, yes."

She took a deep breath, as she returned the phone to its cradle.

Grabbing a notepad and a pen, she began

explaining to Carter, "Father Silva has the Opening Benediction for Eucharistic Adoration in about five minutes at the Holy Cross Chapel."

Was she speaking English?

She scrawled quickly, but paused to look up at Carter and ask, "Are you Catholic?"

"No."

She frowned, returned her attention to the notepad, and crossed something out then began scribbling more instructions.

She tore the page from the notepad, handed it to him, and said, "Outside of this building, you'll find the Directory. Father Silva will be at the Holy Cross Chapel, which is through the church grounds."

She angled herself and pointed her finger in a zig-zagging shape, as if Carter would be able to visualize how to get to the chapel based on her pantomiming.

She sighed. "Just look for St. Christopher's statue and make a left, then head towards Our Blessed Mother." She waved her hand and rolled her eyes, mentioning, "It doesn't matter that you're not Catholic, the Virgin Mary is *your* mother, too!" She let out a little laugh, then told him, "The Holy Cross Chapel is past Mary. You won't miss it."

Carter turned on his heel and said, "Thanks," as he eyed the chicken scratch she had provided him with.

"Wait!" she whispered. "Once you go inside the chapel, wait at the back. Father will find you after he finishes the Benediction. Oh, and please don't speak inside the chapel. It's *Eucharistic Adoration.*"

When Carter clearly hadn't a clue as to what that

meant, she clarified, "The body, blood, soul, and divinity of Jesus Christ is present within the Holy Host—the *wafer*—on the altar. So, no talking during Adoration, because Jesus is there."

Riiiiight.

"I'll speak with Silva outside."

"*Father* Silva," she corrected him.

"Thanks," he said dryly before leaving the rectory.

There was no way in hell that Carter was going to call some guy he didn't know 'father,' but the receptionist didn't need to know that.

Locating the Holy Cross Chapel wasn't nearly as complicated as the receptionist had made it out to be.

That being said, Carter was surprised when he found the statue of Saint Christopher.

The Catholic saint had the head of a dog.

He stared at the fangs and the wolfish dog-face of the statue.

It looked like a monster.

Creepy as that was, it hardly factored into the investigation, so he continued walking.

After less than a minute of following the cobblestone path that twisted through the grassy, tree lined church grounds, Carter found the Holy Cross Chapel.

The free-standing chapel was made of stone, covered in thriving ivy, and had small, stained glass windows all around. As a chapel, it was tiny, with a rounded dome roof. But Carter didn't realize how tiny the chapel was until he stepped inside.

Lit only with candles, the interior of the Holy Cross Chapel was so dark that Carter had to wait a moment to let his eyes adjust.

When they did, he saw that he was standing at the back of the sanctuary. The altar was on the far side. The stone walls had alcoved nooks where candles sat glowing. The entirety of the chapel was five pews deep.

On the altar was a golden, sparkling monstrance, shaped like a giant star. He got the impression that the thing was important.

A priest, who could only be Father Silva, was kneeling on a padded kneeler, facing the golden monstrance, and reciting a prayer that sounded like Latin to Carter's untrained ears. Silva was wearing a purple vestment with a shiny, white cross embroidered on the back.

Beside the altar where the monstrance sat was a metal ball—a thurible—which was smoking with incense.

Carter sat down on the rear pew.

For a tiny chapel, it wasn't exactly crowded. There were a few elderly Catholics praying up front. Other working class types. And a couple of disgruntled looking Catholic school boys in the back. Carter figured they had been sent here as some kind of punishment.

He felt eyes on him and heard the chapel door thud closed behind him.

When he turned, he awkwardly touched eyes with a Catholic school girl. A teenager. She was wearing a plaid skirt, a thin black tie, and a cardigan sweater over a button-down shirt. Her huge eyes were stuck on Carter, probably because he was so out of place there.

She started up the aisle, having torn her

attention away from the muscular African-American seated at the back of the chapel.

It was then that Carter realized her hair was tied up in a perfect, slick bun, exactly how the ballerina, Tracy Jones, had worn her brown hair.

The teenage girl tossed her school bag onto the wooden pew at the very front of the chapel, which earned her a scowling glare from Father Silva. Then she dropped to her knees in the pew, bowed her head, and remained unmoving in prayer.

"Genitori, genitoque laus et jubilatio. Salus, honor, virtus, quoque sit, et benedictio. Procedenti an ubtroque, compar sit laudatio. Amen," said Father Silva, concluding the benediction.

He rose from the kneeler, took the thurible of burning incense, and swung it towards the monstrance, as he walked around the altar.

It was then that Carter gained a decent impression of the priest.

Silva appeared to be in his late 60s or early 70s. His hair was white and wispy, nearly bald on top. His posture was frail but erect. He struck Carter as a typical Italian-American Catholic priest. There was nothing especially remarkable about him.

Next, Silva returned the thurible to its hanger, made the sign of the cross, and then disappeared into a room adjacent to the altar at the far side of the chapel.

Carter straightened his spine, thinking the priest had given him the slip. But a moment later, Silva emerged again, having removed the purple vestment. He looked more like a priest now, dressed all in black and wearing a white, clerical collar.

Silva walked up the aisle and neared Carter at

the back of the chapel. He greeted the detective without words and gestured towards the exit, inviting Carter to lead the way outside.

The bright sunshine blinded Carter as he exited the chapel, coming along the cobblestone path.

Silva followed after him, and suggested they talk in a shady area.

Farther along the cobblestone path was a bubbling fountain with a huge statue of another saint, Carter presumed.

"Welcome to St. Christopher's," said Father Silva, as his black eyebrows lifted, a smile forming on his aged face.

His attitude was warm. He wasn't shaken to be in the presence of a detective like the receptionist had been.

"Are you discerning the Catholic faith?" he asked.

Carter didn't know what that meant, so he said, "I'm a detective with the 66th Precinct, which serves the Kensington neighborhood. Can I ask you a few questions?"

Silva went from warm to reserved almost instantly.

"May I ask what this is about?"

"I would prefer to tell you after I ask you a few questions," he countered.

As Silva considered how to proceed, the fountain beside them bubbled and pigeons competed for the stone saint's head.

"I would like to be helpful," the priest agreed.

"Do you know Bobby Campopiano?"

Recollection came over him, and Silva said, "Of course. I know all of the Campopianos."

"Can you tell me, do you teach at the school, as well?" Carter asked, interested in getting a handle on Silva's scope of involvement with St. Christopher's.

"I do, but nowadays, it's really only one or two classes."

"Did you teach Bobby?"

Silva smiled. "I taught Bobby, yes. I baptized Bobby, I ordained his confirmation, I heard more than one confession from Bobby." He chuckled to himself. "I've been the Campopianos' priest for as long as I've been in the order."

"Was Bobby an altar boy? Involved in the church?" asked Carter.

"All of the Campopiano boys were," he answered easily. "Jimmy, Bobby, and the cousins. They're a devout Catholic family."

Silva was relaxed and open. Carter had no reason to stop.

"When did you last see Bobby?"

That tripped the priest up for a moment. "Is Bobby missing?"

"No," Carter answered frankly.

"Um, let me think," he said, as he combed through his memory. "Not for months. I definitely saw him on Christmas at the Mass."

"Any time this year?"

"I really can't say," he realized, having failed to remember. "What's this about, Detective?"

"Bobby was murdered. I'm investigating the homicide."

Stunned, Silva breathed, "What?"

"He was found this morning," Carter went on. "My partner and I have informed the Campopianos, and we wanted to talk to you."

"Oh, dear," he said, sinking into the deepest recesses of his concerned mind.

"They haven't contacted you?"

He shook his head. "I don't have a cell phone. It's allowed, I just don't like them. I'm typically unreachable unless I'm in my office, or near one of the phones in the priests' quarters in the cathedral or chapel. Guido probably tried to reach me…"

It hadn't occurred to Silva why Carter was paying *him* a visit. He wasn't behaving like a guilty man. Frankly, Carter couldn't see Silva obtaining a key to the Brooklyn Ballet Studios with rope in hand and plans to murder Bobby Campopiano, but then again, more shocking things have happened in this world.

"This case is complex," Carter began, as he mentally worked out how to bring up the molestation allegation from the fake suicide note.

He would need to broach the topic with extreme caution, or else Silva, like any suspect, could lawyer up.

But Carter used a bold approach and exercised no caution whatsoever.

"I shouldn't divulge the details of the crime, but it appeared to be a staged suicide. The crime scene included what we believe to be a *fake* suicide note. The note explained that the reason for the suicide was because Bobby couldn't live with having been molested by 'Father Silva' at St. Christopher's school when he was growing up."

"Please," Silva interrupted, as he held his hand up, stopping Carter from continuing.

"I have to investigate this angle," he told Silva.

"Please!"

Father Silva paced away from Carter. His hand was pressed over his mouth.

Carter gave him a minute.

The teenage girl with the bun spilled out of the Holy Cross Chapel. As she trailed up the cobblestone path, passing them, she shouted at Silva:

"I'm done doing my penance, Father!"

"Oh, God," breathed Silva. "Eva..."

The girl clomped along, walking away.

"Campopiano?" Carter questioned Silva, as he neared the priest. "That's Eva Campopiano?"

Silva angled his huge, tear-filled eyes up at Carter and asked, "Does she know?"

"No, she wasn't home."

Eva swayed her way along the cobblestone path, heading towards the huge stone Catholic school buildings, the campus of which dominated the city block.

Carter didn't want to miss his chance to talk to a Campopiano without Guido and Jimmy shutting her up.

"Excuse me, Father," he told Silva, as he started off after Eva.

"Eva Campopiano?" he called out.

She slowed her step and turned on her dress shoes.

She wore black leg warmers, and a pair of ballet en pointe shoes were tied and dangling from her school bag. The plaid of her skirt and her cardigan were a maroon color. A Catholic uniform with a few personal touches.

"Who wants to know?"

Carter reached her and said, "Detective Dobbs. I

spoke with your parents this morning, and Jimmy."

"Yeah, right," she balked. A strange grin tugged at the corner of her mouth. "We don't talk to the cops without our lawyers present."

"I don't doubt it," he allowed. "But your parents made an exception this morning."

She must have believed him, because she asked, "They did?"

An innocent glimmer of genuine curiosity filled her big brown eyes.

"What did you talk to them about?"

"They didn't call you?"

"The school holds our phones. We turn them in when we get there and we don't get them back until we leave." She looked him up and down. "Why did you talk to them?"

He suddenly wasn't sure if he had a legal right to tell her anything, and Eva must have sense that, because she informed him:

"I'm eighteen, alright?"

Father Silva was hovering nearby, unwilling to leave if Eva was about to receive the blow of a lifetime. But the priest didn't join them. Silva was probably too scared to receive another blow himself. He didn't want to remain in the alleged molestation spotlight.

"Your brother, Bobby, was found dead this morning," he told her.

It took Eva a very long time to comprehend the news. She didn't react outwardly, but rather seemed to get lost somewhere inside of herself. She shook her head, swallowed, and couldn't seem to pull herself out of the mile-long stare that had come over her.

"How did he die?" she asked after a long moment.

"It's a homicide," he said without mentioning the hanging, the suicide note, or the other bizarre details of the crime. "He was found murdered in one of the dressing rooms at the Brooklyn Ballet Studios."

"My parents know?"

"Yes, my partner and I spoke with them this morning. We'll likely speak with them again and again, as we investigate who did this. When did you see Bobby last?'

She looked up, locking eyes with Carter, and confusion spread across her youthful face.

"Eva?" he asked.

"I saw him this morning. He can't be dead. I just saw him."

Thrilled—the girl could have been the last person to see Bobby alive, and she could have seen someone, the killer perhaps—Carter eagerly asked:

"Where? Where did you see Bobby?"

She barely opened her mouth to reply, and Father Silva was on her.

Silva captured Eva into his arms and pulled her protectively away from Carter, as he insisted:

"Your father would not want you speaking to the police!"

"Let me go," she snapped and shoved Silva off of her.

But he captured her again and began ushering her towards the rectory.

Eva shouted complaints, insisting that Silva should let her go.

Carter stepped in, getting between the priest and

the girl.

"She's not a minor!" Carter told Silva. "If she's eighteen, she can make her own decisions."

Carter had to pry Silva's hand off Eva's arm.

"Get off of me, both of you!" Eva yelled, jerking free and scrambling off the cobblestones and onto the grass.

Silva pointed his finger at her and warned, "I'm calling your father."

As he stomped off towards the rectory building to do just that, Eva suffered some kind of internal mental breakdown. She turned on her heel several times, holding her head with both hands.

Carter approached her and said, "Eva?"

"Don't!" she snapped.

She got her bearings and then took off.

Carter expected her to head towards the street or maybe the parking lot.

But instead, she charged towards the Holy Cross Chapel, threw the door open, and yelled, "Jesus!" as if she actually expected to find the messiah inside the little stone church.

Chapter Four

"I HAVE MY S.I.A. meeting tonight."

"Carter," Kathy warned, as the kids piled into the back of the family minivan.

The Dobbs' most athletic son, Christopher, tore himself away from a solo game of hoops. With his basketball under his arm, he crawled into the rearmost seat of the minivan.

Amanda, their fifteen-year old teenage daughter slid the door closed, shutting all three kids inside, while Kathy and Carter had words in the driveway.

Carter did the math for his wife. "The session ends at 8pm, my meeting with S.I.A. starts at 8:30pm. There's more than enough time for me to drop you and the kids off and drive into Lower Manhattan."

"Having enough time isn't the issue," she argued.

At the risk of infuriating her, he asked, "Then what's the issue?"

Her blue eyes widened and her eyebrows shot up to her hairline.

"Is that a real question?" she challenged.

Carter didn't have it in him to do this with her. He started for the minivan and caught sight of his youngest son, Matty, on one of the seats. If anything was traumatizing their son, it was this. Constant bickering.

"Carter!" she hissed, but he didn't stop.

He opened the driver's side door and climbed in behind the wheel, knowing full well that Kathy wouldn't dare make them late.

She took a good long moment to make her

point, though.

Folding her arms, she glared at him from where she stood in the driveway.

Carter turned the engine and flipped on the headlights as the minivan growled to life.

Behind Carter, Matty asked, "What's Mom doing?"

"Auditioning for Il Trovatore."

"What's 'ill travel torn'?" Matty wanted to know.

As Carter turned on the high beams, blinding his wife, he told Matty, "It's an Italian opera that's so dramatic, it doesn't make any sense."

Matty screwed his face up. "But Mom's a terrible singer."

"She knows that," he allowed. "But she also knows she'll always get cast for her beauty."

Carter dared to honk the horn, startling Kathy, and she gaped at him.

He told the kids over his shoulder, "It's time to yell at Mom."

Christopher and Amanda did not hesitate.

"Mom!"

"Let's go Mom!"

"Maaaaa'ooooom!" sang Christopher again, overlapping his sister's volume.

Matty got in on it, too, and finally Kathy shook her head, neared the minivan, and threw the passenger side door open.

Carter waited for her to close the door and buckle up.

As he backed out of the narrow driveway, shifted gears, and started down the street, Kathy asked the kids, "Who wants to go to the Cheesecake Factory after therapy?"

Carter knew what she was doing. He wasn't pleased.

But Christopher said, "I have a homework Zoom date with Ziggy."

Ziggy was Christopher's new *friend*, who looked like Pocahontas but was actually Filipino, an exchange student. She was some kind of math genius, so the jury was still out on whether Chris was truly interested in her or just using her to get better grades.

Amanda also declined, "One meal at the Cheesecake Factory is, like, literally three-thousand calories."

Kathy sank into a lump of quiet rage.

"Another time," Carter told her with a huge grin on his face.

"When will you be home?" she asked.

"Around ten."

"That sounds late to me," she complained.

"I got assigned a complicated case," he informed her, only slightly changing the subject. "Ten o'clock should sound early compared to the long hours I'm about to work."

As Kathy shook her head, Carter enjoyed his victory, guilt-free.

He had a right to maintain his boundaries. Dr. Murphy had taught him that. He had a right to live freely without walking on eggshells, and he had a right to dedicate as much time as he wanted to the Survivors of Incest Abuse meetings, and also to whatever S.V.U. case he was assigned.

If Dr. Ling had opened Carter's eyes to the master-slave dynamic he had been stuck in with Kathy, Dr. Murphy had broken the chains and set

Carter free.

Dr. Murphy's private practice was located in a brick office building on the southeast side of Kensington, nearly in the Midwood neighborhood of Brooklyn.

Situated on a tree lined street, the office building had its own parking section.

Dusk gradually darkened the skies, pulling the warm day towards an even warmer night, as Carter angled the minivan into a vacant parking spot right in front of the glass entrance doors.

As he killed the engine and pulled the key from the ignition, Kathy unbuckled, turned in her seat, and told the kids:

"Dr. Murphy is a very nice man. You can tell him anything, speak freely, and be honest. It's really important that all of us get as much as we can out of this meeting. We all have a lot to heal from after what happened to Matty."

"I'm fine, Mom," said Matty, but Kathy disagreed.

"Seriously, Mom," Christopher insisted, as he tried to spin his basketball on his finger. "We're kind of over it."

"Yeah," Amanda chimed in. She was so unenthusiastic about going inside that she hadn't even unbuckled yet. "Can't we just move on and live our lives?"

Kathy frowned, but admitted that she hoped they were right.

The family climbed out of the minivan.

As they made their way into the building, Carter checked his cell phone.

He hadn't been able to follow Eva Campopiano

back into the Holy Cross Chapel earlier that afternoon. Father Silva had essentially thrown him off of the St. Christopher's property and had made it clear to Carter that he wasn't welcome back. Technically, Silva couldn't prevent that. All Catholic churches maintained an 'open to the public' policy. Not to mention that any time Carter had official police business, of course he could return to St. Christopher's. But today, he hadn't pushed it.

He *had* updated Danny, however, who had experienced her own surprises and challenges with the ballet company.

Both detectives had yet to hear from Jill Andover, the M.E., though they had gotten word that the body had been transported to the morgue. Carter imagined that Jill was currently in the throes of conducting a thorough autopsy on Bobby Campopiano.

At the moment, he didn't have any missed calls or text messages, so he set his cell phone on silent and followed Kathy and the kids into the waiting area that served Dr. Murphy's patients as well as the patients of the other therapists in the complex.

They spent the fifty-minute session focusing on Matty and the kids. Dr. Murphy did an excellent job of keeping Carter and Kathy's issues off the table. Kathy was the only one who tried to bring up their strained dynamic, but Dr. Murphy wouldn't allow it. There was a boundary that divided parents from children, and in his professional opinion, the husband-wife relationship and tensions therein must remain private, hidden from the children.

The kids spoke freely, but Carter noticed it wasn't to Kathy's liking. Christopher boasted about his demanding sports schedule. Matty first proudly showed the therapist his spy pen, a toy gadget that Carter had bought for him when Matty had shown interest in being a private investigator. The pen was really an audio recording device. Kathy didn't like it. Nor did she like Matty 'wasting time' by going on and on about his spy pen.

Perhaps to please his mom, Matty began to open up about the fact that he had been having a hard time with a bigger boy at school and was struggling to maintain his other friendships, which was news to Carter. The way Matty told it, he had gradually become an outsider among his classmates. He felt strongly that his spy pen would get him back into the 'in crowd.'

Dr. Murphy offered practical advice to Matty. Amanda took the opportunity to tell her mom that she needed more space, and Dr. Murphy delicately led Amanda through the process of setting healthy boundaries with her mother, right then and there.

By the time the therapy session was over, Kathy's eyes were full of tears.

Carter touched her shoulder, but she shifted away, rejecting him.

Dr. Murphy noticed.

The kids were practically out the door, so Carter shouted, "Hey, Chris!"

When his son turned, he tossed the car keys and Christopher caught them.

"We'll be out in a minute," he told his son.

Matty followed Christopher out. Amanda was at their heels and closed the door without fully shutting it behind her.

Dr. Murphy asked Kathy, "Where is this reaction

coming from?"

"I feel ganged up on."

"Your children are healthy. They're dealing with normal everyday issues that come with being kids. They're not focused on what happened to Matty. Matty's not focused on what happened to him. He's concerned with trying to get along with a boy at school who sounds like a bully. Your children are happy, well-adjusted kids. This is good news, Kathy."

She put her foot down and directed her response to Carter.

"I don't want you to be a cop anymore. It's killing us. I want you to quit."

HAVING DROPPED Kathy and the kids off at the house, Carter drove into Lower Manhattan.

Earlier that month, Carter had been introduced to the Survivors of Incest Abuse meeting through a man named Wallace Bronson. He had been pursuing a lead, and Wally had turned out to be, not only one of the witnesses, but also one of the criminals in a triple homicide and two child abductions. One of the children had been Matty.

Wally had ended up behind bars, along with the true mastermind and killer, Damian Payne. But the victory had been a tragedy. Wally and Damian had become what their abuser had intended. Pedophiles who perpetuate the cycle. Carter hadn't, even though all three of them had been abducted as babies, held captive in a basement, and tortured for years until the police had eventually kicked the door down.

The case was closed. Carter had no investigative reason to continue attending the S.I.A. meetings that were held in the musty basement of a church in Lower Manhattan. Except that he wanted to. Other adult members here at S.I.A. had survived the Kensington basement with Carter. Carter liked spending time with them a few nights a week in the controlled setting of these anonymous meetings.

He also couldn't deny that attending S.I.A. had done more good for him and his mental health than a thousand marriage counseling sessions with Kathy ever could.

He could not believe that Kathy wanted him to resign from the force.

In fact, he refused to believe it.

He wasn't in the mood for coffee and donuts, but he poured himself a coffee anyway, pressed a lid on the disposable cup, and grabbed a chocolate glazed donut.

The meeting room was filling up. The folding chairs were already in a circle and most of the men had claimed their seats. There were a few new faces, but the majority of members were familiar to Carter.

As Carter found a chair, set his coffee and plated donut on the seat, and draped his suit jacket over the back of the chair, Football Forty—otherwise known as Marcus Stevens—entered the room.

In the triple homicide case, Marcus Stevens had been used by Payne as a pawn. Stevens had even been arrested for his brief involvement, but the charges were quickly dropped. Ultimately, Stevens had been innocent.

Stevens sat on one of the folding chairs across

from Carter. Carter shot the man a nod and Stevens returned the sentiment.

Soon the meeting got underway. With Wally in prison, there was a new man who ran the S.I.A. meetings. He also ran another S.I.A. group in the Bronx. Caucasian and probably in his 50s, Chuck Barnhardt looked like a long-haul truck driver. He smoked cigarettes outside every chance he got. As far as Carter had learned about the guy, he had been sexually abused by his aunt growing up, and because of it, Chuck couldn't hold a job or keep a woman for very long.

He had one hell of a sense of humor, though.

When it was Carter's turn to share, he realized that five minutes would not be enough time to clean out all the cans of worms inside of him. Kathy had put him in a pressure cooker. The Campopiano case was not going to solve itself. And his investigative partner was harboring a secret that Carter sensed would eventually bite both of them in the ass.

"I'm not religious. I never think about stuff like that," he began, surprising himself with the topic that was tumbling out of him. "But earlier today, I saw a statue outside of a church. It was a statue of a saint. But the saint didn't have a human head. It had the face of a dog. The body of a man. The head of a dog. Like some kind of monster. Like he had been cursed, and his human face had been replaced with a snarling snout, fangs, black soulless eyes, and coarse fur. He was some kind of animal...

"Maybe he had always been an animal..." he trailed off, wondering.

Carter pondered further, remembering the statue for a long moment, then asked himself, "How can a monster become a saint?"

CARTER LEFT THE church, stepping out into the warm night air. He carried his suit jacket instead of wearing it. He found his cell in the front pocket of his slacks. There was one missed call from Danny. She had texted a message, as well.

The city hummed with traffic, as he made his way up the sidewalk.

He had parked along the curb, and when he reached his wife's minivan, he read the text message.

'Just left you a voice message. Jill has a preliminary report. Meet me at Kings County Hospital?'

He checked the time, unlocked the minivan, and sent Danny a fast reply—*'On my way.'*

Kathy wasn't going to like it, but frankly, he would rather come home to her already asleep than come home to another argument.

As he cued up his wife's cell number, Marcus Stevens caught up with him on the sidewalk.

"Hey, Dobbs!"

S.I.A. was anonymous, but Carter had lost that privilege the second he had arrested Stevens. At least he would never have to explain his holstered police-issued gun when he wore it under his arm at the meetings.

"What's up, Marcus?"

"This belongs to you," he said, as he produced an antique pocket watch.

Carter had forgotten about the pocket watch. He had used it as bait to draw out the killer of his last case. But the killer, Payne, had sent Stevens to retrieve the watch. In the chaos of the arrest, Carter had lost sight of where the pocket watch had ended up.

"I figured this was in Evidence," he mentioned off-handedly to Stevens, as he took the pocket watch and turned it over in his hands.

"The police returned it to me when I was released," he explained. "But it's yours. You had the balls to face Daughtry. He gave it to you."

"Thanks, man," he told Stevens sincerely.

Carter felt his cell phone vibrating in his hand.

Stevens started off and said, "Have a good night."

"Take it easy," he replied.

It was Kathy calling.

Carter rounded to the driver's side of the minivan and climbed in behind the wheel. Once he shut the door, he answered the call.

"Hey—"

"I'm really sorry, Carter," she interrupted. She sounded emotionally drained. "I had a glass of wine and realized that the only person who has been negatively affected by what happened is me. I think I feel alone, or something. But I was wrong to try to drag you and the kids into a problem that doesn't belong to you. I'm sorry."

It sounded like Kathy had drank more than *one* glass of wine, but at least her heart was in the right place.

"I appreciate that," he promised. He went on to reassure her, "You and I still have our weekly meetings. You don't have to be alone with what you're feeling."

She sighed. "Thanks. Are you on your way home?"

"Danny called. I have to stop by the Medical Examiner's office. There's been a development."

"Are you kidding me?!"

Carter pulled the phone away from his mouth so his wife wouldn't hear him groan.

Her voice came shrill and distant through the line.

"How is this different from when you were gone working undercover for weeks on end?"

Carter could list about a dozen ways that his current position was different.

He found the courage to return his cell to his ear just in time for Kathy to split his ear drum.

"I'm sick of this, Carter! I'm sick of falling asleep in bed without my husband beside me!"

"I don't know what to tell you, Kathy! Wal-Mart's still processing my application to be a crappy manager! Keep your fingers crossed!"

"Are you getting cute with me?!"

"No, I'm hanging up now—"

"You better not!"

"I will see you later!"

"I'll be asleep!"

"Bye!"

He ended the call, tossed his phone on top of his suit jacket on the passenger seat, and ran his big hand down his face.

After taking a brief moment to compose himself, he started the minivan and pulled out into the street as soon as the steady stream of traffic cleared.

The ride over the Brooklyn Bridge that

connected Lower Manhattan to Brooklyn Heights took no time thanks to the late hour.

Traffic thinned out and the avenues were open with green lights once he hit Boerum Hill.

When he turned onto Flatbush Avenue, which cut through breezy Prospect Park, he rolled the windows down.

Warm wind slapped his face from all directions. The crisp scents of grass, trees, and blooming flowers livened him. It was that time of year. The Brooklyn Botanical Gardens had opened to the public, and the smell of flowers, especially dogwood, filled the park.

As he exited Prospect Park, he closed the minivan windows, trapping the fragrance.

It wasn't long before he reached the Kings County Hospital.

Carter found Danny inside the hospital, waiting for him in the corridor outside of the morgue.

Police Officer Quinlan was standing post, which piqued Carter's interest.

"Quinlan," he greeted the officer.

"Detective," replied Quinlan with a nod.

Danny explained, "Franco assigned Quinlan to stay with Jill for protection." She shrugged, adding, "It's probably overkill."

"Franco's looking at the big picture," Carter surmised, recalling the potentially dangerous elements of this case—the mob and a dirty judge. "It's probably a good idea."

Officer Quinlan looked over the moon, as he explained, "Cops will be stationed outside of Jill's apartment building every night, too. We're on round-the-clock protection detail orders."

"Congratulations," Carter told him, and Quinlan's cheeks turned pink. He pulled the door open for Danny and said, "Shall we?"

Deep inside the morgue, Jill was standing near a stainless steel table where a cadaver lay, covered with a white sheet.

"Did you get past my security detail okay?" Jill joked, but she was annoyed.

She wore a white lab coat and looked fresh, all things considered. She had been working with the body all day.

Carter told her, "Quinlan's a good guy."

She shot him a funny look then rolled her eyes at Danny.

"What?" asked Carter. "Any other cop would be checking his cell phone, unconvinced that anything was going to happen. Quinlan will take the assignment seriously."

"That's the problem," Jill pointed out. "He's been a little *too good* at his job. He's been on me all day. He's driving me nuts."

"Better safe than sorry," he reminded her, but Jill didn't seem to agree.

Jill pulled the white sheet down, revealing the cadaver's face, which belonged to Bobby Campopiano.

Though dead, Bobby resembled his older brother, Jimmy. He had the same thick, black hair. Same nose and jawline. Cheekbones that could cut glass.

Jill began walking them through her discovery.

"Bobby was found hanged, as you know. But he did not die by hanging."

Carter and Danny touched eyes then returned

their attention to the Medical Examiner.

"It takes between two to four minutes to hang to death. Many physiological processes go into motion, as the brain is deprived of oxygen, and those processes leave all kinds of evidence in the body."

Jill was doing an excellent job of keeping the details straightforward without any forensic jargon so that the two detectives could understand.

Carter had to ask, "He didn't die from the hanging?"

"No, and get this," she said, as a sideways grin spread across her face. "I can't rule out suicide."

"What?" asked Danny.

Jill cut to the chase. "He died of cyanide poisoning. I found the capsule, cracked, in his mouth."

"*What?*" Danny asked again, totally thrown.

She locked eyes with Carter.

Carter insisted, "There's no way this was a suicide."

Danny asked, "Jill, can you give us any kind of timeline between death by cyanide capsule and the hanging?"

Carter clarified, "How long between Bobby's cyanide-induced death and him being hanged?"

"That's the thing..." said Jill, perplexed. "It could have happened all at the same time or it could've happened in the span of twenty minutes. All I know is that the cause of death was cyanide poisoning, not hanging."

"Cyanide poisoning..." Danny breathed, thinking to herself.

"Cyanide capsule?" Carter asked himself, trying to wrap his head around the cause of death.

Jill reiterated, "Crazy as it sounds, this might have been an instance of suicide under duress."

Chapter Five

THE CAMPOPIANOS were seated around the dinner table at their mansion, not that anyone had an appetite.

Chandeliers overhead sparkled, reflecting the soft lighting.

The dining room had marbled floors, mirrored walls, gold trimming, and one very pissed off Italian-American family.

Guido Campopiano had been percolating with quiet rage ever since he had learned that his youngest son had been murdered.

Eva was a trembling shell of shock and disbelief.

Baby Rosa gurgled in Catherine's arms then grasped hold of Eva's hair, clamping her little fist around a brown lock.

Eva hardly noticed.

At eighteen years old, Eva Campopiano felt like she had one foot out of this family. In a matter of weeks, she would graduate from St. Christopher's Catholic School. Bobby had paved the way for her. He had succeeded at leaving the estate and making a life for himself. He had shown Eva that it was possible to be more than a Campopiano. Bobby had shown her that it was possible to be free.

But Bobby was dead.

He had gotten far, but his freedom hadn't lasted.

Eva looked around the table at her family. Every one of them had been furious that Bobby had left. Any one of them could've killed him, except for Lorenzo, obviously. He was only eight. And baby Rosa hadn't done it. But still...

She studied their faces.

At the head of the table, Guido Campopiano refreshed his wine glass with Merlot. His forlorn wife, Maria, was seated at the opposite end of the table. She hadn't touched her food.

Guido's elderly parents, Pasquale and Roseanna, were on one side of the table. They spoke Italian and had never given up their dream of returning to Sicily. Bobby's murder had hit them hard.

Beside them sat Jimmy, Catherine and the baby, and finally Eva.

On the other side were Maria's brother, Tony, and his wife Alice, both in their late 50s. Then there was their adult son Nico, who the kids called 'Cousin Nico,' Nico's wife Bianca, and their eight year old son, Lorenzo.

Ordinarily, Eva regarded her eight year old cousin as the most annoying thing in the world, but tonight she felt sorry for him.

Lorenzo kept looking at Eva for answers. She didn't have any. Every time she felt those tight brown eyes of his staring at her from across the table, she glanced at him and offered the slightest smile of reassurance.

Her father, Guido, was going to absolutely slaughter whoever had taken Bobby's life.

Whoever had done this to the family was going to pay.

Everyone around the table knew it.

And everyone was scared.

Including Father Silva.

The priest was seated between Lorenzo and Maria.

Eva was not pleased to have Father Silva with them.

She didn't like him.

Baby Rosa tugged Eva's hair, yanking her sideways, then the baby shrieked with joy, piercing everyone's ears.

"Rosa," Eva complained, as she tried to pry the baby's fist from her hair.

Lorenzo barely let out a chuckle.

Catherine helped, and soon Eva was free, which Rosa found very upsetting.

Jimmy suggested, "Why don't you take the baby upstairs?"

Catherine bounced Rosa to prevent an eruption of baby screams.

"She's okay," she softly sang, bouncing and rocking Rosa. "You're okay. She's okay."

Eva reached for one of the wine bottles that was on her side of the long table, but her mother, Maria, scowled.

"I'm just going to have a splash," she argued.

"No, you aren't, Eva," said her mother.

Eva folded her arms, unsurprised.

Maria asked everyone, "Are we ready for dessert?"

No one was enthusiastic, not even Maria.

Never-the-less, she pushed away from the stately dinner table and started for the kitchen.

As soon as she was out of sight, Eva poured herself more than a splash of Merlot, but had the good sense to get silent permission from her father before she brought the glass to her mouth.

Guido gave her a nod from the head of the table, and no one dared to object.

As Eva gulped the wine, Father Silva thanked Guido for dinner and broached the very sad subject at hand.

"The Requiem Mass for Bobby can be scheduled as early as tomorrow evening, or the day after?"

Guido scratched his chin and touched eyes with Jimmy.

"Day after tomorrow will give the family more time," Guido decided.

"Very good," said Silva. "Eva and Lorenzo are, of course, excused from classes. I'll handle those administrative aspects with St. Christopher's. This won't negatively affect Eva's graduation."

"I appreciate that, Father," said Guido, as Maria returned with a large tray of Italian desserts, serving utensils, and a stack of porcelain dessert plates.

The women with the exception of Catherine and the baby hopped up. Roseanna, Alice, Bianca, and Eva made room at the center of the table and helped Maria to set the large silver platter down. She had brought silver serving utensils, which the women used to begin cutting the various desserts.

Soon tiramisu, sultana cheesecake, and orange polenta cake were plated and passed around.

Father Silva eyed the desserts in front of him, picked up his fork, and had a bite of tiramisu.

"This is delicious," he told Maria.

"I can't take credit," she replied. "It's from Rocco's."

"Wonderful none-the-less," he complimented.

Eva wondered how Silva had an appetite, except that she was convinced the priest didn't care that Bobby had been killed. Father Silva hadn't liked Bobby anymore than he liked Eva, and frankly, Silva *didn't* like Eva. He was always on her case at school.

Father Silva went on, speaking to everyone but

addressing Guido, "I want you to know, I'm available twenty-four hours a day. All of St. Christopher's and the Diocese of Brooklyn are here for your emotional support and well-being. I will personally offer bereavement counseling, either here at the home or at the parish center. We've added Bobby's name to vespers, and with your permission, St. Christopher's would like to schedule a vigil for tomorrow evening."

Maria's eyes filled with tears. It was hitting her all over again.

Guido thanked the priest.

Father Silva stiffened on his chair. After a tense moment of thought, he offered, "I'm also available to hear confessions."

Tension rose in the air.

Guido narrowed his eyes on Silva.

Jimmy hardened and looked at his father.

After a moment's consideration, Guido told his family, "You all will make private arrangements with Father for Confession, understand? Every one of us is going to confess our sins before the Funeral Mass."

When Guido softened, Jimmy followed suit.

Guido said to the priest, "Thank you, Father. Let me walk you out."

Father Silva and Guido rose from the table.

As Guido walked the priest out of the dining room and through the grand foyer, Eva relaxed and there was a sense of relief around the table. The Catholic formality was over for the evening.

Baby Rosa started acting up. Catherine didn't need her husband, Jimmy, to suggest that she leave the table.

She scooted her chair backwards.

"She's getting fussy," she whispered to Jimmy.

Once Catherine left, there was no one between Eva and Jimmy.

Jimmy draped his arm across the back of the empty chair and squeezed Eva's shoulder.

She shot him a look.

"What are you looking at?" said Jimmy.

"What are *you* looking at?" she echoed, as they often did.

He squeezed her shoulder again, and she had to grin, but it still felt sad.

"Why don't you eat your dessert?" he asked.

"Why don't you pour me some wine?" she countered.

"Eva," Maria warned.

"I'm eighteen."

"That's right," said her mother.

"Nonna Roseanna," Eva said, speaking to her grandmother in Italian. "Qual è l'età legale per bere alcolici in Italia?"

Grandmother Roseanna told them, "Diciotto."

"See?" Eva said to her mother. "*Eighteen.*"

Maria shook her head and objected, "It doesn't matter what the legal drinking age in Italy is. This is America, and you're not twenty-one."

Jimmy, who had noticed Guido had permitted Eva a glass of wine earlier, took hold of the wine bottle and refreshed Eva's glass.

Maria pressed her mouth into a hard line and didn't look at either of her children.

Eva grinned at Jimmy.

But as she tried to sip her wine, Jimmy squeezed her shoulder, which made it hard to drink without giggling.

"You have to stop," she playfully warned him.

"*You* have to stop," he teased.

"Don't start," she said, lighthearted.

"I didn't start nothing, Eva," he joked, as he gave a lock of her brown hair a little tug. "Drink up. Pop wants to talk to us."

That got Maria's attention.

"Now?"

"He said after Father leaves, he wants to talk to us," Jimmy explained.

Eva gulped her wine then pushed away from the table with Jimmy.

As they made their way out of the dining room, the rest of the family started cleaning up.

Eva would've liked to have changed out of her Catholic school uniform, but at least she had let her hair down.

She walked through the large house with Jimmy.

Guido was still speaking with Father Silva in the marble foyer.

They came into their father's study, a large office with plush carpeting, mahogany furniture, and leather sofas and settees. It smelled faintly of cigar smoke and cologne.

Jimmy eased the door closed, but didn't shut it. Guido would join them soon.

He asked his sister, "You okay?"

"Why would I be okay?"

"You know what I mean."

She did.

He reminded her, "Nobody saw Bobby since Christmas. I think we would all be falling apart if we saw him yesterday, you know?"

She was guarded with her agreement, because it was a lie. "Right."

"Hey, sit down," he told her.

The options were a Remington Chesterfield leather sofa or a matching leather armchair, so she took the corner of the sofa. Jimmy sat next to her in the armchair.

"Did you talk to the cops at all?" he asked her.

Jimmy knew that a detective had told her the news of Bobby's murder. She knew what his question meant.

"No," she said.

"Did that detective say anything weird about Silva?"

"Silva was there with me," she reminded him. "They say anything weird to *you* about Silva?"

"Yeah, that's what Pop is going to talk to us about."

"What about Silva?"

"Wait for Pop," he told her. "Did that detective tell you what happened to Bobby?"

She shook her head, *no*.

They heard footsteps approaching the study. Guido was about to enter the room.

Jimmy insisted at a whisper, "Don't talk to the cops, you got that?"

She needed to know, "Aren't they going to find who did this to Bobby? Wouldn't talking to them help?"

"Don't push it, Eva," he warned, as Guido eased the large, mahogany door open, coming into the study. "Are you going to listen to me?"

"Yes," she hissed before they both gave their father their full attention.

Guido closed the door behind himself and told them, "Your mother won't be joining us."

As their father neared them, Jimmy knew to sit beside Eva on the leather sofa, making room for Guido to sit in the armchair.

Jimmy draped his arm behind Eva, across the back of the sofa.

Their father unbuttoned the cuffs of his button-down shirt and rolled his sleeves up.

"We have a big problem," he told his children.

He produced a cigar from his breast pocket. The glass coffee table in front of them had a cigar clipper, ash tray, and a lighter. Guido proceeded to clip and light his cigar, as he further explained:

"I don't know what the hell happened to Bobby, but let me tell you. Bobby wasn't collateral damage. This has nothing to do with *the restaurant*."

"How do you know that, Pop?" Jimmy asked, tense.

Eva didn't know what to think. She was still working on believing the fact that Bobby had in fact been killed. It made no sense. She had *just seen him* that morning.

Doubt filled Guido's mind. But he maintained, "I know because it makes no effing sense, that's how I know."

Guido puffed his cigar and thick clouds of smoke billowed up all around him.

He asked his daughter, "What do you know about it?"

"I don't know anything."

"Did the detective talk to you?" Guido pointed out.

"He didn't tell me anything," she promised. "He

told me Bobby had been killed."

Guido leaned forward and pointed his thick finger in Eva's face.

"If I find out the cops told you something that you're not telling me, or if I find out that you told them something that you're not coming clean with right now, you're going to be in very big trouble, young lady."

Eva felt her heart rate spike. Her cheeks flushed hot and her mouth went dry.

She had seen Bobby that morning. She had told the detective. And her father didn't know about either.

Jimmy pushed, "Eva?"

She swallowed the lump in her throat. When she spoke, her voice sounded thin and weak.

"I don't know anything."

Jimmy insisted to their father, "She doesn't know anything, Pop."

Guido leaned back, accepting her answer. "Okay."

He puffed his cigar, thought long and hard, and told them:

"Bobby was hanged. Definitely a homicide, but there was a suicide note that the cops think is fake."

Eva gaped and looked at Jimmy.

Her brother didn't seem surprised.

Jimmy told her, "I was here when the cops told Pop all that."

"Hanged?" she breathed.

Guido went on. "The suicide note implicated Father Silva. Alleged that Father had abused Bobby. Crazy."

"Crazy," Jimmy agreed.

It didn't sound that crazy to Eva, but she held her tongue.

"What this tells me," Guido went on, "is that whoever did this had some kind of *impression* of Father Silva, if you know what I mean."

Jimmy pulled his arm from around Eva. He clasped his hands together and didn't look his father in the eye when he stated:

"I don't see Bobby speaking ill of Father, I don't."

"Calm down, Jimmy, we need to think this through."

"You think Bobby *lied* about Father to someone, and then that person killed *Bobby*?" Jimmy questioned.

"Like I said, son, I don't know what the hell to think," Guido admitted. "But I'll tell you this, between the three of us, we're going to find the son-of-a-bitch before the cops do. And we're going to deal with it ourselves, you understand?"

Jimmy complained, "I wouldn't know where to start. Bobby had cut ties with us. What are we supposed to do here? Eh? It's not like he was going to St. Christopher's. He graduated, what? Five years ago? He wasn't going to Mass, either."

Guido figured, "It's starting to sound like someone from the ballet world did this, what do you think?"

Jimmy shook his head. Like his father, he didn't know what to think.

"What if Bobby's murder was part of a set up? What if the killer only killed Bobby to frame Father?"

"Who would do that?"

Again, Jimmy shook his head. He ran his fingers through his black, slicked hair.

"Someone from the church?" he guessed, unsure.

"Give me a name," Guido pushed.

"I can't," Jimmy admitted.

Guido gave it a rest. He puffed his cigar and thought deeply to himself.

Then he told Eva, "This is why you don't leave the family, you understand?"

Jimmy told his dad, "Let me get her to bed."

Eva slid off the sofa and gave her father a kiss on the cheek.

"Night, Pop."

"Love you, princess."

Jimmy walked Eva out of the study, through the house, and up the wide staircase to the second floor of their huge home.

Her bedroom was at the rear of the mansion, between their grandparents' bedroom and Lorenzo's bedroom. She had her own bathroom and enough space to have a portable ballet floor with a ballet barre fit in front of the large picture windows.

Jimmy followed Eva into her bedroom, as Lorenzo zipped through the hallway on his energetic way to his parents' bedroom.

"Sleep well, Lorenzo!" Eva called out just before Jimmy shut the door.

In the privacy of her bedroom, her brother took hold of her shoulders.

He told her, "Bobby wasn't like us."

"I know."

He stroked her brown hair off her shoulders and tucked the locks behind her ears.

He searched her eyes for a long moment.

"Go to Confession like Pop said, but don't open up as if you can trust Silva. You can't."

"I know," she agreed.

"Good."

He relaxed a bit, pulled her in, and kissed her forehead.

When he urged her back again to look her in the eye, he asked, "Do you still have it?"

She knew exactly what Jimmy was referring to.

She neared her huge vanity desk that had an oval mirror, drawers, and several jewelry boxes.

Jimmy came up behind her, as she opened the top drawer, found a little pill box, and opened it, showing her brother that inside, she still had the little glass cyanide capsule that their grandfather had given her long ago.

Their great-grandfather, now deceased, had fought in the Second World War under Mussolini. Italian soldiers had been supplied with cyanide capsules in case they were captured by the Russian Soviets, who had been notoriously torturing POWs after the Stalingrad disaster. Their great-grandfather had given their grandfather, Pasquale, the cyanide capsules. When Pasquale had come to the U.S., he had brought the suicide capsules, and years later, when he had fully grasped the family business that Guido had gotten tangled up in, Pasquale had a bizarre moment of clarity and secretly gave his grandchildren all of the suicide capsules.

"You need to keep the capsule with you at all times," he said.

"You're scaring me."

"Eva, listen to me. If anyone comes for you, you

have to kill yourself."

Chapter Six

O'TOOLE'S WAS packed, loud, and rowdy.

For a Thursday night, this was unusual.

But the weather was warmer. Residents of Kensington didn't have to hole up in their apartments to avoid rain storms or bitter winds. The rainy months had passed. Summer would soon press in with brutal heat and humidity. Anyone who wanted to enjoy fair weather and a fun night had to get out while the *gettin' was good.*

O'Toole's bar sat on Caton Avenue just shy of Ocean Parkway. As an Irish pub, the bar mainly served cops, firefighters, and other working class locals. But on nights like tonight, a younger crowd had piled into the place.

It was great for business.

Young women wobbled on high heels, thrilled about their upcoming college graduations. Shouting over each other and competing with the loud sea of voices, these girls draped themselves around each other and sloshed their pints of beer, while men from all walks of life lined up to buy them drinks.

Tommy O'Toole was glad he had hired more bartenders and barbacks, but that didn't mean he was in a good mood.

Ordinarily, he would spend busy nights like this carrying cases of beer out and running around. Or he would get stuck behind the bar, cracking open bottles and collecting cash non-stop.

With the additional hires, Tommy could afford to take it easy, have a beer, and spend the majority of the evening in his office in the back, which he was doing now.

The crowd, those overlapping voices, and the loud bar music sounded muffled through the walls.

Tommy sat behind his desk. There was a computer, vendor folders, a mug full of pens, and a few stacks of cash on the desk.

He had been nursing a longneck bottle of beer for so long, the alcohol was room temperature. He didn't care. He was trying to make sense of all the wrong turns he had made in life, especially recently.

He couldn't tell which had been a bigger blow to his happiness, Danny walking into his life, or her walking out of it.

Wrestling with hard emotions wasn't Tommy's strong suit.

He had genuinely thought that they could be a family—Danny, Tommy, and the baby.

But wrapping his head around what had happened felt impossible.

He'd had no knowledge that he had gotten Danny pregnant until after their infant son had died.

Tommy shook his head, brought his beer to his mouth, and drank.

Danny hadn't told him that he had gotten her pregnant. Nine months had lapsed, and during that period, they hadn't seen one another.

But when they got back together, he had forgiven her for that. He had recovered from two consecutive shocks—the existence of the baby and his subsequent death. He had even made a fresh start with her, having decided deep down in the pit of his soul that the choice to love her would bring meaning to his life and happiness into his heart.

It had.

But it hadn't lasted.

Nora had killed their son. Danny had found out and done nothing about it. She hadn't told Tommy. She hadn't reported the crime. And from where Tommy had been standing, all of this came to light when Nora, herself, had confessed the infanticide to him.

'I wasn't about to let that bratty baby come between me and my daughter,' she had sneered at Tommy. *'Do you really think I'm going to allow you to be with her? Stay away from her.'*

He felt his eyes widen at the memory. Nora's almost cartoonish threats. She was a frail, little old woman who wore cardigan sweaters and used too much hairspray.

Appearances could be deceiving, evidently.

Tommy concluded that Danny's appearance had been deceiving, as well. Had to have been. She was an endless abyss of secrets and lies. But damn if she wasn't beautiful, fun, and rough around the edges. Danny was more than his type.

She was perfect.

He had to wonder what the hell was wrong with him. He should have been able to write her off by now. Damn, he should've gone to the police himself to have Nora arrested. But he hadn't.

Why?

The screensaver on his desktop computer appeared—a photo of Gregory that Danny had given him.

He nudged the computer mouse, and the screen came back to life. His bookkeeping software was open, showing a profit and loss report.

O'Toole's had dipped into the red last month when the rains had kept customers away. But the past week or so had more than made up for it.

He took hold of one of the stacks of cash, eyed the Capital Investment line item on the P&L, and used his calculator with his free hand to figure out the value of last month's 'investors' draw.'

That's what he was calling it so his tax filings would make sense to the I.R.S.

An *investors' draw*.

But that wasn't what this was.

After crunching the numbers, Tommy counted out seventeen crisp one-hundred dollar bills and fought the urge to drive his fist through a wall.

If anyone had warned him this would happen, he would have never opened O'Toole's. A little Irish pub in a sleepy corner of Kensington should not have been a target. But over the years, as the neighborhood had turned and new businesses had shown up and the market value of every slice of real estate had increased, so had the risks.

There came a loud knock at the door.

"Yeah?" Tommy called out, as he stuffed an envelope with the cash he had counted.

One of his barbacks opened the door and poked his head into the office.

"Got a guy here to see you, Tommy. He said the back door was locked."

"Right," he replied, improvising. He wasn't expecting anyone until tomorrow. "Let him in. Thanks, man."

The barback pushed the door open for Jimmy Campopiano to enter. As Jimmy stepped inside the office, the barback returned to the loud, busy bar.

"How you doin', Tommy?" the slick Italian-American asked.

The gel in his black hair was as shiny as the three-piece suit he wore.

As Jimmy closed the door behind himself, Tommy kept a lid on his anger.

"Busy night," he said dryly.

"It's no problem," said Jimmy, as if Tommy had apologized.

He had a look around, as he crossed the room.

Tommy stood, but stayed on the business side of his desk. The envelope of cash was already in his hand.

"I was expecting you tomorrow before opening," he mentioned. "The date stays the same. That's the deal."

Jimmy shrugged. "It *is* tomorrow."

"It's one minute past midnight," Tommy pointed out.

The man smiled. "Like I said."

Tommy stooped and used his mouse to click his way through printing the profit and loss report for his unwanted overlord.

Jimmy softened and mentioned, "I had to come tonight. Found out I won't be available tomorrow. There's a family matter I have to focus on."

As the printer came to life and the one-sheet began stuttering out of the machine, Jimmy remarked, "Business looks good."

"Now it does," he allowed. "The rainy months put us under."

When the report finished printing, Tommy handed it to Jimmy with the envelope.

Jimmy eyed the report, skimming quickly, then folded it in thirds, tucked it into the envelope, and slid the envelope into the inner pocket of his suit jacket.

All the while, Tommy kept a lid on his boiling rage.

Jimmy explained, "In the coming days, I'll be hard, but not impossible, to reach. Your bar is in good hands, though. We'll keep an eye on it."

"I'm sure you will," he seethed between clenched teeth.

Tommy had been paying the mob for protection in the neighborhood, not that he needed it.

They both knew that Tommy had really been paying the Campopianos every month so that his bar wouldn't mysteriously burn to the ground or get shot up in a drive-by shooting or suffer any of the other consequences that the crime family was capable of exacting against O'Toole's.

"Cute baby," Jimmy remarked when the desktop screensaver of Gregory filled the screen again. "My wife and I have a two month old."

"That's my son. He's dead," Tommy said darkly.

As Jimmy grew serious, a glimmer of compassion filling his brown eyes, Tommy could tell he was moments away from losing it.

He had been losing control for years without realizing it. The cold, hard truth was staring him in the face now, though. Impossible to ignore. He had lost control of his bar, lost control of his emotions, lost control of his life, and the list went on. He couldn't get Danny out of his head, which proved he had lost control of his mind.

He knew it was only a matter of time before he completely lost control of his fists.

"I'm sorry to hear that," Jimmy said earnestly.

"He was killed..."

Tommy had no idea what he was doing. Maybe rubbing his own personal hell in Jimmy Campopiano's face would distract him from the madness that was hijacking his personality.

"What are you talking about, O'Toole?"

When Tommy sat down on his office chair instead of answering, Jimmy reminded him, "Listen, Tommy, what do you think we're doing here, eh? We're here to protect you. Did someone threaten you?"

"No—"

"Someone killed your son? What do you think we're here for? Nobody messes with you. Who did it? Do you know?"

Tommy stared at Jimmy for a long moment.

Jimmy told him, "I can tell by the way you're looking at me that you didn't know I've got your back. But I do. Our relationship isn't just about your bar, Tommy. It's about you and me. Tommy O'Toole and the Campopianos. What happened?"

Mulling the situation over, Tommy sank into deep thought.

Jimmy leaned over the desk and promised him, "You're part of my family, Tommy. You want someone dead, all I need is a name. You don't have to share the planet with someone who killed your baby, you understand? You give me a name, I'll remove the guy from the face of the earth."

Chapter Seven

AS THE ORANGE sun dawned over Brooklyn, harsh light cut through the bathroom window and cast shadows across Danny's face, causing her reflection in the medicine cabinet mirror to look grotesque.

On the porcelain sink counter in front of her were a slew of makeup bottles and concealer wands. She couldn't afford to suffer another day of everyone at the 66th asking her what had happened to her face.

The scratches had flattened and faded. No longer red and raised, the marks that her mother had given her weren't impossible to mask under a thick layer of taupe foundation.

She dabbed the liquid makeup onto her skin, caking on another coat to cover the worst scratch that spanned her cheek. Her chin didn't look quite as bad.

She took a step back and studied her reflection. She looked washed out, but otherwise normal.

After streaking rose-colored blush across her cheekbones and smearing pink lipstick onto her asymmetrical mouth, she decided that would do and trailed into her bedroom where she shoved her police-issued Glock into the holster on her hip, threw on a thin, black blazer, and ran out the door.

When she reached the lobby, the building super, an old Russian man by the name of Camil Usov, stepped aside. He was sweeping. The glass entrance door was wide open and fresh spring air breezed through.

"Доброе утро," Camil said in Russian, giving her an easy smile.

She returned a smile. "Good morning to you, too."

She was nearly out the door when Camil asked, "I haven't seen your mother in awhile. Is everything well?"

People tended to 'mind their own' in Kensington, but Danny had developed a rapport with Camil over the years, going out of her way to be polite to compensate for her mother's cold regard for the man.

She slowed her step, turned on her heel, and told him over her shoulder, "If she tries to enter the building, don't let her."

His friendly demeanor stiffened and the cheerful smile on his face fell flat. Turning serious, he locked eyes with her and nodded.

"We have saying in Russia. 'Лояльность бесплатна, но ее можно заработать'."

She raised her eyebrows, waiting for a translation.

"Loyalty is free, but earned."

"Yeah," she agreed. "But who pays for betrayal?"

He frowned and shrugged. "Everyone."

She nodded. "See you later, Camil."

The warm, spring air antagonized Danny's low mood, as she walked north on Ocean Parkway, making her way towards Prospect Park.

The sun was shining, birds chirped in the tree tops, and all of Prospect Park smelled of sweet dogwood flowers. She jogged across an intersection when the traffic light was in her favor, and used one of the cobblestone walking paths that cut through the park to get to the Brooklyn Ballet.

While Carter reconvened with Jill and the forensics unit this morning at the Kings County Hospital Medical Examiner's Office, Danny had to pursue the possibility that one of the dancers from the ballet company was responsible for Bobby Campopiano's bizarre, 'staged suicide' murder.

Danny had barely scratched the surface with the ballet dancers, Eric MacDermott and Tracy Jones. There were more ballet dancers to question and angles to explore. She planned to hook up with Carter at the precinct after her visit to the Brooklyn Ballet.

Situated on the northwestern corner of Prospect Park, directly beside the Brooklyn Botanical Gardens, was the Brooklyn Center for the Performing Arts, a modernist travertine glass and stone venue that hosted theatrical stage plays, traditional operas, and of course classical ballets.

The tremendous venue reminded Danny of a poor man's Lincoln Center, but that wasn't the first thought on her mind, as she crossed the grand plaza, coming towards the glass entrance.

The most promising lead they had at this point was the fact that Bobby had died of cyanide poisoning.

Had Bobby taken his own life, a desperate act committed under the duress of realizing he was about to be murdered?

Jill had not ruled out the possibility.

But had that been the story?

If so, had the killer noticed?

What if Jill was on the right track, but not entirely correct? What if the killer had forced Bobby to crack the cyanide capsule between his teeth? The crime scene had been a staged mess of convoluted clues, after all. A hanging. A suicide note. Hands tied behind the dead man's back, which had practically screamed that this had been a homicide...

And what about the knot that had anchored Bobby's dead, hanging body to the masonry hook on the brick wall near the floor?

Danny wondered if she should be looking for someone who enjoyed recreational sailing...

The outdoor marquees were flanked by giant Romeo & Juliet posters, advertising the upcoming ballet. In the advertisements, two exquisitely posed ballet dancers, romantically wrapped around one another, seemed to leap off the poster. Romeo and Juliet, she presumed.

Danny entered the building and stepped into the cold, dry air of the Brooklyn Center for the Performing Arts.

There was a long, sleek receptionist's desk on the far side of the gleaming, marble lobby.

Danny had her badge in her hand by the time she reached the woman behind the counter who looked as slick and polished as the building itself.

"I'm Detective Foster," she said with authority. "Where can I find the Brooklyn Ballet?"

"The Box Office is around the corner. When you leave the building, turn left and you can't miss it," she said, as a smug look came over her otherwise pretty face.

"I'm investigating a homicide."

"I'm doing my job," the woman countered.

"I don't need the Box Office, and I think you know that."

"I don't work for you. You work for me. I pay your salary, and I happen to know that no one is ever obligated to speak with the police." She shot Danny another smug smile and added, "The door is behind you. Have a nice day."

It had been awhile since Danny had felt beneath someone, not that that was how she felt now. But it did occur to her that she was attempting to infiltrate a high level of society that knew she didn't belong. If a low-rung receptionist could treat Danny like the dirt beneath her designer heel, Danny had a feeling that the higher up the food chain she climbed, the more resistance she would be met with.

She formed a wicked smirk on her face, glaring down at the snobby girl, and told her, "I will have a nice day, thank you."

With that, she continued through the lobby, heading straight for the bay of elevators.

"Hey!" shouted the receptionist. "Excuse me? You can't interrupt the ballet company!"

The second elevator dinged, and as the doors whooshed open, the receptionist yelled, "Opening night is less than a week away! You can't bother them!"

Danny ducked into the elevator, turned around, and smiled to herself as the elevator doors whooshed closed.

It didn't take a degree in rocket engineering to find the Brooklyn Ballet's rehearsal space on the fifth floor.

The double-doors of the rehearsal room were open. Professional ballet dancers were seated in the hall, massaging their feet, inhaling protein bars, stretching their muscles, and otherwise refueling their energy.

There was excitement in the air, but to Danny it felt like quiet tension. The dancers were serious, focused, and blocking out the world, in a sense.

When one of the female ballet dancers glanced up at Danny, Danny asked, "Have you seen Eric MacDermott?"

"Friar Lawrence and the Nurse are rehearsing with Jasper."

Jasper was the choreographer, and the artistic director was another strange, petite fellow that Danny had met briefly the day prior.

As she peeked her head into the rehearsal room where Eric and Tracy were passionately flinging each other around the room, the ballerina on the floor said, "I wouldn't interrupt them if I were you."

Regarding the girl with the same brazen attitude that she had used on the receptionist, Danny kindly pointed out, "You're not me."

She slipped into the room, stepped softly onto the gray marley floor, and ignored the ballerina when she muttered, "Thank God."

"Can I help you?" asked the choreographer, Jasper, obviously angered at the detective who had dared to enter his rehearsal.

"Detective Foster," she informed him. "I'm with Homicide," she stated quickly, because it would trigger the least questions. "I spoke with the artistic director yesterday, but I have some questions for you, too. And I would like to talk to Eric and Tracy again. This is about Bobby Campopiano's murder."

Tracy and Eric were fighting to catch their breath. Jasper crossed the floor in his bare feet. He was a petite man, probably a retired ballet dancer himself. He wore thin, tight sweatpants and a very annoyed expression on his glowing face.

"I regret that Bobby was cast in Romeo and Juliet," he told Danny frankly, as if the man's death had sabotaged Jasper's entire career. "And if I'm being honest here, I strongly disagreed with the Brooklyn Ballet's decision to hire Bobby for the ballet company in the first place."

"Because he wasn't a very good ballet dancer?" Danny asked, having learned as much from the other dancers.

Jasper winced as if a sudden thought had pained him. "Good, not good, doesn't matter. *I* can make *anyone* look good. You should see what I do with my high schoolers every winter when they're cast in the Nutcracker."

Eva Campopiano came to mind.

"Bobby Campopiano… What can I say? Bad luck followed him wherever he went," said Jasper.

Being born into the Campopiano crime family was the first explanation that came to mind, but Danny didn't want to assume anything.

"What do you mean?" she asked.

Jasper shook his head. "It was that boyfriend of his. Drama queen," he grumbled.

"Boyfriend?"

"It was always something with him," he ruminated, having fallen into such deep thought that he hadn't noticed Danny's surprise to learn Bobby had been gay. "You know, when someone is toxic, you have to get them out of your life. But Bobby couldn't see it. Paul showed up unannounced and unwanted less than a handful of times. Not much, right? But Paul put Bobby into a bad frame of mind.

Paul was a toxic, controlling, manipulative lover."

"Paul?" Danny said to herself as she found her notepad and pen that she kept in the pocket of her blazer. "Can you tell me Paul's last name?"

"Decker," he told her. "He works next door at the Brooklyn Botanical Gardens. Don't let the pretty face fool you. He was way too old for Bobby. My God, Bobby was a baby. Only twenty-five years old. What the hell was he doing with a controlling, narcissistic old man like Paul?"

"How old is Paul?"

"At least fifty years old."

"That's quite an age difference."

"He was one hell of a mean sugar daddy."

"Sugar daddy?" Danny questioned.

Bobby didn't need a sugar daddy. He belonged to the wealthiest family in Kensington, maybe the wealthiest family in all of New York City aside from the Rockefellers, Bloombergs, and Murdochs.

"If it hadn't been for Paul, Bobby would've been sleeping on the street. His family had totally cut him off, or at least that was the impression he gave."

All of this was news to Danny. Valuable news.

"Do you know if Paul and Bobby had a serious fight before he was killed?"

Jasper's eyebrows shot up to his hairline. "Do I know if they had a serious fight? Honey, all they did was have serious fights. Their entire romance was a passionate fling of rage, break ups and make ups, black eyes and broken bones."

Danny turned her attention onto Eric and Tracy. "Why didn't you mention this to me?"

Tracy held her head high and admitted, "Bobby did not want his family to know he was gay. You're investigating the murder. It's obvious you're talking to the Campopianos. If I had told you, and you used that information to get the Campopianos to, I don't know, tell you more stuff..." she trailed off, shaking her head.

"Bobby might be dead, but I'm still going to respect his wishes," she concluded. "And you should, too."

BACK AT THE 66th, Danny headed straight for her desk. She fanned the thin tee shirt she was wearing in an attempt to cool her slick skin. The blazer had caused quite a sweat during her walk, but she had stubbornly kept it on.

Carter was seated at his desk. Brutal sunlight seared through the windows. The old, loud air conditioners in the precinct couldn't compete.

"How did it go with Jill?" she asked.

Carter glanced up at her, but his attention was stolen.

She hadn't even pulled out her chair when Detectives Crouse and Toliver ambushed her from behind.

"We need to talk, Danny," said Crouse.

Carter screwed his face up and demanded. "Are you going to tell me what's going on?"

"That's what we would like to know," Toliver added like a smart ass.

Danny wasn't about to make a scene, not when keeping a lid on this thing was the only thing keeping her sane.

"It's fine, Carter," she told her concerned, confused partner. "I'll just be a minute."

She followed the homicide detectives through the bullpen. She didn't have to guess that they were taking her into one of the interview rooms. It was a foregone conclusion.

As they entered the small interrogation room, Toliver having held the door open for Danny as if he could pass for a gentleman, and Crouse keeping at her heels like a nipping hound, Danny reminded them, "You boys know I'm not going to talk to you, and by now you should know that I'm also not going to let you make a scene in front of my partner and the rest of the Special Victims Unit."

"Have a seat, sunshine," said Crouse.

He pulled out a chair for her. Danny folded her arms, refusing. She would rather stand for a thousand years than get comfortable.

"Fine," said Crouse.

The homicide detectives sat down. There was a laptop computer on the table, which was open. Detective Toliver clicked a few buttons, as his older, basset hound partner told Danny:

"There are some things we know, and there are some things we don't know. There's one thing we care about, and another thing that we're curious about, but we don't really care that much. We want to 'make nice' here, Danny. Do you believe me?"

She stared at him, dead-pan and unemotional.

"You look pretty, by the way," he added, referring to the thick makeup she wore. "It doesn't even look like your mother had to claw your face off to prevent her own murder."

Danny refused to be rattled.

Crouse chuckled, and finally Toliver cued up whatever files he had been looking for.

Detective Crouse sobered up, not that his sense of humor had been very funny.

"We're homicide detectives. We care about homicides. Attempted homicides are less interesting. Consider yourself off the hook... for now."

Detective Toliver told her, "We talked to Jill. Your son was killed. That's what we're investigating at the moment."

He tapped a key on the laptop, and soon Nora's worried sounding voice played through the speakers.

Danny recognized what she was hearing.

The detectives were playing Nora's 911 call from the night that Danny had come home and discovered her son dead in his crib.

Emotions surged, tearing Danny's chest wide open. Tears stung her eyes, listening to the call, and her mind started reeling.

Unlike the night itself when Danny had held her lifeless infant, now that she was listening to Nora's 911 call, Danny realized that her mother sounded... *unaffected.*

It was a struggle, but she found her voice and said, "Stop."

"Pardon?" said Crouse, delighted to have gotten a rise out of her.

"Stop the recording."

Detective Crouse told her, "Nora lied to us about several things. She was there that night. Are you going to tell us what happened?"

"What do you think?" she snapped.

Crouse and Toliver exchanged a look, and Danny knew what would come next.

Hardball negotiations.

Toliver laid their cards on the table. "This is what we're after, Foster. We think your mom killed Gregory. And considering that you tried to strangle Nora to death, we're willing to bet that you think your mom killed Gregory, too. You're going to cooperate with us, as we pursue this."

"Help you put my mother in prison?"

"If you don't, then honey, you're going to look like an accomplice to murder. A career-focused mother who didn't give a damn about her own kid—"

Danny lunged at Toliver, angled her finger in his face, and raged, "You don't know the first thing about me, Toliver! You keep your damn mouth shut, or I will shut it for you!"

"Easy, Foster, easy," said Crouse, as he laid his big hand protectively across Toliver's chest, urging his partner back against his chair.

She pressed her mouth into a hard, crooked line, and forced air into her lungs, inhaling deeply through her nostrils, as she paced away.

Crouse pointed out, "You have to admit, sweetheart, if you don't want your son's killer caught, and you were there that night... It really doesn't look good."

"I don't give a crap how it looks," she said, as she threw the door open and stormed out.

She heard Crouse call after her, "We gotta bring it to Franco, honey! The captain after that!"

She paused, slowing her step.

The threat slammed into her like a two-ton anvil, and she was surprised the blow didn't send her flying down the hallway.

She would've loved to turn on her heel, charge back in that room, and show them what she was made of. But if her objective was to stay out of jail, she had no choice but to keep walking and let the chips fall where they may.

The second she reached her desk, she told Carter, "We need to go, now."

"Now?"

"Right now," she insisted.

Carter was on his feet in a blink. He grabbed his suit jacket from the back of his chair, and they crossed the bullpen and were out the door before Homicide could chase after Danny, pull her into Franco's office, and tighten the figurative noose that was already clamped around her neck.

The Crown Vic was parked in front of the precinct.

Carter jumped in the driver's seat. Danny threw the passenger side door open, climbed in, and as soon as Carter started the engine, a wall of stagnant heat punched her in the face. She rolled her window down the first chance she got.

As Carter pulled into the street, he mentioned, "Can't wait for August when the scalding heat and humidity drives everyone in Brooklyn to murder each other out of irritability and impatience."

"Yeah," she said, matching his sarcasm. "That's pretty much my Christmas."

"The cyanide detail gives us an excuse to talk to the Campopianos."

She agreed and suggested, "Rocco's?"

"Rocco's Italian Restaurant, it is," he confirmed.

As they made their way through Brooklyn's tight grid of crawling traffic, Danny pulled herself together mentally.

Crouse and Toliver weren't bluffing. In fact, the detectives had been going easy on her. They could've gone to Franco from the jump, reported to the captain, and made Danny's life a waking nightmare. They hadn't done that. Not yet. They had given her a day, hadn't they?

But the grace period was over.

She cursed under her breath.

Carter grumbled, glanced at her, and couldn't hold his tongue any longer.

"Are you going to let me help?"

"Help what?" she asked even though she knew exactly what he was referring to.

"Homicide has been on your ass, and it's not because it's shaped like a peach."

She burst out laughing and stared at him, wide eyed with tickled horror. "Don't you go noticing my ass, Carter."

He hadn't meant to be funny. He found none of this funny.

"Why are they talking to you?"

"Give it a day," she darkly promised him.

He couldn't tear his attention away from her. But when the traffic light turned red, he squeezed the brakes and came to his senses.

So did she.

"Bobby was gay," she said out of the blue.

"How do you know?"

"The ballet dancers and the choreographer, the whole ballet company in fact, they all knew. It was common knowledge."

"Okay...?"

"He had a boyfriend. An older man named Paul

Decker. I got the impression that Paul was controlling and violent."

"Possible suspect?"

"He's worth checking out," Danny said. "He works at the Botanical Gardens, but I didn't swing by."

Carter ruminated, turning quiet, as the grid of streets tightened. Now every street was one-way.

The detectives looked at the numbers. Danny leaned forward on her seat.

"Hook a left at the next intersection," she suggested. "We'll have to circle around to get to Rocco's since it's on a one-way street."

Carter squeezed the brakes and flipped on the turn signal, while a thick stream of traffic flowed in the opposite lanes. He would have to wait for traffic to clear in order to make the left.

The sedan behind him wasn't happy about it.

The driver honked, and Carter glared at the guy in the rearview mirror.

"The Catholicism," he said, thinking out loud, while they waited for a chance to turn. "The machismo Italian-American attitude… I doubt the Campopianos were happy to have a gay son."

"According to the ballet dancers, the family didn't know. They had cut Bobby off in fact."

"Financially?"

"That's what Eric and Tracy told me. Was that really the case? I don't know," she allowed. "But I believe them. I believe Bobby told them that his family had cut him off. As far as the dancers knew, Bobby kind of had to shack up with his toxic lover, Paul, to keep a roof over his head."

Carter glanced at her. "I doubt it."

"There are lies, and then there are secrets and lies," she allowed.

Finally, traffic cleared. Carter zipped across the intersection and started around the block.

"What if one of the Campopianos found out that Bobby was gay, and killed him?"

"That would make Bobby a 'special victim'," she acknowledged.

"That would make this a hate crime."

"Let's not get ahead of ourselves."

"The killer certainly knew how to paint a confusing story." Carter concluded. "I'll give him that."

Danny felt a strange grin come over her.

"Are we admiring killers now, partner?"

He touched eyes with her and said, "I think everyone knows, deep down, what they're really capable of, and it scares them."

She felt the smile slip off her face and turned her attention to the little shops that lined the narrow street.

She wasn't going to acknowledge Carter's point.

It had cut far too close to home.

Rocco's Italian Restaurant sat on the corner of St. John's and First Place. Rocco's had a red and white awning, sidewalk seating out front, and all the charm of a classic, New York City Italian restaurant.

By some miracle, there was a parking spot just shy of the restaurant. Carter parallel parked with expert precision, and they climbed out of the Crown Vic, stepping into the warm aromas of garlic and herbs that seemed to hover over the entire block.

It was barely noon, but Rocco's was already serving lunch. Customers sat outside in the sun, happy to have survived the months of rain.

Inside, the restaurant was occupied, but not too crowded. White table cloths, place settings, and folded cloth napkins described every vacant table. But where customers sat, the tables were covered with large, Italian, family-style plates, full wine glasses, and a general air of warm-weather cheer.

Danny and Carter reached the hostess stand, but no one was there.

She scanned the restaurant, looking for a waitress.

Jimmy Campopiano breezed onto the dining room floor, having entered through a swinging door that probably led to the kitchen. He did a bit of a double-take when he saw the detectives, and wasted no time meeting them at the front of the restaurant.

"Would it be too optimistic to assume you're here for lunch?" he asked them, good-naturedly.

"I wish," Danny told him easily.

Carter wasn't nearly as amicable. "There's been a development, and we would like to ask you some questions."

A look of grave concern washed over Jimmy's handsome features. He raked his fingers through his slick, black hair, as a helpful thought crossed his mind.

"My dad and the family are in the lounge. Well, except for Eva," he added, as he began leading them through the restaurant. "My sister is a very devout Catholic. With the loss of our brother, she's been spending all of her time at St. Christopher's, not at school. At the chapel, for prayer."

As Jimmy pushed open an elegant, wooden door, leading them into the lounge, Danny couldn't help but sense that Jimmy was full of crap.

Or maybe that was her own rotten mood she was sensing.

Guido Campopiano was seated in the lounge with the other Campopiano men, Danny presumed.

There was a lot of cigar smoke. Glass tumblers full of hard liquor were on the low tables in front of the men.

If Danny didn't know better, she would've guessed they were celebrating.

Guido quieted his family members and stood to greet the detectives. Many of the men around the lounge also stood and joined Guido.

Making formal introductions, Guido said, "This is my father, Pasquale, and my wife's brother, Tony, and their son, Nico."

"The men of my family," Guido concluded. "The rest here are our closest friends. We're getting things in order for Bobby's memorial that will take place after the Mass tomorrow."

"I see," said Danny gently. "Mr. Campopiano, can we speak with you privately?"

It appeared the man understood, but when he asked the men in the room for privacy, only the non-relatives left, which left Pasquale, Tony, and Nico in the room with Guido, Jimmy, and the detectives.

Danny invited everyone to have a seat. Carter and she sat on a brown leather sofa that was adjacent to the leather armchairs that the Campopianos eased into.

"Mr. Campopiano," Danny began. She was careful to come across as sympathetic, and not like a hard-boiled detective that was convinced someone in the Campopiano crime family had murdered Bobby. "Bobby's autopsy report shows that his cause of death actually was not the hanging."

Jimmy's ears pricked up. His brow furrowed, and he leaned forward on his chair.

"Bobby died of cyanide poisoning," she stated plainly and keenly studied each man's reaction to the information.

They all seemed to freeze, but it was Jimmy who looked like a ghost.

Pasquale, the elderly father of Guido, started speaking in Italian. He was clearly confused. His English wasn't good enough to understand what Danny had said.

Guido held his father by the arm and said, "Pappa," before translating for Pasquale in Italian what Danny had said.

Pasquale's eyes widened, and he blurted out, "Capsula di cianuro?!"

The elderly man launched out of his chair and it took both Guido and Jimmy to capture him, as he flew into an emotional outburst, spitting Italian words through his teeth. Tears streamed down his face.

"Dalla guerra, di Mussolini?!" Pasquale asked his son desperately before turning his horror onto his grandson. "Di Mussolini, Jimmy?!"

Danny definitely understood 'Mussolini,' but couldn't begin to imagine what the old man was flipping out about.

Guido barked at Jimmy, "Get him out of here! Now!"

Jimmy immediately ushered his grandfather out of the lounge, steering him into some other room deeper inside the restaurant.

Guido and his brother-in-law, Tony, stared at each other for a long moment. Then the bereaved father told Tony and Nico, "I can't with this."

"Get some air, Guido."

"I can't with this!" Guido shouted.

In a similar fashion to how Jimmy had lovingly yet forcefully removed Pasquale from the lounge, Nico now removed Guido from the lounge, leaving only Tony.

Tony was a thick man. Rough around the edges. His suit didn't fit quite right. His dark hair didn't sit on his scalp quite right, either.

Tony explained to the detectives, "You'll have to excuse Pasquale. His father fought on the wrong side of World War Two."

Carter remarked, "I thought I recognized 'Mussolini'."

Danny and Carter touched eyes, and she knew that he was thinking the same thing she was.

The cyanide capsule that had killed Bobby obviously hadn't come from the ballet company. Pasquale had known what Danny had referred to. Pasquale must have known how Bobby had come into possession of a cyanide capsule.

Carter asked, "Did Pasquale bring cyanide capsules to the U.S. from Italy?"

Tony nodded.

"How did Bobby get one?" Carter asked.

Danny felt her cell phone vibrate in the back pocket of her jeans. If anyone else had been calling her, she would've ignored it.

But it was Franco.

Damn, she hissed through her teeth. "I have to

take this."

Tony went on to describe for Carter what he could about Pasquale's father and the Second World War, as Danny slipped out of the lounge, coming into the restaurant.

She did not want to have to deal with this.

But there was no point in delaying the inevitable.

She accepted the call, pressed her phone to her ear, and, figuring that Crouse and Toliver had painted her in the worst possible light, she asked, "What do you want me to do, Franco?"

"If you think we're going to square this away over the phone, you've got another thing coming, Foster."

"Fair enough."

As Franco insisted that she get back to the 66th Precinct *ASAP* and proceeded to rip her a new one, all Danny could think was that no matter how bad things were with Tommy, she needed him now more than ever.

Did she want her mother in prison?

No.

But she didn't want herself there, either.

Somehow, some way, she needed to come out of this thing alive.

And she would need Tommy to make a formal statement, vouching for her, if she wanted that to happen.

Chapter Eight

"HAVE A SEAT, Danny," said Franco, as he pulled out a chair on the near side of the table in Interview Room One.

Detectives Crouse and Toliver were standing at the back of the room, conspiring.

Sarah Hovey, the district attorney, stood with a leather bound, legal-size, executive notebook in her rough hands. Sarah had all the polish of an experienced prosecutor, but her crusades had aged her prematurely. She smelled faintly of cigarettes.

Danny didn't like how the D.A. was looking at her.

Reluctantly, Danny sat down, and seeing no way out, she tried to control the situation.

Addressing Sarah, she said, "Campopiano's cause of death was cyanide poisoning. Jill Andover's report notes a capsule found in Bobby's mouth. Carter and I just learned from Tony Campopiano that the Vic's paternal grandfather, Pasquale, had given all the kids Nazi cyanide capsules that Pasquale's father had passed down, having fought alongside Mussolini in World War II."

"Danny—"

She wasn't going to let Franco interrupt her.

"We need a warrant for the Campopiano residence in Kensington. We have other leads, but we would be idiots not to search that mansion."

Sarah looked down, sighed, and frowned, as if a bitter taste had formed in her mouth.

Danny told Franco, "We need a warrant."

"That's not why I called you here," he reminded her.

Sarah lifted her head, pulled out the chair directly across from Danny, and sat down.

"We need to talk about the infanticide," she informed Danny.

Detectives Crouse and Toliver migrated towards the table, but didn't sit down.

"What's happening right now," Sarah went on, "is that your mother is gunning for your arrest. She made a big mistake when she insisted that you killed Gregory, because now that's what Homicide is focused on. Danny, it doesn't help that Nora also insists that you tried to strangle her to death."

It felt like a tangle of flaming barbed wire was twisting in Danny's chest.

She gritted her teeth together and admitted, "It isn't lost on me how bad things sound."

Sarah and Franco touched eyes, and then Franco had the floor.

"We talked to Jill. We know you ordered the autopsy."

Franco placed a compassionate hand on her shoulder, and Danny fell apart.

Tears filled her eyes, betraying her determination to remain stoic and say nothing.

"Danny," Franco whispered. "Did she kill your baby?"

As tears spilled down her cheeks, smearing her caked makeup, she breathed, "Yes."

"What tipped you off?" asked Detective Toliver, as he inched towards the table.

"I don't even remember," she answered honestly.

Crouse questioned her. "You don't know what made you decide to exhume your son for the purposes of an autopsy."

"My mom said something weird to me… But I don't remember."

She sniffled and wiped her cheeks.

Crouse told Franco, "She wouldn't be here if Nora Foster hadn't accused her."

Danny snapped, "What's that supposed to mean?"

"You know what it means, Foster."

"You think I was going to let my mom get away with it?" she barked.

Crouse planted his fist on the table and leaned over Danny. "Yeah, I do. I think you wanted to take justice into your own hands. I think you tried to kill your mother. You're not a cop. You're an animal, and if I have anything to do with it, you're not going to be working here very much longer."

Franco said nothing.

Sarah and Toliver were silent.

Danny was in a pressure cooker.

Crouse leaned in and whispered in her ear, "You're done, Foster."

"That's enough," said Franco.

The heavy-set detective eased off and joined Toliver, but Franco had no further use for the homicide detectives.

"You're excused, both of you," he told them.

"Let's go," said Detective Crouse to his younger partner. "It *stinks* in here."

No one said a word until the detectives had left, shutting the door behind them.

Sarah started thinking out loud, asking Franco, "We don't have anything that actually nails Nora. We need a confession. At this point, it's not even a 'she said, she said' situation that might zero out. It's a damn homicide, and if Nora maintains that Danny did it, best case scenario, Nora brings her daughter down with her."

Danny's heart plummeted, pulling her into darkness. But she refused to stop fighting. The light of hope was dimming, but she would be damned if she let herself slip into the black abyss of no return. Yes, she had lost her son. She had lost Tommy. She would probably lose her career. But she would never lose her freedom.

Never.

Remembering what Tommy had told her, she cleared her throat and said, "Nora confessed."

"What?" asked Sarah, darting her attention from Franco to Danny. "Who did she confess to? You?"

"No, not me," she promised them.

"Who?" Franco pushed.

"Thomas O'Toole. Nora confessed to Tommy, my baby's father."

Sarah shot Franco an easy smile. "Now we're getting somewhere."

"He owns the bar, O'Toole's, on Caton Avenue," she added and then offered, "I'll ask him to come in and make a statement."

Again, Franco placed his hand on her shoulder and said softly, "I'm going to get you out of this, as long as you stay out of trouble."

She nodded and pulled herself together.

Then she told Sarah, "I'm still a cop. Get me that warrant."

There wasn't a shred of kindness in Sarah's tone when she replied, "I'll see what I can do."

※

DANNY LEFT THE 66th Precinct, having noticed that Carter still hadn't returned.

As she stepped outside into the glaring sunshine, she rolled up the sleeves of her blazer, pulled her cell phone out of her pocket, and sent a call through.

A ring tone blared in her ear as she briskly walked down the sidewalk. Hailing a cab was a luxury that the residents of Kensington rarely enjoyed, so she didn't even bother.

O'Toole's wasn't far. She reasoned that a walk in the sunshine would do her some good, if not give her a chance to work out her thoughts.

Carter's voice came through the line. "Foster?"

"Yeah, are you still at Rocco's?"

"Where the hell did you disappear to?"

"Franco needed to see me. I pushed for a warrant on the Campopianos' mansion."

"Good," he said. It sounded like he was on the go, as well. "I'm at St. Christopher's. Bobby's Funeral Mass is tomorrow. I'm trying to see if I can catch Eva at the Holy Cross Chapel. Father Silva is on the grounds, too, so I might get kicked out again."

"This is quite a life we live."

"I wouldn't change it for the world."

"I'll see about meeting you at the church. I have to do something first," she told him, as she came to a busy intersection.

"Yeah, yeah," said Carter, sick of her secrets, but willing to roll with the punches.

Pedestrians spilled around her. A teenage bicycle gang zipped around cars that were idling at the light. All of Brooklyn took on a wild, almost reckless spirit when the weather was beautiful like today.

Danny didn't trust it.

Maybe Carter had gotten to know her too well, but he didn't say 'see you later.'

"I'll see you at the Mass tomorrow," he said instead. "Better yet, I'll pick you up. How's that?"

"Carter," she groaned. She wasn't about to let a rift form between them, even if she was the one that was causing it.

"Holy crap," he blurted, but not at Danny. "Sheesh."

"You good?"

It sounded like he was taking a moment to steady his racing heart on the other end of the line.

Finally, he told her, "The dog-man statue at St. Christopher's sets my teeth on edge."

"Dog-head man?" she asked, as a faint glimmer of recognition flashed through her mind.

"There's a stone statue here of a saint, but it has the head of a dog. It startled me."

Mention of the dog-headed saint rang a distant bell, and she knew who he was talking about.

"That's Saint Christopher," she told him.

"*That's* Saint Christopher?"

"The saint with the dog's head," she confirmed. "Yeah, that's Saint Christopher. He was a monster."

"Catholics give me the creeps, man."

"Hang in there," she encouraged, as she weaved through a thick cluster of pedestrians, having turned onto Caton where the stores were bustling with shoppers.

Carter let her go, and she returned her cell phone to her pocket.

O'Toole's Irish Pub sat on the corner, up ahead.

Danny slowed her step.

The huge wooden sign with 'O'Toole's' etched artfully across its glossy surface gleamed in the sunshine, shining a light on the darkness that had clouded Danny's soul.

Filled with nervous jitters, she forced one foot in front of the other, continuing up the avenue until she came to the large picture windows. The glass reflected the sunlight, and Danny saw herself instead of the bartenders and patrons within the establishment.

She looked like hell.

The last time she had seen Tommy…

God that felt like it had been a lifetime ago, but in reality, it hadn't even been a week. He had looked at her like she was a monster, like she had chosen her murderer mother over her own dead son…

That's why Crouse had touched a nerve with her. He had twisted his finger in a fresh wound.

Nothing hurt like the truth.

Maybe Danny was some kind of monster, some kind of maniac.

Maybe her life would have been easier if she *had* killed her mother.

Maybe…

But if she had, then Danny would be fully dead inside.

Because she had restrained herself, there was still a spark of life within her soul.

No matter what, she couldn't let that spark go out.

Danny threw the heavy O'Toole's door open, promising herself that this didn't have to go *well*, it just had to happen. But deep down she felt that she wanted nothing more than for Tommy to forgive her...

When would Nora be done ruining Danny's life? She didn't know.

Inside, the bar was dim, though sunlight cut through the windows.

Music played softly through the speakers, some laid back rock band. Patrons filled almost every table, but it wasn't packed. A good crowd for good weather.

Danny stepped aside and scanned the room.

Tommy wasn't behind the bar, but she recognized the bartenders that were. The familiar faces were too focused on their pints to have noticed her arrival, which suited her just fine.

Then she spotted Tommy standing at one of the tall, round tables, and talking with the gentleman that was seated there. Tommy's back was to Danny, and she couldn't see the customer, other than his arm, leg, and shiny leather dress shoe. The man wore a tailored suit, not typical of O'Toole's usuals.

She was here to ask for Tommy's help. She knew that.

But she was also here to win Tommy's heart, and she knew that if she didn't succeed, it would be a worse blow than getting locked up for a murder she should've committed and an infanticide she had nothing to do with.

Tommy stepped away from the suited gentleman he had been talking to. Recognizing the man, Danny felt the wind get knocked out of her.

Dressed in the same three-piece suit she had seen him wearing earlier at Rocco's, Jimmy Campopiano studied the amber I.P.A. in his frosted glass then knocked the beer back.

She froze.

What was Jimmy Campopiano doing at O'Toole's?

She made the mistake of staring at him for too long.

Jimmy must have felt her eyes on him, because the next thing she knew, he was staring right back at her.

She was so thrown by these two worlds of hers colliding that she didn't even notice Tommy approaching her until he said:

"What are you doing here?"

She swallowed the lump in her throat and desperately searched for the right words to say.

"Can we talk?"

His gray-blue eyes contained a world of pain. He looked as rugged as ever, and refreshed, as though barely a week without the burden of Danny in his life had given him a hopeful new start.

She couldn't hold his gaze, and ashamed, she glanced away.

"I don't know if that's a good idea," he said in a low tone.

"I'm not a saint, Tommy."

"Yeah, I noticed."

She sensed Jimmy was still staring at her, and when she glanced across the room, she saw she was right.

Shifting gears, she stuffed all the hard emotions down into the pit of her stomach and told herself to do what she had come here to accomplish.

"I need to talk to you about Nora. It's serious."

"I don't want to talk about her, Danny. I don't even think I want you here."

She searched his eyes, having heard the lies in his deep tone.

Tommy wanted her here. She could see it written all over his face. She felt magnetized to him. If she had her way, she would be melting into his arms right now.

"Either you talk to me now, or you talk to the police later," she informed him.

It gradually dawned on him. "The cops found out about Nora?"

He was referring to the infanticide.

"Can we talk somewhere private?"

"I really don't know, Danny. I might just wait for the police and talk to them if you're saying that's inevitable."

"Why is Jimmy Campopiano sitting in your bar?"

"What the hell does that matter?" he said, in perfect defense of himself, considering her tone of voice had been an attack.

"Do you know who he is?"

"A paying customer," he answered easily. "Not that that's any of your business."

Jimmy was watching them from his mobster perch at the round table.

She didn't like it.

"Tommy, let's cut the crap."

"Oh, you want to cut the crap?"

He grabbed her by the upper arm and walked her briskly through the bar. Danny shuffled to keep up and tried not to knock shoulders with the customers. He used his free hand to slap open the 'Employees Only' door that separated the bar room from the business.

When they reached his office, he tossed her across the threshold and slammed the door shut behind himself.

He barked, "You want privacy! You want things your way! You want, you want, you want!"

He was furious, but her attention had been stolen by the screensaver on Tommy's computer.

It was a photo of their infant son, Gregory.

Seeing it, Danny died inside just a little bit more.

"What about what I want?" he demanded. "What about what I went through? What about the fact that to be with you, Danny, I had to bend over backwards so hard and fast that it broke my back? And you show up here, and you want more? I don't have anything else to give you!"

Her vision blurred with tears, but she found the strength to face him.

He crumbled seeing those tears, seeing her overcome with emotion.

"Don't," he warned her. "Don't you dare fall apart and make me feel sorry for you."

Pulling herself together and knowing that this was her last chance, she blurted out:

"She went to the police. She's framing me. She's trying to get me locked up for killing our son!"

Tommy froze, stunned.

It took a very long moment for the information to work its way through his rattled brain.

When he had finally made some semblance of sense out of the unfathomable, all he said was:

"What?"

"Nora is out of her mind." Danny put her hands up for the purposes of composing herself and sticking to the objective. "According to what you told me, she approached you and confessed to taking Gregory's life that night?"

"You're asking me?"

"Yeah, I'm asking you, Tommy. Tell me that's what she said to you. She confessed?"

He nodded his head.

"You have to get me out of this," she begged. "You have to tell the police."

Tommy advanced on her, pulled Danny into his arms, and held her tightly.

"You have to, Tommy," she cried, letting out the hard emotions. Her shoulders quaked, but Tommy squeezed her more. "Promise me."

Danny didn't know whether Tommy agreed, or if he even said a word, she was crying so hard.

The next thing she knew, her emotions took on the form of words and the dark truth that had been rotting her insides came tumbling out of her.

She didn't recognize herself, as she cried:

"She turned me into a monster! She destroyed me! I can't live with myself like this! I hate what she turned me into! I wish she was dead!"

Chapter Nine

CARTER EASED THE Crown Vic towards the curb and rolled to a stop in front of Danny's apartment building. The clock on the dashboard read 9:59am then flipped to 10:00am.

Sunlight sliced between the buildings, brightening the sidewalk in patches.

He had a feeling the weather would get hot and humid today. He was wearing a dark suit, dress shoes, and a nice tie. He looked respectable, appropriately dressed for a Funeral Mass, not that he had ever attended one before.

A moment passed then Danny came out of her building with a man, a tee shirt and jeans type. It took Carter a second, but he recognized Tommy. He had met the bar proprietor a few times, but Tommy looked different in the sober light of day.

Carter watched them descend the stoop.

Danny wore a knee-length black dress with her usual black blazer. A purse was slung over her shoulder. The high heels and panty hose were what really threw him for a loop.

When they reached the sidewalk, Tommy took Danny's face in his large hands and kissed her. Then they parted ways. Tommy headed down Ocean Parkway towards O'Toole's, and Danny crossed the sidewalk and opened the passenger side door of the idling Crown Vic.

As she climbed in, he told her, "You look nice."

"Thanks," she replied.

He pulled away from the curb, and as they drove off, he off-handedly asked, "How's Tommy doing?"

She shrugged and smiled to herself, and he

knew a real answer wouldn't come.

They drove in silence through Kensington, heading towards St. Christopher's Cathedral.

Danny had been keeping things from him. Whatever secret she was harboring obviously wasn't hidden. Homicide knew, and as of yesterday, Carter was certain that the lieutenant and the district attorney had also discovered Danny's secret. The skeleton wasn't in the closet anymore, but Danny was keeping Carter in the dark?

It didn't sit right with him.

But pressuring her to clue him in hadn't been working either.

Out of the blue, she mentioned, "I spoke with Franco and Sarah Hovey yesterday. They're going to see about getting us a warrant to search the Campopianos' mansion. There could be more cyanide capsules. It'll give us an in."

He shot her a skeptical glance then returned his attention to the road.

She wasn't thinking straight.

He challenged her, "You think the judge that's been taking bribes from the Campopianos is going to sign a warrant, authorizing us to search the Campopianos' house?"

"Harlan Ellsworth isn't the only judge in Brooklyn."

"Ellsworth is in a position to intercept a warrant request like that."

"We have to try, Carter."

There was an edge of desperation in her tone.

"Franco said he would get us a warrant?" he asked, softening.

"Sarah said she would see what she can do," she

said, sounding unconvinced.

"I shouldn't be a naysayer," he apologized. "Let's see what they can do."

She touched eyes with him.

"You look better, Danny. Does Tommy have something to do with that?"

Her silence was enough of an answer.

"I'll take that as a 'yes'."

He turned onto Church Avenue where St. Christopher's towering cathedral loomed over the block.

The bell tolled in the vaulted, stone steeple, as Catholics dressed in black made their somber way into the cathedral. Older women wore black veils over their faces.

As Carter and Danny crawled past in the Crown Vic, heading towards the church parking lot where they would actually have a chance to find a parking spot, Carter caught sight of the ballerina, Tracy Jones.

"This should be interesting," he remarked.

"Two worlds colliding," Danny agreed.

Carter turned into the parking lot and found a spot at the very back of the lot. They climbed out of the Crown Vic, stepping into a warm breeze. There was enough vegetation—trees, bushes, and grass—to cool the church grounds. The air smelled fresh and crisp, as they walked across the parking lot, found the cobblestone walking path that led to the cathedral, and came around to the side entrance.

As Carter had come to understand it, a Catholic Funeral Mass, or *Requiem*, was always open to the public unless otherwise specified, and non-Catholics could attend even though the rites of an ordinary

Mass were also performed.

He could see the appeal, he realized, as they entered the beautiful cathedral with its high vaulted ceilings, glimmering stained-glass windows, and tremendous marble altar. There were polished, marble statues around the perimeter and a number of votive candle stations.

What a luxury it must be to trust in some external God to solve all of life's problems, thought Carter. No external God had saved him growing up. If there was a God and he truly was all-powerful and he truly did want people to be good and not evil... Then he was a contradiction, an oxymoron... A paradox...

...because as far as Carter could tell, most days evil prevailed.

Must be nice to worship a God that made no sense...

Danny elbowed him. "There's Guido and Maria," she whispered, indicating that the parents of the deceased were seated at the front of the sanctuary. "We should sit in the back, though."

Keeping to the side aisle that hugged the perimeter, Carter followed Danny to the back of the cathedral. Her high heels clicked over the polished, marble floor.

As they chose one of the long, wooden pews and sat in the middle of it to have a decent vantage point to spy Guido and Maria Campopiano, Eva entered the church, holding a young boy's hand. Behind her, Jimmy and Catherine Campopiano trailed in. Catherine was holding the baby, whose name was 'Rosa' if Carter's memory served him correctly.

Baby Rosa giggled and shrieked, as she glanced at the high ceiling and tugged her mother's chocolate-brown hair.

Carter watched them get settled next to Guido and Maria. He scanned the pews. The cathedral was filling up. He spotted Tracy Jones and Eric MacDermott, and assumed that the other unfamiliar faces they were sitting with belonged to the rest of the Brooklyn Ballet Company.

A few pews ahead of where Carter and Danny were sitting, an older gentleman dressed in a suit, who happened to be standing and facing the back of the church while he helped his wife get settled, blurted out, "Oh, for Christ's sake."

He wasn't annoyed with his wife. His attention was fixed on whoever had just entered the cathedral.

Carter turned to see what had caused the older man's unrestrained reaction and found a middle-age man dressed in a magenta pink, seersucker suit. He wore a very tall top hat that was just as pink, and the cane in his hand glimmered with encrusted rhinestones.

Carter nudged Danny with his elbow.

"Get a load of this guy."

She turned just as more Catholics throughout the cathedral took notice of the pink man who looked like he had arrived to mock the dearly departed. There were gasps, and murmuring ensued. When Jimmy Campopiano took notice, he leapt to his feet and started quickly down the aisle.

From where Carter and Danny were sitting, they had a front row seat to the confrontation. By the time Jimmy reached the pink man, they guy hadn't made it very far into the sanctuary.

"You can't be here dressed like that," Jimmy told the pink man firmly.

They didn't appear to know each other.

When the pink man responded, he sounded, to Carter's ear, like a flaming homosexual.

"As I understand, this Requiem Mass is open to the public," the pink man sang, as he removed his comically large top hat and tossed his shaggy white hair off his shoulders.

"I'm going to have to ask you to leave," Jimmy told him firmly.

Jimmy reached for the pink man's arm, but pinky jerked away and asserted, "I loved Bobby, and Bobby loved me!"

One of the ballet dancers hissed, "Paul, you're making a scene!"

Carter asked Danny, "What did you say the lover's name was?"

"That has to be him," she agreed. "Paul Decker."

Jimmy's face went pale, as he insisted, "Get out."

Paul angled himself closer to Jimmy, looked him dead in the eye, and told him, "Bobby was my lover. He hated you people."

Jimmy grabbed Paul, taking his lapel into his fists, and shook him hard.

"My brother wasn't gay," he spat through clenched teeth.

Nico and Tony rushed up the aisle to help get the situation under control, but Jimmy was already shoving Paul, two-fisted, out of the cathedral. Paul shuffled his feet as quickly as he could to keep himself from tripping.

Nico and Tony seized Paul, as well, just as they spilled out of the sanctuary and into the small lobby.

One of the Campopianos hissed something in Paul's face, but Carter couldn't make it out.

Paul's response, however, was as clear as a bell.

"Bobby was a beautiful lover! I love how he made love to me!"

When Carter heard the distinct sound of a balled fist connecting with Paul's jaw, he jumped up, tore through the cathedral, and found the Campopiano men beating the living crap out of Paul on the stone entrance in the bright light of day.

"Lay off him!" Carter shouted, as he grabbed Tony and peeled him away from the poor guy.

Paul was on the ground. His nose was bleeding. He tried to use his sparkling cane to defend himself. His top hat tumbled towards the sidewalk.

Jimmy had a knee on Paul's chest. He delivered one hard blow after the next.

Carter had to get Nico off first. Once he had, he hooked his muscular arm around Jimmy's throat from behind and locked him in a choke hold. He jerked Jimmy up and away from Paul.

As Paul rolled and curled up into the fetal position, laughing like a madman, Carter barked at the Campopianos, "Leave him! He's disturbing the peace. I can do something about it, but don't touch him."

He released Jimmy.

Jimmy sucked snot back into his face, raked his fingers through his greased, black hair, and took a slow lap around Paul.

When Jimmy spat on Paul, Carter knew it was over.

"Let me handle this," he told Jimmy, and he knew that to Jimmy's ears it sounded like a promise.

The mobster nodded and told Tony and Nico, "Come on. Today is for Bobby. We'll take care of that piece of garbage later."

Carter didn't like the sound of that, but he left it alone, as the Campopiano men returned into the cathedral.

Danny stepped aside for them to enter the church, as Carter helped Paul to his feet.

"You're not going back in there," he told Paul, as he presented his detective's badge.

"Oh, that's rich," Paul scoffed.

As Danny neared them, Carter explained to Paul, "This is Detective Danielle Foster and I'm Detective Carter Dobbs. We're investigating Bobby's murder."

That seemed to amuse Paul.

He took a moment to fetch his top hat, dusted the thing off, and then fit the ridiculous hat onto his head. He wiped blood off his cane next.

Maybe Paul's attire *wasn't* meant to mock Bobby's funeral. It occurred to Carter that the guy's Willy Wonka style might be his authentic wardrobe.

Danny asked him, "Can you tell us the last time you saw Bobby alive?"

Paul snorted a strange laugh. "Forgive me if I'm not thrilled to help you."

Blood streaked down his nose, mouth, and chin, so Danny found a packet of tissues in her purse and offered him several.

He told them, "I didn't kill Bobby."

"We don't assume you did," Danny assured him. "Don't you want us to catch who murdered Bobby?"

"That family murdered him," he said with another snort. "They murdered his spirit. They never accepted him. Bobby was half alive when I met him. I brought him back to life. I *resurrected* his dry bones."

Paul inhaled deeply and held his head high.

"I was the one who encouraged Bobby to leave his father's house, as they say," he went on. "I believed in him. I also encouraged him to audition for the ballet company. Bobby didn't think he was good enough, because those Campopiano men were always criticizing him and putting him down. I built Bobby up!"

"Were you living together?" Carter asked.

"Of course," said Paul.

"In Kensington?" asked Danny.

He shook his head. "No, we were living at the seaport in a manner of speaking." When Danny formed a funny look on her face, Paul clarified. "I live on my sailboat at the Brooklyn Marina."

Carter and Danny glanced at one another. The professional sailor's knot that had been used to anchor the lynch rope to the mason's hook at the crime scene immediately sprang to Carter's mind.

He asked Paul, "You're a sailor?"

"Have been my whole life," he said proudly. "But I'm ending this conversation. You two might think you're investigating Bobby's murder, but Bobby was a Campopiano. I promise you, all you're really doing right now is working for the Campopianos, and the second you step out of line, you're going to wind up at the bottom of the East River."

Carter wouldn't have suddenly felt worried if he hadn't believed the guy.

Paul said, "Good luck. You're going to need it."

Then he turned on his patent leather loafer and started for Westminster where he disappeared around the corner.

"A sailor," said Danny.

Carter was already having his doubts. "If he killed Bobby, why would he come here?"

"You think a guy who intentionally buys a bright pink seersucker suit and wears it to a Catholic Funeral Mass has *good* judgment?"

"Point taken."

If the conflict between the Campopianos and Paul Decker had been teeming with unbridled hatred, and it *had*, the confrontation that occurred directly after the Requiem Mass was even worse.

Tracy Jones approached Maria Campopiano outside, after the majority of the funeral guests had gathered in the sunshine in front of the cathedral.

"I'm so sorry for your loss," said Tracy and all of the ballet dancers behind her nodded in solemn agreement.

Maria scowled at the young ballerina. Beside Maria was her daughter, Eva. Eva held her mother's arm and told Tracy, "Thank you."

Guido had taken notice.

From where Carter was standing, it appeared Tracy was interested in pushing it.

"He was a valued member of our ballet company," she went on. "We'll really miss him."

Maria took a powerful step towards Tracy and said, "You never knew my son. You never saw the *real* Bobby."

A smirk spread across Tracy's face. "I think it was the other way around."

Eva attempted to steer her mother away, but

Maria dug her heels in.

"I was his mother. I knew him his whole life," she hissed, as tears filled her eyes.

Tracy sneered in the older woman's face. "He had to hide who he really was from you. From all of you."

Eric took hold of Tracy's arm. "Let's go."

"Come on, Tracy." said another ballerina.

"No," she stated, keeping her attention locked on Maria. "I'm not going anywhere until she admits that Bobby was gay."

"Aye!" Maria cried, as she threw her hands into the air. She started shouting expletives in Italian.

Jimmy and Catherine rushed over, but Catherine couldn't help much with her shrieking baby in her arms.

The next thing Carter knew, Maria had taken two fist-fulls of Tracy's brown hair. She started jerking the ballerina and tossing her around like a dirty rag doll, while Tracy screamed bloody murder and the other ballet dancers looked on in horror.

Catherine doubled back and shoved baby Rosa into Danny's arms.

"Take her, please!"

Confusedly, Danny accepted the squishy baby who immediately started patting Danny's face.

Catherine joined Eva as they tried to pry Maria off of Tracy.

All hell broke loose after that.

Carter threw himself into the mix, but it was a cat fight of clawing nails and hair pulling. Separating the women was more complicated than untangling a wad of Christmas lights.

Tracy kept shrieking, and though the

Campopiano men shouted, "Ladies!" and angled into the dramatic cluster, they didn't exactly get *involved.*

Carter wedged himself between Maria and Tracy, breaking the women apart. For her own good, he shoved Tracy towards the ballet dancers and they caught her.

Eva pulled her mother into a hug and began saying something comforting in Italian, while Jimmy shouted at the dancers, "Go on! Get out of here! You've done enough, haven't you?"

Guido muttered between his teeth, "Filthy liars," as the ballet company, led by Tracy and Eric, made its way down the sidewalk.

Tony agreed. "They poisoned Bobby's mind. Probably killed him, Guido."

A furious look hardened the older man's weathered face. "We're going to find out, aren't we?"

As the Campopianos composed themselves, Nico comforted a boy, probably his son, who looked badly shaken up.

"Bastards," said Guido before he spat.

Then Tony spat, Nico spat, elderly Pasquale spat, and even the boy spat on the ground.

When Carter glanced at Danny, tears were streaming down her cheeks and her lower lip was quivering. The baby in her arms was breaking her heart.

"Hey," he said softly to Danny, having neared her.

He took baby Rosa from Danny.

"Danny," he said when he caught sight of her chest. Two dark stains had formed in the black cloth of her dress. Holding the baby had caused her to start lactating.

"Oh, my God," she breathed, as she pulled her blazer closed in front.

"There's a bathroom inside the cathedral," he reminded Danny.

As she excused herself to get cleaned up, Catherine swooped in, took Rosa, and asked, "Is she alright?"

"Her son died," he told Catherine honestly. "Died as a baby. It wasn't too long ago."

Catherine bounced Rosa on her hip. "That's terrible," she said, but she was distracted.

Jimmy and Eva had stolen her attention.

Jimmy had his arm around Eva. He rubbed and squeezed her shoulder.

A strange frown of animosity formed on Catherine's pretty face, and she shook her head to herself.

As Carter wondered what that was about, Catherine left him in favor of approaching her husband.

"Eva's fine," Catherine told Jimmy, as if she could air a grievance privately.

Jimmy barked, "My sister was just sucked into a brawl, Catherine! Don't start with me!"

The Campopianos made their slow way around the side of the cathedral, presumably heading towards the private parking lot. Jimmy kept his arm around his younger sister, Eva, while Catherine trailed behind like some kind of second class citizen.

The dynamic gave Carter pause.

He ran his big hand down his face and realized he was dripping with sweat.

Father Silva emerged from the cathedral, and

Carter would've approached him, but his cell phone vibrated in the front pocket of his slacks.

It was his wife, Kathy.

He didn't want to take the call.

But he also didn't want to come home to an angry wife.

"Kathy, now's not the best time," he told her the second he answered his phone.

"Fine." She sounded mad and cold. "When will you be home?"

"I'm working a case, Kathy. And I have S.I.A. tonight."

"This is too much."

He wasn't about to fuel her fire by engaging unnecessarily.

"Carter?" she barked. "When you get home, we're going to talk about this career of yours."

Their previous therapist, Dr. Ling, had been right, and it was starting to scare the crap out of Carter. His wife had married a slave, someone who had needed a master to lord over him. That's who Carter had been, and he took responsibility for that. He had acknowledged it, and he had faced his demons.

He wasn't that subservient man anymore.

And Kathy literally could not stand it.

That's why she had convinced Carter that they needed a new therapist, one who could also help the kids here and there. Well, that had been her argument. But now he could see what leaving Dr. Ling had really been about. Ling had seen right through Kathy, right through both of them. And she had spoken the truth. She had helped Carter to see that he had been shackled by his own low self worth. But Ling hadn't freed Kathy from her entitlement. A master without a slave wouldn't last long in this world.

"Carter!"

"Let me tell you something, Kathy," he asserted. "There's nothing about my career that's negotiable. Do not make me choose between being a cop or being a husband, because I promise you, honey, you won't like my choice."

When he hung up on his wife next, he knew that if Kathy didn't change, he would have to leave her.

Chapter Ten

EVA HAD SURVIVED the bizarre attack that had occurred after her brother's Requiem Mass. She had held herself together during Bobby's informal memorial and the reception, both of which had been at the family's restaurant, Rocco's.

Father Silva and a handful of close family friends had returned to the Campopiano residence for further consolations and mourning, but Eva had been through enough. She didn't have it in her to endure one more hug. Her brain was totally fried, and she knew if she didn't use her last ounce of energy to take a shower and brush her teeth, she would collapse into bed, dirty and depleted.

"Goodnight, Pop," she said, as she kissed Guido on the cheek.

He was seated in the sitting room, smoking a cigar with the other men.

Eva kissed her mother next, then took Lorenzo by the hand. The eight year old had been gently snoring on the sofa, draped sideways across his mother's lap, while his dad, Nico, listened to Father Silva offer more assurances that Bobby was in heaven with Our Blessed Mother.

"Let's get you into bed, Lorenzo," she told the groggy boy.

Lorenzo sleep-walked, holding Eva's hand, as she led him out of the sitting room, through the marble foyer, and up the grand staircase.

On the second floor, she brought Lorenzo into his bedroom, let go of his hand, and threw the covers back.

Lorenzo was about to roll into bed, but she said, "Ut-ut, get changed into your pajamas and brush your teeth."

She left him to change his clothes in privacy and entered the bathroom, leaving the door open.

While she waited, she brushed her own teeth then brushed her hair.

She felt grimy.

Lorenzo pitter-pattered into the bathroom in his pajamas and bare feet. He rushed through the chore of brushing his teeth.

After rinsing his mouth with water, he asked her, "Bedtime story?"

"I'm beat, but I'll tuck you in."

She made good on her promise. The boy climbed into bed. Eva pulled the thin comforter up to his ears and tucked him in all around like a single sardine in a tin can.

"I can't move," Lorenzo said.

"Good, that means the Boogie Man won't get you."

Lorenzo smiled like he knew more about it than she did. "Papa said if the Boogie Man comes for me, I have to off myself before he can do his worst."

Eva stared at him for a very long moment.

Lorenzo didn't even know what he was talking about, or what those expressions meant. But that's how it was in the Campopiano household. As children, each one of them had been trained to 'off themselves' at the first whiff of danger, even though, as children, they didn't comprehend what 'offing themselves' inferred.

"Don't do that," she whispered, as she stroked his feathery hair off his forehead. "Promise me you won't do that."

She tickled her fingers down his forehead, nose, and chin. He closed his eyes and a sleepy smile spread across his young face. After soothing him with gentle caresses, her fingertips grazing down the length of his face, she rose from the bed and closed his bedroom door on the way out.

Exhausted, she dragged herself into the bathroom where she took a long, hot shower, scrubbing every inch of her body and washing her hair in a thick lather of shampoo.

When she felt satisfied, she turned off the water, stepped out of the shower, and wrapped her long, brown hair up into a towel turban. She wrapped another towel around her body and stepped out of the steaming bathroom into the hallway.

Jimmy had just reached the landing, having climbed the stairs.

"Pop wants to talk to us."

"I'm in a towel, Jimmy."

"Everyone's gone except for the family."

Eva cocked her head and the huge towel turban shifted.

"You're fine. Two minutes," he insisted. "He just wants to talk to us."

With water still dripping down her arms and legs, she made her way downstairs with her brother.

When they reached the study, Jimmy pushed the door open for Eva and she padded in.

Guido was seated in one of the leather armchairs. His burning cigar was down to a stump.

Jimmy closed the door behind himself.

"Have a seat," he told them, completely unfazed that his daughter was only wearing a towel.

Eva and Jimmy sat beside one another on the adjacent leather sofa.

"Now that your brother is in the ground..." Guido began, as he studied his burning cigar, the tendril of smoke that whirled and twisted towards the ceiling. "We have to deal with some things."

Jimmy nodded, poised.

Eva felt nervous.

"The cops know about the cyanide capsules, and I got word that they're pushing to search the house—"

"That'll never happen," Jimmy interrupted.

"Of course, it'll never happen," Guido agreed. "Never-the-less, Tony's in a bit of trouble with me for his big mouth in that regard, but I'm handling things with him. If things seem tense, don't worry about it."

Guido stared at Eva for a long moment then concluded, "I got one family member with a big mouth, and I got another who don't talk enough when she's told to."

Eva froze.

"Is there something you want to tell me, Eva?"

She felt her eyebrows shoot up to her hairline. Rather than respond, she pressed her mouth into a line.

Guido asked his son, "You see what I mean?"

"What's Eva not telling you?" Jimmy asked, genuinely curious.

Here it comes, she thought. *Damn.*

"Eva, do you remember when I told you that if you keep anything from me, there would be hell to pay?"

Jimmy pushed, "Did you keep something from

Pop?"

Guido chucked his stumpy cigar onto the ashtray on the low table and lunged at her.

He grabbed her face with both of his meaty hands and shook her, hard.

"Did you forget to tell me you saw Bobby that morning, eh?!"

"Pop! Stop!" Jimmy yelled, jumping off the sofa to have a better angle to pull Guido off his sister.

Guido elbowed him away and seethed at his daughter, "What did I tell you?!"

Shaking her so hard that her towel loosened, he yelled, "You saw Bobby that morning?!"

Jimmy gave up trying to help his sister.

"Yes," she wheezed out the admission.

Guido threw her sideways and she spilled across the sofa.

As he paced away, she covered herself up.

"Why didn't you tell me?" he asked in a tone of voice so unemotional that she feared he would murder her next. He angled over her and shouted, "You're getting sloppy, Eva. You told the Black cop that you saw Bobby that morning. But you didn't tell me any of that."

Jimmy offered, "Let me handle this, Pop."

"I'm calm," he stated. "I got it out of my system."

He sat back down in the armchair.

"Eva, do you know who killed Bobby?" he asked her point blank.

"No," she lied.

"Okay," Guido said. "We're going to get past this. I want the cops out of our hair. By. All. Means. Necessary."

"Yes, Pop," Jimmy agreed without hesitating.

"Tony's big mouth might be a blessing in disguise. Those detectives *must conclude* that Bobby took his own life. Best case scenario, I want the case to go cold. Plan B, I want that fruitcake Willy Wonka bastard going down for this. You know, I think that guy *did* kill Bobby, but even if he didn't, he has to be punished for having the audacity to wear that pink suit."

The image seemed to fill Guido's mind, haunting him. He found the stump of his cigar and figured out how to light it.

Jimmy tried to assure his father, "Bobby wasn't gay, Pop, I promise you."

The old man screwed his face up. "Son, are you retarded?" He shook his head, looking away, then had to return his attention to Jimmy just to quench his curiosity. "Bobby was as queer as a two-dollar bill, you couldn't see that?"

Jimmy hung his head. Of course, he had been able to see it. But he hadn't liked seeing it.

Guido ran through the math out loud. "He was shacking up with that guy. But I know my son. He knew the difference between right and wrong. He knew he was queer, and I bet you anything, he woke up one morning next to that filthy bastard and couldn't stand it. He probably told the guy he wasn't going to do this anymore, and the guy retaliated, tried to hang him, but Bobby killed himself right then and there."

Jimmy and Eva touched eyes.

Jimmy asked their dad, "You think so?"

"That's what my gut is telling me, yeah." Guido leaned forward and looked Eva square in the eye.

He yelled, "Are you some kind of lesbian? Eh?"

"No."

"Are you? You some kind of dyke, Eva?"

"No, Pop!"

"You sure you're not a *lipstick lesbian*? Answer me!"

"I'm answering you! I'm not a lesbian!"

Guido leaned back. "Good. You need to get yourself a Catholic boyfriend. I want you married by this summer, and you'll live under *my* roof where I can keep an eye on you. Agreed?"

Eva pressed her mouth into a hard line, refusing to agree or even look at her father.

Jimmy said, "Let's give it a rest for the night. I'll deal with the cops. I'll see about the fruitcake."

He helped Eva off the sofa.

The moment they left the study, emotions rose up through Eva and her vision blurred with tears.

Jimmy whispered, "Keep it together until we get upstairs."

It was the hardest thing she ever had to do, but she choked down the raging sobs that were clawing up her throat, as they climbed the stairs.

When they reached the landing, Catherine was standing in the open doorway of her bedroom with baby Rosa on her hip. She was wearing her white, gauzy nightgown and a very concerned look on her face.

"I heard yelling," she said softly.

Jimmy told her, "I'll be there in a minute.

"Is everything okay?" she needed to know.

"Catherine, get back in the bedroom!" Jimmy barked, his patience having run out.

He took rough hold of Eva's upper arm, and

Catherine didn't like the sight of it.

"I've held my tongue long enough, Jimmy, I'm still your wife."

Jimmy glared at her over his shoulder and warned, "Don't stick your nose where it doesn't belong. I'm dealing with my sister. I told you, I'll be back in a minute."

Whether Catherine had a problem with that or not, they didn't stick around to find out.

Jimmy walked Eva into her bedroom and closed the door.

Eva totally broke down, but she had been living in this household her entire life. She knew how to sob without making a sound.

Jimmy pulled her into a hug and held her.

She was hanging on by a thread. Her shoulders quaked as she let out hard, muffled sobs and gasps. Her towel fell, pooling around her bare feet.

Jimmy pushed the towel turban off her head. Her wet hair tumbled down her nude back where her brother stroked and caressed the length of her spine.

"I feel like I'm losing my mind," she breathed.

"It's going to be okay," he whispered.

He urged her back, drank in the sight of her, and then searched her eyes.

He leaned in and planted a long, sweet kiss on her cheek.

Eva wished she could live in this moment forever.

Chapter Eleven

BRIGHT SUNLIGHT filled the bedroom, gently rousing Tommy from deep sleep. The room looked too big to be his, and then he remembered he had gone to Danny's apartment after he had closed the bar last night.

He could feel her body heat behind him. He was lying on his side, but rolled onto his back and turned his head.

There she was, sound asleep. Her brown mop of hair spilled over her pillow, those shaggy bangs of hers falling across her forehead.

For the second night in a row, he had held her while she had cried herself to sleep. This time, her geyser of tears had sprung because of some Italian woman's baby. Danny had held the baby and doing so had caused another break in her heart.

Tommy had promised her that he would go to the 66th and speak with the homicide detectives that had been gunning to destroy Danny's life.

Today was the day. Nora had to be stopped. It wasn't lost on Tommy that this was a lose-lose situation for Danny. From where Tommy was standing, Danny losing her mother to prison would be better than her losing her career and possibly her freedom. But it was obvious that to Danny both outcomes would be equally devastating.

She could probably use more sleep, but he wanted to hold her before he left for the precinct.

She was lying on her back. He slid his muscular arm under her neck, placed his other hand on her soft stomach, and curled up into her ear.

He could smell the warm sunlight on her unwashed skin, and realized it might be his favorite scent.

Tommy loved her.

And though her flaws scared him, when he had taken her back this time, he knew it had been for good.

He lingered, savoring the moment for just a bit longer, and then released her and eased out of bed. He found his jeans in a heap on the floor. His tee shirt had gotten bunched up under the bed.

After throwing his clothes on, he found his sneakers near the apartment door, wriggled his feet into each one, and then dared to make a pot of coffee at the risk of waking Danny up.

He found a bag of ground coffee in the cabinets, as well as coffee filters. A few moments later and the coffeemaker started percolating, while he gazed out the kitchen window.

There was nothing but blue skies above. The ordinarily hectic energy of the city felt sleepy this morning, relaxed, as if everything would be okay.

He didn't trust it.

As he grabbed a mug and filled it with coffee, he considered everything that had gone wrong in his life, and all the control he had lost.

Gulping coffee to wake his mind up, he realized that the only good thing he had left in this world was Danny. He didn't even have his bar anymore, not with Jimmy Campopiano lording over him and bleeding him dry.

He drained the rest of the coffee from his mug then walked up the hallway and peered in at Danny from the bedroom doorway. She was still sound asleep.

It was a little after 7am when Tommy left Danny's building. The air was warm and fresh. He descended the stoop, sensing more than seeing the neighboring apartment building where Nora lived. He had a flickering idea, but told himself not to go there.

Starting in the opposite direction down the sidewalk, he headed south towards the 66th Precinct. Danny had asked him to speak with Homicide first thing in the morning, before her partner, Carter Dobbs, would arrive at the station.

The Kensington Police Precinct was a two-story brick building with narrow windows and an American flag angled over the entrance door. Truth be told, Tommy had found himself at the station once or twice over the years. If a bar brawl had gotten out of hand or if Tommy had tied one too many on, he had wound up in the basement jail.

However, this morning the precinct intimidated him for an entirely different reason.

If he screwed this up, he might lose Danny forever. Their whirlwind, lust-driven romantic rollercoaster would definitely not survive a prison stint, no matter how much Tommy felt he loved her.

He threw the door open and checked the directory in the shallow lobby to make sure he knew where to find the Homicide Department. Located on the first floor, he found it alright, approached the front desk there, and pulled the handwritten names Danny had supplied.

"Can I speak with Detectives Crouse and Toliver?" he asked the uniformed police officer behind the desk.

"Your name?" replied the cop, as he clamped a phone between his ear and shoulder and dialed an extension.

"Thomas O'Toole," he said. "I'm here about the infanticide of my son."

The seriousness of the statement gave the cop pause. When the line opened up, he relayed the information to whichever detective was listening. "The detectives will be right out," said the officer, as he returned the desk phone to its cradle. "You want coffee?"

Tommy declined and backed away from the counter, but felt too nervous to sit down.

He glanced through the open doorway and across the lobby to the Special Victims Unit on the other side.

Danny came to mind.

What kind of little girl grows up to want to be a cop? And one that works grisly, disturbing cases no less?

The kind of little girl that had been raised by a woman like Nora, he surmised, as two detectives approached him from the bullpen, having come around the front desk.

One was older and bloated with bloodshot eyes and a cheap suit. He introduced himself to Tommy as Detective Crouse. The other guy—younger, taller, and slimmer—was Toliver.

"Let's chat somewhere private," Detective Crouse suggested, and the detectives walked Tommy into what appeared to be a windowless interrogation room. "Have a seat."

Tommy pulled out a chair, as Crouse sat across from him, and Toliver shut the door.

"Did Foster ask you to come speak with us?"

Detective Crouse asked, as his partner settled onto the chair beside him.

"Yeah, that's right."

"We're all ears," said Crouse. He folded his arms, disinterested in taking notes apparently.

"Danny and I had a son a few months back. Gregory. I wasn't exactly in the picture so much, so Danny's mom was helping her with the baby."

"Nora Foster?" Detective Toliver asked, but to Tommy's ears it sounded like the cop just wanted him to keep things formal, use names, and stick to the facts.

"Yeah, Nora Foster," he confirmed.

Crouse was already unconvinced. "How do you know Nora was helping with the baby if you weren't in the picture?"

"Look, I'm not here to give you a whole song and dance. I'm here to tell you that Nora came to me and she told me that she killed my son, Gregory."

Crouse and Toliver looked at one another, then Toliver leaned in. "Why would she tell you that?"

"She's a sick woman, and in her mind, she thought the information would keep me away from her and Danny."

"How do you know what was in her 'mind'?" Crouse wanted to know.

"Come on, you know what I mean."

"She could've been lying to you," Crouse suggested.

"Don't you have an autopsy that proves my son was killed?"

The detectives weren't going easy on him, but Tommy had a feeling he had convinced them, especially the younger cop, Toliver.

Crouse asked him, "You're Gregory's dad, Danny's boyfriend?" When Tommy nodded, confirming as much, he pointed out, "What if it looks like you're just trying to clear your girlfriend of suspicion? You have a vested interest in keeping your girlfriend out of prison."

"Nora looked me dead in the eye and admitted she smothered Gregory to death, alright?"

Toliver softened up. "You want to make a formal statement? We'll get you a pen and paper."

"Great."

Crouse added, "You need to know something about that woman, your girlfriend. She's not good. Call it bad genes or the apple not falling far from the tree, but she has a killer inside of her, too."

"What are you talking about?" Tommy asked, annoyed. "She didn't kill our son."

"She didn't report it, either," Toliver told him, and Tommy couldn't argue. "And she tried to kill Nora."

Tommy screwed his face up. "Get out of here."

"Did you notice the scratches on her face?" Detective Crouse cut in. "The fact of the matter is that Danny wasn't going to do a damn thing about Gregory's murder, and I think you know that. *That's* who she is. Okay? Do you get that?

"From our perspective, " Crouse went on as he touched eyes with his partner, "Danny was about to let her mother get away with murder, but Nora, we suspect, got in her face or got pushy or tried to keep Danny under her control, *something* happened. And Danny's solution was to try to strangle the woman to death. The only reason any of this has come across our desk is because *Nora* came in to report the attempted murder."

Toliver added, "Now, Nora's trying to get Danny put away, Danny's trying to get Nora put away, you're in the middle of it, and we're having a hard time sorting out who did what and how culpable Danny might be, even if she *didn't* take her own son's life."

Tommy challenged them, "You're telling me that you would be quick to turn your own mother in?"

Detective Crouse frowned and had a good, long think on that.

Then he said, "As a citizen? No, I wouldn't be quick. As a cop? Yeah, I would have my mother arrested faster than you can say, 'happy mother's day'."

Tommy didn't believe the guy for a second.

Crouse referred to himself and Toliver as he explained, "We aren't built like everyone else. Cops, that is. We don't think the same way regular people do. We don't operate the same. We put the law above everyone and everything, even our own families. If a person doesn't have it in them to put the law above all else, then they don't have it in them to be a cop. And that's our problem with Foster."

"Alright, Crouse," said Toliver, as if his partner had said too much already. "Let me get you that pen and paper," he offered, rising to his feet.

While Detective Toliver fetched a pen and paper for Tommy to write down what Nora had confessed to him, Tommy asked Crouse, "What are you going to do about Nora?"

"We'll talk to her."

"That's it?"

"You're not exactly giving us hard evidence," he pointed out.

Tommy gained the distinct impression that the cops weren't going to do a damn thing about Nora. Danny had been right. The detectives were gunning to have her removed from the force. That was their objective.

Who the hell was fighting for Gregory?

Tommy didn't know, but he wrote up a statement never-the-less when Toliver returned.

If they didn't have enough to get Nora based on Tommy's statement, then it stood to reason that they didn't have enough on Danny to get her, either.

But what about those scratches…?

Tommy tried to push the thought from his mind, but the possibility nagged at him.

Had Danny tried to take her own mother's life?

Again, he shoved the idea out of his head, signed his full legal name at the bottom of the statement, and got the hell out of the police precinct.

As he stepped outside into the clear light of day, he knew that Nora was never going to stop…

…unless someone stopped her.

Tommy was walking up the sidewalk, heading towards O'Toole's, when a black sedan with dark, tinted windows came to a screeching stop in the street right next to him.

Nico Campopiano jumped out of the back of the sedan with another man, grabbed Tommy, and pulled him into the car.

The next thing Tommy knew he was wedged between Jimmy and Tony Campopiano in the backseat of the sedan, and staring down the barrel of a gun.

Jimmy lifted the gun and pressed the barrel against Tommy's cheek, while Tony held him.

"What were you doing at the police station, O'Toole?" Jimmy asked.

"It had nothing to do with you," he promised, as they drove off down the street.

"Why should I believe you?"

"Come on, Jimmy, I'm not stupid!" he yelled, losing it.

Jimmy eased off, but kept the gun on him. "What were you doing there?"

Tommy didn't want to open up his private affairs to the mobster. But he also didn't want to get whacked for a betrayal he hadn't committed.

"It's about my son," he told them.

"Why don't you let me handle that?" Jimmy asked him, as he tucked the gun into his suit jacket. "Talk to me, Tommy."

"I'm handling it!" he barked, coming undone.

"What are you handling?" the mobster pushed. "Who did it?"

When Tommy shook his head, refusing to answer, Jimmy told him, "You don't know how to handle something like this, O'Toole, look at yourself. You're coming apart at the seams. You went to a police station. You think those cops give a damn about your boy?"

"No," he darkly admitted.

"You think you can take matters into your own hands, Tommy, but you're not made for it."

"Let me out of the car," he growled.

"I can handle this for you," Jimmy promised. "I

take dirt bags out like it's trash day all the time, it's nothing for me, Tommy!"

"Let me out of the car!"

"Why won't you let me help you?"

"Goddamnit! Stop the car!" Tommy yelled.

Jimmy told the driver, "Pull over. Let him out."

The second the car pulled along a row of parked cars and Jimmy climbed out, Tommy jumped out of the car and rushed down the sidewalk, walking as fast as he could and clipping shoulders with pedestrians that were too slow to move out of his furious way.

Jimmy called out after him, "Don't do anything stupid, Tommy!"

Tommy's vision began tunneling badly. A deafening ringing sound filled his ears.

He told himself to get a grip and to slow down, but the part of him that was capable of reason felt like it was sinking down into a deep, dark pool within his racing mind.

Nora had taken everything from him.

She had taken everything from Danny.

She was never going to stop.

Tommy told himself to go to the bar and drink, but that wasn't where he went.

Blocks later, he found himself standing outside of Nora's building.

This ends now.

He took the stoop steps two at a time to catch the door as a corporate-looking woman breezed out of the building. She thanked him, assuming he had meant to help her with the door.

In the lobby, he came to the mailboxes on the wall. He had never been to Nora's apartment, he didn't know the number. But each mailbox had the resident's name and apartment number. He scanned them until he found 'Foster.'

With the apartment number in mind, he took the stairwell, raced up the stairs, his blood boiling all the while. A strange rage-induced euphoria filled him.

He pounded on the door. His heart punched hard in his heaving chest.

The memory of Danny sobbing in his arms surged to mind.

"She turned me into a monster! She destroyed me! I can't live with myself like this! I hate what she turned me into! I wish she was dead!"

Danny *had* lost control.

"She turned me into a monster!"

She *had* tried to take Nora's life.

"I wish she was dead!"

He pounded on the door again and heard movement on the other side.

"Open up, Nora!" he shouted and pounded. "We have to talk!"

Brazen and fearless, Nora opened the door.

Tommy towered over the frail woman, as she looked up at him with a weirdly victorious smirk on her face.

"You're too late, Tommy, I've spoken with the police."

"So have I," he said, as he entered her apartment, forcing her to back up, not that there was anywhere to go. One quick glance, and Tommy gleaned that she was some kind of hoarder. It didn't matter. He told her, "I don't know what game you're playing, but you're going to back off."

"Game!" she laughed. She lifted her chin to show him her neck. "Danny did this to me," she snapped. "I have cancer, you know. I'm dying."

"You're willing to risk it all, even Danny's life, her happiness! You don't care, you have cancer, you're as good as dead, is that it?"

Nora gazed up at him as if she found him pathetic.

"I'm going to end up with my daughter," she informed him. "If we have to go to prison together in order for that to happen, then so be it."

Restraining himself was nearly impossible.

"You killed my son! You threw it in my face! *You're* going to prison, Nora! You're going to come clean to the cops, or else!"

Nora slapped him clear across the face.

Tommy saw red.

His vision tunneled even worse.

If he had been hanging on by a very thin thread before, the thread had just snapped.

He plummeted into a black hole, lost all control, and had no way of stopping what happened next.

Chapter Twelve

DANNY KEPT HOPE alive, but she was still looking over her shoulder.

When she woke up that morning, Tommy had already left for the precinct. His mug had been placed in the sink. The coffee pot was nearly full.

Danny clung to the kernel of relief that had formed in her heart and kept her head down when she arrived at the 66th. Whether Tommy was still there or had already spoken with Crouse and Toliver, she had no way of knowing.

At the precinct, she regrouped with Carter. There were no updates in terms of the warrant, and their biggest lead was the sailor's knot.

As they drove northwest, heading towards the Brooklyn Marina, Carter behind the wheel and Danny seated in the passenger seat, Carter reasoned:

"Even if the Campopianos' estate is chock-full of cyanide capsules, that's not going to automatically flush out the killer. Besides, I'm starting to consider that Bobby *could have* offed himself."

"Suicide under duress is still murder," she pointed out. "But I'm with you. Let's run down the suspects and motives, no matter how thin."

"Eric MacDermott. Motive, to get the role of Friar Tuck."

"Friar *Lawrence*," she corrected him.

Danny pulled her notepad out of the inner pocket of her black blazer. There was a pen in the glove compartment. She jotted the male ballet dancer's name down, wrote a hyphen, and added *'power'* as a motive. The motive was weaker than 'thin,' but people have killed to advance their own careers. It wasn't beyond the scope of reason.

"Paul Decker," she listed next, as she wrote the toxic lover's name down.

"Motive?" Carter asked her.

"Let's hope we find out when we talk to him today," she replied, as she glanced at him. He touched eyes with her then returned his attention to the tight grid of traffic they were caught in. "All that comes to mind is the sailor's knot," she admitted.

"All we've got is loose, flimsy circumstantial evidence... We could add Father Silva to the list, but why? We've got nothing, Danny."

Carter shook his head and squinted into the harsh, late morning glare.

She couldn't argue with him, but she kept pushing.

"The fact that Bobby was gay..." she began thinking out loud. "That puts the Campopianos at the front of my mind. But I'm just going with my gut and indulging assumptions," she admitted, as she checked the side view mirror in case there were any unmarked police cars following them.

She had been looking over her shoulder ever since Detectives Crouse and Toliver had ambushed her at the crime scene days ago. Considering that Tommy had spoken with them, Danny knew that police procedure would dictate the cops would either talk to Danny next or Nora. Given that Crouse and Toliver seemed to hate Danny's guts, she had to figure they would come to grill her ass next and spare her murdering mother the anxiety.

"Which Campopiano?" Carter asked, but the question was directed at himself more than anyone.

"Which Campopiano could've gotten into the ballet studios?"

He knew where she was going. But Carter didn't like it. It didn't square right with him. "I can't see Eva Campopiano hanging her brother."

"But she, more than anyone, would have a key."

"Same goes for every ballet dancer in the company, and Paul Decker, for that matter."

"Why would Decker have a key?"

Carter shot her a look and questioned her, "Tommy doesn't have a key to your place?"

"Sure, but he doesn't know my locker combination," she countered. "Does Kathy have a copy of every key to all your locks?"

"Yes, as a matter of fact." He started brooding as if *that* was a new dilemma to solve.

"You know the hardest case to prove?" she asked him.

He did. The fear had been on his mind. He replied, "Conspiracy."

"Conspiracy," she confirmed with a soft echo, as she turned her attention to the piers.

"Danny, I think we have to build a case for conspiracy," he told her.

She touched eyes with him. "And don't forget about exposing that dirty judge."

He chuckled and pointed out, "At least if I get fired for failing, my wife will throw me a party."

Danny felt her smile flatten. "Kathy doesn't want you to get fired," she said.

"You want to bet?"

"Are you kidding me?"

He shrugged but distinct anger rolled off him like heat from an engine. Danny left it alone, as the

Crown Vic bounced over cobblestone streets, coming to Pier Zero where a tight row of sailboats were docked along the East River.

Carter steered the Crown Vic left on the one-way even though the Brooklyn Marina would be behind them.

"Hydrant," she pointed out, and Carter eased the car into the space in front of the fire hydrant.

They would have no chance of parking otherwise. The entire block was lined with a wall of bumper to bumper cars that were parked so close, Danny doubted a piece of paper would fit between one vehicle and the next.

As they climbed out of the parked Crown Vic, she glanced up and down the street for Homicide, but the detectives hadn't followed them. Traffic was slow and lazy at best. Though the neighborhood had become a gentrified, pricey area thanks to the museum, it was mostly residential and therefore relatively tame during the daytime.

According to Decker's boat registration, his sailboat was docked at the Brooklyn Marina, Slip 112, which Carter had discovered at the precinct that morning.

Danny and Carter headed down the cobblestone street, keeping close to the parked cars since there wasn't a proper sidewalk.

Seagulls soared in circles high in the sky. Other gulls gracefully swooped in low over Danny and Carter's heads. Their curious, aggressive manner told her that these gulls were accustomed to being fed. She was in no mood. If one of them pooped on her, she would shoot the damn thing. As they briskly walked, Carter looked up at the hovering gulls, thinking the same thing it seemed.

Luckily, they reached the wooden docks of Pier Zero at the Brooklyn Marina unscathed. The marina had an office building on the East River. A two-story glass structure, the office had all the trendy charm of the developed waterfront itself.

Danny and Carter didn't need to go inside. She scanned the docks, looking for the slip numbers.

"This dock covers the 80s," she pointed out.

The slip nearest them started at 80, followed by 81, 82, 83, and so on. Carter looked north and the neighboring dock, while Danny looked south, checking the numbers.

"South," they said simultaneously.

They headed south, walking over the wooden boardwalk, their heavy heels clunking over the boards. Underneath them, the briny waters of the East River slapped against rocks. Harbored sailboats bobbed and knocked against buoys. The area smelled of salty sea air, and the humidity made Danny's skin feel sticky.

"This way," Carter said when they reached the dock with Slips 100 - 125.

"Paul wanted us to be afraid of the Campopianos," Danny began ruminating. "But I don't get the feeling he's afraid of them. I think he's smart."

"What do you mean?"

"I think he knew Jimmy and the rest would kick his ass if he showed up at the funeral and rubbed in their faces that Bobby had been living with him, you know?"

"So, Paul wanted to get his ass beat?" Carter asked as they came to Slip 112 where a 40-foot sailboat with a towering mast tipped and bobbed on the water.

"What if Paul knew the cops would go to the funeral. I don't think he *wanted* to get beaten up. I think he wanted the cops to witness the Campopianos' short fuse and their violent inclinations."

"But Paul saw it coming from a mile away when Jimmy and his boys faced no consequences even though you and I were there, as cops," Carter pointed out.

Danny squinted, thinking long and hard. "I think there's something to it. It has the feel of a staged performance, or a set up."

"Like the phony suicide note and implicating Father Silva," Carter surmised. He snorted a laugh and shook his head. "This whole case has the feel of a set up."

"Check this out," she said, as she came to the massive rope that was anchoring the sailboat to the dock. There was an equally massive metal bar bolted into the dock, which the thick rope was tied around. "Is that the knot?"

Carter looked down and studied the professional sailor's knot that had been used to anchor Paul's sailboat to the dock, as Danny found her cell phone and sent a quick call to Jill Andover.

"It's Danny." she said, as soon as Jill's distinct voice came through the line. "You took a photo of that knot from the crime scene, right?"

"You have to get Quinlan off of his protection detail," she blurted out, deaf to Danny's request. "He's driving me crazy!"

It took her a moment to place what in the hell

Jill was talking about. "Oh, Officer Sean Quinlan?"

"He never leaves me alone," Jill complained, as Danny locked eyes with Carter.

Danny covered the mouthpiece and told Carter, *'Jill's annoyed with the police detail.'*

Jill went on, "It would be one thing if he sat in his cruiser outside of my building all night. But, oh, no, he won't do that. He stands out in the hallway, makes me feel guilty because he's out there, and what do I do, Danny?"

"I have no idea," she replied.

"I feel bad for the guy. So, I let him in. Then he's on the couch, then I'm making him coffee, and now I can't get rid of him!"

"Are you telling me Quinlan crossed a line?" she asked, suddenly curious.

"No, he hasn't crossed a line," Jill sighed. "I wish he would, because then I could get him fired. He's just constantly around me."

"And you like it?"

Furious, Jill barked, "What do you want, Danny?"

"I thought you would never ask," she said, as she stooped down in front of the sailor's knot. "Could you text me the crime scene photo of the knot that was used to tether the rope at the crime scene?"

"The Clove Hitch?"

"That's what it's called?" she asked.

"Looks like a figure-eight, or an infinity sign?" Jill suggested.

"Yes," she confirmed, studying the knot.

"Will do! Anything else?"

"Nope, just the knot," said Danny.

She was about to hang up when Jill begged,

"The sooner you solve this case, the sooner Quinlan will be out of my life!"

"We're working as fast as we can, Jill," she promised and ended the call.

"How's Jill?" Carter asked.

"She's in love with Officer Quinlan."

"How long before she realizes that?"

Danny smiled and shook her head.

Her cell vibrated with the text message from Jill containing the crime scene photo. Danny swiped the image open and angled her cell phone so that Carter could also see the screen.

"Same knot," he pointed out.

"Same *rope*, if I'm not mistaken," she added.

"We've got circumstantial evidence coming out of our ears at this point."

She wondered, "How do you knock on a sailboat?"

Carter neared the side of the boat as it tipped and dipped in the warm breeze.

"Paul Decker!" he called out, then he told Danny, "That's how. Hey, yo', Paul!"

"Mr. Decker!" she shouted. "Detectives Foster and Dobbs, here!"

Carter took hold of the sailboat railing to steady the boat and said, "At least on a boat, there's no such thing as *breaking* and entering."

Carter helped Danny up onto the stern of the sailboat, and as she climbed farther up onto the cockpit landing, Carter made his way onto the stern and followed up after her.

"Mr. Decker!" she shouted down into the darkened cabin beyond the cockpit.

The only thing separating the cabin from the

cockpit was a brown curtain. Danny descended three steps, pulled the brown curtain aside, and again called out, "Paul! It's the police!"

She told Carter, who was right behind her, "I don't think he's here."

When they entered the cabin, they discovered she was right. Paul wasn't there. No one was.

The cabin provided very tight quarters. Danny couldn't imagine two grown men living down here. There was a cot-size bed. A wooden desk had been built into the headboard of the bed. It seemed like every piece of wooden furniture was an outgrowth of another furniture piece if not the siding of the boat itself.

But that wasn't what gave the detectives pause.

The place looked like it had been ransacked. Clothes that should've been in the dresser were strewn across the floor. Books, journals, magazines, and other publications were scattered everywhere. It looked like someone had been here and had torn the place apart in search of something.

"Hey, Danny," said Carter. He had eased past her and was now standing in what appeared to be the 'living room' of the cabin. "It looks like there was a struggle."

She joined him, fighting the woozy feeling in her gut. Her every step felt like it was on unsteady ground since the sailboat was rising and dipping with the swells of the East River.

Carter was right. There was blood on the table and upholstered benches that made a cramped square.

He insisted, "We have to get Jill down here. We gotta call Franco."

Danny already had her cell phone in her hand, but neither Jill nor the lieutenant would be her first choice.

"Let's see if Paul made it into work," she said, as she looked up the main number for the Brooklyn Botanical Gardens.

"This has *'mob hit'* written all over it!"

"Don't jump to conclusions," she told him, as she concentrated on putting a call through. "Hi, yes, can you connect me with Paul Decker?" Danny asked the woman who had answered.

Carter found his own cell phone, moving ahead.

Danny covered the mouthpiece of her cell and reminded Carter, "We can't justify being here."

"That's the least of my concerns," he grumbled.

"Yes?" Danny said into the line.

On the other end, a different woman began explaining, "Paul has yet to arrive. May I help you?"

"This is Detective Foster with the Kensington P.D. When are you expecting Paul?" she asked.

There was hesitation on the other end, then the woman said, "He should've been in at nine this morning, but he didn't show. Has something happened to Paul?"

"That's what I'm looking into," said Danny. "Let me give you my cell number, and please call me if you hear from Paul, or if he shows up for work."

As Danny recited her cell phone number for Paul's supervisor at the Brooklyn Botanical Gardens, Carter was barking his way through his own rocky phone call.

"The gay lover has gone missing. We're at the Brooklyn Marina, Slip 112, at Paul Decker's sailboat."

Danny could hear Lieutenant Martin Franco's loud, unamused reply coming through the line.

"Tell me you didn't set foot on his boat, Dobbs!"

"There's blood in the cabin," Carter told the lieutenant, shamelessly.

"Carter," Franco warned, just as Carter switched his cell to speakerphone for Danny's benefit. "Don't touch anything. Don't tell me anything else. I'll see what I can do about Decker's boat and get you the authorization to enter, alright? In the meantime, I need you both back at the precinct."

Carter and Danny glanced at each other, and Danny argued, "We need to circle back to the dancers and question the Campopianos, one at a time if possible. Today was the day we were planning to strike hard since Bobby's Funeral Mass is over."

Franco told them, "I got you a warrant."

"No way," said Carter under his breath.

"We need to reconvene in my office," Franco said with such conviction that Danny could hear the lust for justice in his voice. "Get back here, now."

"Right away, Lieutenant," said Danny, and Carter seconded the affirmation before hanging up.

Carter started out of the cabin. Danny followed after him up the little stairs. When they crossed the cockpit, coming to the stern of the sailboat, a huge wake rolled through the East River.

Where it had started was anyone's guess. Carter nearly lost his balance standing on the stern as the sailboat suddenly plummeted then popped up, bouncing with the hard wake. But he managed to jump off the stern and onto the wooden dock.

When it was Danny's turn, the sailboat bounced

with the next hard wake, and the momentum caused the boat to slam against the rubber buoys on the wooden dock. That was exactly when Danny jumped, but when she pushed off, the boat was already ricocheting against the dock and coasting away in the opposite direction.

It wasn't until she was in the air and saw the look of certain horror on Carter's face that she knew she wasn't going to reach the dock.

"Ahh!" she screamed before smacking into the shockingly chilly waters of the East River.

Freezing water stung every inch of her, as she plunged deeper into the brackish water. Above the surface, Carter shouted her name, but his voice was muffled and distant. Water rushed in her ears and she kept sinking until eventually the deep waters decided to spit her out again.

She rose up, floating to the surface, and when her head broke through, she gasped for air.

"Danny! Jesus! Swim over!" Carter yelled.

He was on his knees on the dock.

"Thanks for not jumping in to save me!" she complained, as she paddled over.

"I'm wearing a new suit."

She would've rolled her eyes if she hadn't been determined to hoist herself up onto the dock.

Carter grabbed hold of her upper arm and pulled her. She rolled onto the dock, soaked and miserable.

"Ready to see the lieutenant?" he asked her cheerfully.

She groaned.

"Come on," said Carter, as he helped her to her feet.

Salt water cascaded off of her and her sneakers squished, water-logged.

"I have to get changed."

"I'll drop you off."

"Go to the precinct. I'll catch a cab."

"Danny, it'll take two minutes."

"It won't, Carter, I have to shower, and if I sit in the Crown Vic, the car will smell like fish for the next ten years."

After some hemming and hawing, they parted ways once Carter had hailed her a cab. The driver was hardly pleased that Danny had taken a spill into the East River, but flashing her badge helped open the guy's mind.

During the ride, she sat uncomfortably in the back seat, her jeans shrinking around her thighs as they dried. Her Glock dripped with water when she released the magazine and slapped it back into place again. Fifteen agonizing minutes later, the driver pulled the cab in front of Danny's building on Ocean Parkway.

She paid the fare, flung herself out of the back, and fought her wet, restricting jeans with each step, as she came to her stoop and made her way inside the apartment building.

There was a janitorial closet at the back of the lobby that doubled as the super's office. Camil was back there, smoking a cigarette and dealing with something, but Danny barely noticed as she threw the stairwell door open.

A couple flights later, she stepped out onto the landing of her floor, opened the stairwell door, and made her way down the hallway.

Her apartment door was open by a few inches

when she reached it.

She froze.

Tommy had left *before* her that morning. Danny had definitely locked up. Why was her apartment door *open?*

She pulled her police-issued Glock from its holster on her hip. The thing was still wet with the East River stink on it, but she flipped the safety off and used her elbow to ease the apartment door open enough to slip inside.

The shallow entryway looked undisturbed. Her shoes were where they always had been. The jackets were hanging on the rack. Nothing appeared out of place or disturbed, but neither had Paul's boat until they had reached the cabin below.

She crept into the living room, quickly aimed her gun one way then the next, confirming that the room was clear with a wide sweep. It was. Nothing was out of place, she realized, and the kitchen was equally undisturbed.

As she tip-toed past the kitchen, coming down the short hallway that led to the bathroom, her bedroom, and what had been the baby's room, Danny heard a very faint tapping sound.

It was coming from the baby's room.

She used long, silent strides and then filled the doorway of the baby's room, swiftly aiming her gun into the room. She looked one way then the other, but the room was empty.

The window was wide open and a warm breeze was causing the venetian blinds to smack against the wall.

She definitely hadn't left the window open. She hadn't left the door of the baby's room open, either.

She had been keeping it closed for emotional reasons.

What the hell was going on?

She wasted no time confirming that no one was in the bathroom or her bedroom. Nothing had been disturbed, so she returned to the baby's room and holstered her gun.

Tommy wouldn't do this, but she grabbed her phone to give him a call anyway. As soon as she did, water dripped out of her cell phone. She cursed under her breath.

She was about to trash the broken thing, shut the apartment door, and get changed for the precinct, when she noticed the baby's crib.

A note was lying inside the crib.

Danny's blood ran cold.

The note was typed on eggshell cardstock. High quality. The letters were big and blocky—an elegant font.

'I'm sorry about Gregory.'

Danny's heart leapt up her throat.

"Nora!"

Whether she had thought it or yelled it, she didn't know. All Danny knew was that her mother had been here.

Enraged, Danny tore through the apartment, slammed the door out of her way, and as it bounced off the wall, she charged down the hallway. She couldn't see straight. She couldn't think straight, but when she spilled out into the lobby she had the good sense to ask Camil:

"Was my mother here?"

"What?" he asked with a burning cigarette between his teeth.

He was seated at a cluttered desk inside the janitor's closet.

"Was Nora here today?" Danny demanded.

"No? I don't know," he told her honestly.

She turned on her heel and charged through the lobby, slapped the glass door aside, and rushed down the sidewalk to her mother's building.

After keying in and throwing the door open, she ran across the lobby and didn't even consider waiting for the elevator.

This had to stop. Nora had to leave her alone. This had to stop.

Danny's mind raced with those two thoughts, as she charged up the stairwell stairs.

When she reached her mother's apartment, the door was ajar just like her own had been.

Her mind went blank.

There was a smear of blood on the door. She touched it, confused, then pushed the door open and stepped inside.

Something was wrong. She could feel it.

The warm, stuffy apartment air smelled of hot, wet pennies—iron.

Blood?

She drew her gun and padded as quietly as possible through the labyrinth of hoarded boxes.

When she approached the kitchen, she saw her mother's shoes, then her legs. Nora was on the floor, Danny realized, as she rushed over.

Lying on the kitchen tiles, Nora was covered in blood.

"Ma?!" she blurted, her hand loosening from its grip on her gun.

She dropped the gun and it clattered against the

floor, as Danny rushed over to her mother and dropped to her knees.

It looked like Nora had been stabbed multiple times. There was a bloody knife on the kitchen floor.

Danny took the knife by the handle, dumbfounded, and then slid it away across the tiles. She focused on her mother and tried to find a pulse. Her mother was *warm*, but dead.

Overcome with emotions, she scooped Nora's dead body into her arms, held her close, and wailed, letting out a guttural cry of anguish that felt like her soul was trying to escape her body.

Her vision blurred with a wall of tears, as she screamed and cried and screamed.

"What happened?" she whined, crying and rocking her dead mother.

"Who did this? What happened?" she wheezed out, as she sucked in breath after breath and cried, her mind fracturing into a thousand fragments.

There came a pounding knock at the apartment door, but Danny was a million miles away.

"Mrs. Foster? Hello! It's Detectives Crouse and Toliver! We would like to speak with you again. Are you home?"

Heavy footfall filled the apartment, as the homicide detectives entered the living room labyrinth.

"We spoke to Tommy O'Toole, Nora, and it's very important that we have a word with you now!"

Danny sensed more than saw the detectives step into the kitchen.

Through blurry tears, she looked up at the men, as they came to tower over her.

Her face contorted with anguish, as she cradled her mother in her arms and told them, "Someone killed my mom."

Detective Crouse asked her, "Was it you?"

Chapter Thirteen

CARTER ENTERED Lieutenant Martin Franco's office at the 66th Precinct.

The district attorney, Sarah Hovey, was present. Standing in front of the cool air conditioner breeze, Sarah was back lit by the strong afternoon sunlight.

Franco stood on the business side of his desk. His arms were folded and the atmosphere felt tense despite the good news.

"Where's your partner?" Franco asked as if Carter had already messed up.

"She took a spill into the East River," he explained before greeting Sarah. "Good to see you."

"Likewise, Dobbs," said Sarah.

Franco's lip curled, but he tried to suppress his amusement. "Danny fell into the river?"

"At the marina," Carter clarified. "She's getting washed up at her place."

"Alright, this can't wait," Franco stated. "Close the door and have a seat."

Carter did exactly that, giving the lieutenant his full attention.

Franco glanced at Sarah then he laid the recent development on his newest S.V.U. detective.

"We obtained a search warrant for the Campopianos' mansion, like I told you. There's one major restriction. We can't seize electronic devices."

Carter furrowed his brow. "Why the restriction?"

Sarah responded on Franco's behalf. "The real question is, why the warrant."

As her thin eyebrows drifted up to her hairline, Carter said, "I don't follow."

Again, Franco and Sarah exchanged a glance.

Sarah told Carter, "Justice Harlan Ellsworth was the judge who signed the warrant, authorizing the search."

"*Ellsworth* did?" he blurted out. He asked Franco, "The dirty judge we're looking into?"

Franco had a grave look of concern, as he nodded.

"Why would Ellsworth do that if he's been taking bribes from the Campopianos and protecting them?" Carter questioned.

"We have a few theories," Franco allowed, as he touched eyes with Sarah. "But for the time being, we're going to act on the warrant. I would like to get you over there now with a unit of police officers and a forensics team."

Carter offered, "I'll text Danny to let her know to meet us there."

As he composed a text message, Franco went on to explain, "We're not going into this naively. Though it's possible Ellsworth saw the light and discontinued his dirty ways, it's far more likely that there's some other plan at work here."

Sarah added, "It's referred to as 'controlled opposition.' Ellsworth might have signed the warrant in order to position himself as the presiding judge over the entire discovery process."

"We can't worry about that now, though," Franco reiterated. "But we all need to watch our backs."

"What about Decker?" Carter wanted to know.

Franco didn't sugarcoat it. "Put Decker on the back burner."

"There was blood on his boat—"

"You weren't supposed to be on his boat!" Franco barked. "Ellsworth has placed a magnifying glass over this investigation, do you get that! No more rogue tactics, Dobbs! I'm warning you!"

Carter showed no emotion. "Yes, Sir."

Franco exhaled like a raging bull, paced away, turned on his heel, and returned, all in the tight space behind his office desk.

Sarah informed Carter, "As long as you stay away from the computers, laptops, tablets, cell phones, and all devices, you can bag and tag anything you see at the Campopiano estate."

"Got it," said Carter.

Referring to the cell phone in the detective's hand, Franco asked, "Did Danny reply?"

"No, I can give her a call on the way," he said as he stood and shoved his cell phone into his slacks.

"Dobbs," Franco warned. "Hope for the best, but expect the worst."

"Always," he agreed.

Carter felt beads of sweat roll down his chest under his dress shirt, as he climbed into the Crown Vic. Danny hadn't replied to his text and she wasn't picking up now. He killed the call he had placed, tossed his cell phone onto the passenger seat, and turned the engine.

Hot, stale air blasted out of the vents. He adjusted the temperature dials, but it didn't help.

There was a cherry siren light in the back seat. From where he sat in the driver's seat, he turned, grabbed the thing, and rolled his window down so he could slap the red light onto the roof of the sedan.

Once the light magnetized in place, he flipped

the switch and the red cherry siren lit up like a lighthouse in hell.

He tore into the street, and as he hit the gas, a caravan of police cruisers followed with lights blazing and sirens wailing.

Brooklyn traffic pulled over to make way from the Crown Vic. Carter didn't wait for red lights. Instead, he squeezed the brakes whenever he came to an intersection, and opposing traffic yielded as he rolled by with a line of police cruisers.

Why wasn't Danny picking up? It wasn't like her, he thought, angered, as he listened to her cell phone ring and ring until her outgoing voicemail message began to play again.

Carter reasoned that the second he saw her next, he was going to have it out with her. Enough was enough. Her secrets had been getting in the way of her police work, and Carter wasn't going to put up with this any longer.

The Crown Vic growled its way down Westminster. Carter spotted the massive church grounds of St. Christopher's and knew that Argyle Road was coming up. The Campopianos' mansion wasn't far.

After a couple turns, the stone lions came into view, marking the grand stoop of the mansion. Carter yanked the wheel, slammed on the brakes, and barrelled onto the curb in his effort to aim for the walkway.

Killing the engine, he yanked the keys from the sedan and jumped out, as the police cruisers came to screeching stops in the street.

With the search warrant in hand, Carter charged up the wide, stone steps of the mansion, grabbed the metal knocker that was probably worth more than Carter's annual salary, and pounded hard on the door.

"Police!" he barked, as he pounded harder. "Campopiano! We've got a search warrant! Open up or we'll break the door down!"

Carter glanced over his shoulder. Two police officers held a long, tactical ram, prepared and ready to break down the front door.

Turning towards the door, Carter gave the family one more chance.

"Open up, Mr. Campopiano! The police have a search warrant signed by Justice Ellsworth!"

Due diligence had been fulfilled, as far as Carter was concerned. He waved the tactical officers over, but as they jogged the steel ram up the stone steps, the front door popped open.

Jimmy Campopiano stood on the other side.

He wore nothing but a white towel wrapped around his waist and a confident grin on his face.

As he pulled a toothpick from his mouth, he told Carter, "You gonna let me see the warrant?"

Carter shoved the folded search warrant against Jimmy's bare, glistening chest, and barrelled ahead into the mansion.

The unit of uniformed police officers followed in after Carter.

Outside, Jill Andover and the forensics unit had shown up and were getting organized on the lawn.

Jimmy trailed back into his house, still wet from the shower he had taken.

Carter directed the cops to fan out, and as they started off, he turned on his heel to face Jimmy and sniffed the air.

"Why does it smell like bleach in here?" he asked Jimmy.

Jimmy grinned and shrugged. "Must be cleaning day."

"I'm going to have to ask you to leave while we exercise our right to search the house."

"I'm not wearing any clothes, Detective, and my wife is upstairs with the baby."

Carter growled under his breath. "Throw some clothes on, get your wife, and get out."

"My pleasure," said Jimmy. As he headed for the stairs, he shouted, "Catherine! We gotta leave for a bit!"

Carter watched him jog up the stairs, just as Jill and her team entered the mansion with Police Officer Sean Quinlan in tow.

"Dobbs," said Jill, greeting the detective. She scowled slightly when Quinlan squeezed through the forensic investigators in order to stand next to her. "Where would you like us to focus?" she asked and then quickly bristled. "Sean, please!" she snapped when the officer had crowded her even worse.

She widened her eyes at Carter, annoyed.

"We're looking for cyanide capsules. We're looking for bloody clothes," he listed, rattling off the dots that he would most like to connect. "Rope, evidence of sailing expertise, keys to the Brooklyn Ballet Studios, anything that can link the Campopianos to the crime scene. But most importantly, we want to narrow this down. Who killed Bobby? If it was one of the Campopianos, which *one*? Or is there evidence that many of them acted in concert?"

"Understood," said Jill.

She began dividing up her team and directing them until there were only a couple of forensic investigators with her, which she instructed to assist her.

"We'll start in the kitchen," she told them, and as they started off, Office Quinlan kept at Jill's heels. "Please, Sean!" she snapped. She put her hands up and insisted, "My life isn't in danger right now. You stay here, I'm going to go over there."

"Okay," he said easily, but Carter could tell Sean really didn't like separating from Jill.

As Jill and her investigators crossed the grand, marble foyer and disappeared into the kitchen, Officer Quinlan meandered after them, as if Jill wouldn't notice.

For a moment, Carter stood alone in the foyer. Warm wind breezed through the open doorway, and Danny's bizarre absence weighed heavily on his mind.

Jimmy made his lazy way down the stairs with his wife, Catherine, and their baby daughter, Rosa.

Jimmy wore a nice suit and smelled of expensive cologne, and his wife and daughter looked just as elite. Even the baby bag that Jimmy was carrying for Catherine had a designer name embossed into its rich, leather side.

When the handsome family reached the foyer, Carter boldly asked Jimmy, "Where's Paul Decker?"

"How should I know?" said Jimmy, hardly rattled, as he steered his wife through the foyer towards the open doorway.

"He went missing," Carter barked, as Jimmy sailed past. Carter was well aware that he was jumping to conclusions, but getting a rise out of

Jimmy could prove beneficial. "What did you do to Paul?"

Jimmy turned on his heel and faced Carter. "I beat the living crap out of him, Detective, but you know that. You were there. And you didn't do a damn thing about it, did you?"

Carter kept a lid on it, clenched his jaw, and watched the family walk outside into the sunshine and descend the stone steps.

"Don't leave town!" Carter warned them.

"Dobbs!" one of the police officers shouted from the second floor. "Got something!"

Carter jogged up the stairs just as the officer shouted, "In here!"

Following the sound of the cop's voice, Carter walked briskly around the landing and came into a little boy's room where two police officers were standing beside a nightstand. The drawer was open. They waved Carter over, and when Carter peered down into the open drawer, one of the cops asked him:

"Does that look like a cyanide capsule?"

"Get forensics," he told them, as he backed away.

His mind began tumbling with disturbed ideas. This was definitely a little boy's bedroom. According to Pasquale, Guido's kids had been given cyanide capsules. That amounted to Jimmy, Eva, and Bobby, the dead Campopiano.

But now it appeared that the youngest Campopiano was also in possession of suicide capsules... What the hell kind of family had secrets like that?

From the basement of the mansion, Jill's faint

voice carried up through the floorboards.

"Carter! You have to get down here!"

He made his fast way out of the boy's bedroom, along the hallway, and down the stairs. Carter swung into the kitchen, but he had been correct. Jill had already found her way into the basement of the house.

One of the police officers was standing at the open doorway of the basement, called for Carter, and waved him over.

Carter barrelled through the doorway and jogged down the stairs, coming into a fully furnished, lounge-like basement that offered more luxury than most Americans' upper-middle class houses.

He followed Jill's voice, as she continued to call for him, until he found her in what appeared to be a large laundry room.

Jill was standing by a sleek hamper, holding a white, men's dress shirt in her gloved hand. It was saturated in blood.

She asked him, "Would you call this a smoking gun?"

He charged ahead. "I want to know whose blood that is… Bobby's?"

"So, do I," she assured him.

Impulse took over, and Carter rushed out of the basement, ran up the stairs, and tore through the house, then he spilled out into the blinding light of day.

He had enough to arrest Jimmy, he frantically reasoned. He wasn't going to miss his shot.

"Campopiano!" he shouted, spotting Jimmy and his family, who hadn't made it very far.

As Carter jogged past a cluster of police officers, he told them. "Put an A.P.B. out on Guido Campopiano, Tony Campopiano, Nico Campopiano, hell, all of them! Arrest all of them, now!"

"Yes, Sir," they said.

Carter was already halfway to Jimmy.

"James Campopiano!" Carter shouted, as he jogged and produced a set of handcuffs, "You're under arrest for the murder of Bobby Campopiano and Paul Decker!"

Jimmy smiled, presented his wrists neatly behind his back, and asked the detective, "Anyone else? Or was it only the homos that I killed?"

He winked at his wife, even though Catherine looked like she was going to puke.

"Shut up," Carter snarled, as he yanked the mobster away.

When he reached the nearest parked police cruiser, he tossed Jimmy in the back, slammed the door shut, and told the cop standing outside, "Book him."

Carter circled back to the mansion steps, feeling powerful and back in control.

His cell phone began vibrating in the front pocket of his slacks. It had to be Danny, he thought, as he pulled his phone out, squinting into the broad light. There was nothing but blue skies above.

It was Franco.

Carter's chest filled with pride, as he accepted the call and told the lieutenant, "The house is teeming with evidence. I just arrested Jimmy—"

"Danny's in big trouble," Franco cut in, his voice thick with urgency. "I need you back here."

Confusion clouded Carter's ability to think. *Danny* was in trouble?

"What?" he asked, refusing to consider that he had heard the lieutenant correctly. "Did you say—?"

"Come to the jails in the basement of the 66th."

"What?!"

The line cut out.

"Franco!"

WHEN CARTER returned to the 66th Precinct, he went straight to the basement where a uniformed police officer was standing watch in front of the jail cells.

The officer knew Carter and let him through with a nod.

He crept past the first set of jails that served as a drunk tank. There were men in the cell on the left and women, mostly hookers, in the cell on the right. After that was a set of empty jail cells, and then Carter found Danny and Franco in the last cell on the left.

Danny was soaked in blood from her quivering chin to her knees where the blood had turned her jeans black. She looked white-faced and shaken. Her eyes were vacant as if a catatonic state had come over her.

Franco was seated on the steel bench next to Danny. The jail cell door was open. Carter stepped inside.

Franco locked eyes with Carter, and the look of unbridled horror on the lieutenant's face said it all.

Whatever secrets Danny had been keeping had just surfaced into the unforgiving light of day, and Carter already couldn't believe it.

"What the hell happened?" he dared to ask.

Danny couldn't seem to lift her gaze to Carter, and it wasn't for shame. She appeared to be in a bad psychological state.

Franco spoke on her behalf, "Danny was arrested for murder."

"What?" Carter breathed.

"Her mother, Nora, was found dead, stabbed to death. Homicide has been tracking Danny on suspicions of attempted murder—"

"*What the hell are you talking about?*" Carter didn't know if he had said it or thought it.

A semblance response seeped out from between Danny's slack lips, "I didn't kill her."

Franco placed his large hand on her shoulder and insisted, "You're being set up, and we're going to get to the bottom of this."

Carter sank onto the bench on the other side of Danny.

Franco continued briefing him, "This is what's going on. Nora killed Danny's son. Danny didn't report it right away. Nora confessed to Tommy. You know Tommy?"

Carter nodded. "Yeah."

"When things came to light, Nora told the cops that Danny tried to kill Nora."

"That's why Crouse and Toliver have been showing up left and right," Carter surmised.

"They're investigating the infanticide," Franco confirmed, "and the attempted murder."

"Where did the murder take place?

"At Nora's apartment. Danny went there, found her mother dead, but guess what? That's when Homicide decided to show up and ask Nora a few more questions."

Carter cursed under his breath and ran his big hand down his sweaty face.

Danny floated back into herself and told them, "Someone was in my apartment. I went home to shower, and the door was unlocked and open. There was a window open, too, and a note in the baby's room. I thought—"

She burst out crying, overcome with emotion.

She had to yell just to get the words out, as she sobbed. "I thought my Ma left that note! I went over to her place to confront her!"

Franco relayed the rest of the story while Danny collapsed into a fit of tears.

"Nora's apartment door was also unlocked and open. Danny entered and the rest you know."

Despite Danny's sobbing, Carter asked her, "Who else has keys to your place?"

From where Carter was sitting, it looked like Danny had an answer, but didn't want to say.

That's when he cursed again under his breath and guessed, "Tommy?" He told Franco, "I saw them leaving together the other morning. Tommy's been staying over, hasn't he, Danny?"

She couldn't admit it.

Carter began thinking out loud. "When will we have an autopsy? If the report includes a precise time of death, I might be able to alibi Danny. She was with me at the Brooklyn Marina. I put her in a cab. The ride couldn't have been longer than fifteen, maybe twenty minutes. Then she's home, finds the note, goes to Nora's... That's quick, you know? Maybe it'll be enough to clear her."

Franco didn't want to be the bearer of bad news, but he had never gone easy on anyone.

"Homicide wants to lock her up," he told his detective, point blank. "I don't see Crouse and Toliver backing off this thing, not now."

There had to be a way to get Danny out of this mess.

Carter promised, "Just tell me what to do, and I'll do it."

Chapter Fourteen

TOMMY WASN'T picking up his phone. Carter had tried Tommy's cell phone countless times, and as he sat at his desk in the 66th Precinct, watching the stark orange sun lower over the cityscape beyond his window, he listened to the ring tone yet again.

After leaving another voicemail message, he depressed the hook switch and quickly punched in the seven digit number for O'Toole's.

"Hi, yeah, this is Detective Dobbs again—"

"Tommy hasn't gotten in yet," said the bartender on the other end of the line.

Carter had already talked to the guy several times, and judging the bartender's tone, the man was starting to get irritated. At least he wasn't concerned. But Carter was.

"I'll let you know when he gets in," he promised half-heartedly.

"Have you talked to him?" Carter needed to know.

The bartender sighed. "No."

Carter sank into a moment of silence, thinking. Where the hell could Tommy be?

Why wasn't he going about his life as usual, managing the bar and otherwise picking up his cell phone?

Unless...

Carter hated to wonder, but it was starting to look like Tommy could've had something to do with Nora's murder.

"Listen, I'll give you a call when I hear from

Tommy," the bartender tried to assure him. "And I'll tell him to call you the second he gets to the bar. Other than that, I can't help you, and we're starting to get busy."

"Thanks, appreciate it," he said and returned his desk phone.

He leaned back in his chair, stared out the window, and as dusk gathered into darkness and the street lights flipped on, Carter contemplated the disturbing possibility that Danny may have snapped, taken Nora's life, and immediately regretted the deed. She may have been so psychologically overwhelmed by the act that the horror triggered some kind of amnesia.

No one but Danny and Tommy had the motive to kill Nora.

How well did he know Danny?

In a sense, it felt like he had been a Special Victims Unit detective for ages, but in reality he had barely been at the 66th for a solid month. Campopiano's murder was his third case with the precinct. He didn't personally know Danny, and he definitely didn't know Tommy O'Toole.

But Franco knew Carter's partner pretty damn well.

Carter considered the decades-long relationship between the lieutenant and the detective. Franco had held Danny's hand like a father down in the precinct jail cell. Franco hadn't questioned her. It hadn't even crossed his mind that she could have committed murder.

The last thing Carter needed was to keep torturing himself. Sooner or later, Tommy would turn up.

Carter had attained a major victory, as far as the case was concerned. Right now, somewhere at the Kings County Medical Examiner's Office, Jill Andover was figuring out whose blood had saturated the white, men's dress shirt that had been recovered from the Campopiano mansion. Jimmy Campopiano had been booked. The 66th had gained a foothold in the investigation, and the ground wouldn't easily be taken back.

Focusing on the positive, Carter pushed away from his desk, stood up, and collected his suit jacket. He stopped by Franco's office on the way out.

"My cell is on if you need me," he told the lieutenant.

Franco nodded. He didn't need to ask Carter about whether or not he had gotten ahold of Tommy.

"Get some rest," Franco told him.

Carter made his way through the bullpen where only a few cops were diligently typing up reports at their desks. The place was otherwise quiet.

Night had fallen, but the air was warm and heavy with humidity, he realized, as he left the precinct and found the Crown Vic that had basically become his personal vehicle.

As he climbed in, turned the engine, and started driving through Kensington, he did some quick math on Paul Decker's timeline. Carter had made a few calls to the Brooklyn Botanical Gardens to see if Paul had shown up or called. The flamboyant, possibly toxic lover had done neither, and so, one of his coworkers had spoken with the Missing Persons department. There was still a day and a half to go before the woman would even be permitted to file a report, however.

Carter needed to figure himself out before he showed up at home. Putting time and space between the 66th Precinct and spending the evening with his family had actually been their new therapist's idea. Kathy hated it, which triggered guilt in Carter whenever he tried the suggestion out. But if ever there was a day *not* to go straight home after work, it was the day his partner had been arrested for murdering her own mother.

Killing time before his regular Survivors of Incest Abuse meeting would begin, Carter drove to O'Toole's and pulled to a stop at the corner of Caton Avenue and Ocean Parkway.

Up ahead, far beyond the intersection was Danny's apartment and Nora's place was one door down. Both were crawling with cops. Red and blue cruiser lights whirled. Somewhere inside, Detectives Crouse and Toliver were building their case against Danny.

Franco had warned Carter not to interfere with Homicide.

Sitting on his hands wasn't his strong suit, but he had parked to stop by Tommy's bar, not the crime scene.

It was a fruitless endeavor, however. No one at the bar had seen Tommy. Carter asked to have a look in the back, but the bartender wouldn't let him. When Carter tried to ask some basic questions, cornering one bartender then the next, they each treated him like a cop and wouldn't talk.

"I'm worried about Tommy," Carter told one of the barbacks in a last ditch effort to get insight as to where Tommy had disappeared to.

"No one here is worried, man," said the young guy. "Just leave it alone."

"Is it like Tommy to not show up and be 'unreachable' for a day?" Carter pushed.

"Sorry, but yeah. Tommy hooked up with his on-again off-again girl," said the barback, referring to Danny. "She lives on the other side of Caton. Why don't you try her?"

The guy had no idea he was describing Carter's partner, and the guy probably hadn't noticed the cop cars.

"Thanks," he said dryly and left O'Toole's.

He could only take a running leap and slam himself against a brick wall so many times.

The drive into Lower Manhattan was a blur. He drove with all four windows down. Hot wind slapped his face yet cooled the back of his neck, but he hardly felt it.

Bobby Campopiano's murder investigation was barely moving forward. Had Jimmy really killed his younger brother? Or was Carter getting fixated on closing the case? Was he determined to catch the killer, or just determined to get Jimmy Campopiano incarcerated?

This was serious, he told himself. Compromising his own integrity was not an option, and Carter knew he needed to watch his step.

What about Paul Decker? Carter's gut was telling him that something was wrong. But Paul could be anywhere doing anything. He could be fine. He could've flown to Fiji to mourn the murder of his ballerina lover, for all Carter knew.

Weighing the most heavily on Carter's mind was the huge question mark of who killed Nora Foster.

When he arrived at the church in Lower Manhattan where his weekly S.I.A. meeting took place, he saw that Kathy had called, left a voicemail message, and had texted.

She never stopped pushing, and it seemed that the more space Carter exercised, the harder Kathy tried to close the gap between them.

It was suffocating.

At least he was able to get a few things off his chest at S.I.A. He pounded donuts and chatted with Marcus Stevens and a few other guys during the break. There was one newcomer, and Carter was reminded of the first night he had come to Group with Wally. Carter had been guarded yet had yearned to share his own story. That's how the newbie seemed.

Chuck Barnhardt, the old trucker who ran the Lower Manhattan Chapter of S.I.A. showed the newcomer the ropes and towed a healthy line between offering the guy 'a warm welcome' and remaining 'cold so as not to cross a line.'

By the time he left Lower Manhattan and was coasting over the Brooklyn Bridge with the windows down, Carter felt alleviated from the crushing stress that had previously threatened to steal all hope from him. He had gained perspective. In his life, he had come a very long way. Nothing was going to destroy him because nothing ever had.

Carter pulled the Crown Vic into his driveway and the motion detector flood light flicked on, brightening the driveway. Matty's bicycle had been discarded next to the door and there was a lone basketball that Christopher must have forgotten to bring inside.

He parked, climbed out, and cleaned up after his kids, returning the bike to the garage and bringing the basketball inside the house.

"Think fast!" he called out before tossing the basketball to his oldest son, Christopher.

Christopher's reflexes were unparalleled. He caught the ball before he even lifted his eyes from his laptop computer. He was seated in the living room on the couch. He twirled the basketball on his finger and told the smart, Filipino girl on the screen, "Did you catch that, Ziggy?"

She giggled.

"Get it?" Christopher grinned. "*Catch* that!"

Ziggy's melodic laugh blared through the laptop speakers.

His teenage daughter, Amanda, breezed by, making her way into the kitchen. Carter caught her by the head, kissed her forehead, then released her fast.

"Calm down, Dad," she said, freely exercising her teenage attitude, rolling her eyes and everything.

She joined her mother in the kitchen, and Carter trailed in after her.

Kathy was stirring boiling pasta in front of the stove. There was a glass of red wine on the counter.

She stroked the stem with a slender finger and didn't look at Carter, as she stated, "I called and texted."

From the kitchen table, Matty twirled his spy pen in his fingers and sang, "Dun, dun, *duuuunnnnn!*"

Kathy scowled. "Mind your own business, Matty."

"Dad's in trouble!" he sang out, disregarding his mother's disapproval. "You called and texted!"

All three of their children sang, "Dun, dun, *duuuunnnnn!*"

As Christopher quickly explained to Ziggy on Zoom what their 'inside joke' was all about, Kathy glared at Carter.

"I'm sick of everyone ganging up on me!" Kathy complained while the kids cackled with laughter and kept singing out *'dun, dun, dun'!*

"I had a meeting tonight that I had to go to," he told her, keeping things as casual and light as possible.

But when he tried to kiss her, she pulled away. Tears filled her blue eyes and color rose to her cheeks.

His heart groaned in his chest, but he wasn't willing to be manipulated.

"Smells good," he commented, smiling at the pasta.

Kathy snorted, shook her head, and lifted her red wine to her pouting mouth.

As she gulped wine, Carter mentioned, "I'm going to hit the shower. I'll be down shortly."

He started through the house and knew he was in trouble when he heard Kathy ask Amanda to take over stirring the pasta.

If Carter had thought sprinting up the stairs, tearing his clothes off, and jumping in the shower would've *prevented* Kathy from starting an argument, he would've done it. But he knew his wife.

By the time he entered his bedroom and pulled his tie off, Kathy padded in after him and closed the door.

But the days of Carter letting his wife ambush him were long gone.

"You don't know what I'm dealing with at work," he warned her, lifting a finger when her jaw dropped to object. "I'm not at your beckon call, Kathy, and if you don't like it, you better find a new therapist who only sees things your way."

"What's that supposed to mean?"

"It means that we left Dr. Valdmanis because you wanted a *better* marriage counselor and then we left Dr. Ling, because again, you wanted a *better* counselor. I have a mind of my own. I happened to notice that Ling pointed out things that were true, and you didn't like it. Now we have Dr. Murphy and—"

"Why are you talking about our therapists? We need to talk about *us*!"

"I'm bringing them up because right now *I'm* doing what *your* new therapist suggested that I should do, and you don't like it!" he hissed. "When I need to take time for myself after work, I will do that, just as Murphy suggested."

"When I call or text, you should always get back to me."

"No, I shouldn't," he told her directly. He pointed his finger in her face. "Don't try to lord over me."

"Oh, I've never lorded over you, and get your finger out of my face."

He returned to the closet, peeled his dress shirt off, and tossed it in the hamper.

"I've had a day, Kathy. Don't push it."

"I will push whatever I want to push, and when I say we need to talk, absolutely nothing else is going to happen until we do!"

Carter stared at his wife for a very long moment

and realized he was holding himself back from hitting her.

"Why are you looking at me like that?" she demanded.

He said nothing. He only kept staring at her and restraining himself from acting on the violence that was boiling through his hot veins.

When he finally spoke, his response sounded like a threat.

"Today my partner was arrested for murdering her mother. I'm not going to let her go to prison."

Horror, confusion, and betrayal—of all emotions—twisted Kathy's pretty face into an ugly knot.

"You would defend a monster like that?" she asked.

He looked her dead in the eye. "I would."

Carter didn't have to tell his wife to back off after that. She didn't say a word, as he removed his dress shoes and slacks. She didn't follow him into the bathroom when he left to shower. And when he finally toweled himself dry, threw on some sweats, and went downstairs for dinner, his wife showed no interest in saying a word to him.

He didn't love Kathy stonewalling him, but it was better than having to deal with her big mouth.

Enjoying dinner with his children afforded Carter enough levity to wash his concerns away, at least for one evening. Christopher had several things to grin about, and he told his dad about every single one, as he shoveled pasta into his mouth to 'carbo-load.'

Matty was still dealing with a subtle bully at school, and Carter determined that if this problem persisted, he would teach Matty how to throw a decent punch. For the time being, he offered his youngest son advice.

Matty clicked the butt of his spy pen and a recording of Carter's advice played for everyone to hear.

"That thing's kind of cool," Christopher told his younger brother.

Matty smiled a big, toothy grin.

Amanda was mostly on her cell phone, which wasn't ordinarily allowed at the dinner table, but Carter went easy on her.

After the meal, Kathy kept her bottle of Merlot close by, as they watched a family movie on TV, and Christopher talked non-stop about how one of the characters was *just like Ziggy!*

By the time the kids were tucked in their bedrooms and it was time for Carter to hit the hay, Kathy was still brooding on the couch with her now-empty bottle of wine and staring at the television monitor even though it was off.

Carter really didn't like having to play hardball with his wife. But if he engaged with her, the monster that he had seen lurking inside of himself might not stay there.

Upstairs, he flipped the lights off, pulled the covers back, and told himself to get a good night's sleep without letting his mind race with worries. All of his problems would be waiting for him in the morning, he reminded himself. He would deal with them then.

He had nearly dozed off when Kathy entered the dark bedroom and asked him, "Did she do it?"

He sighed. "I don't think so."

"What if she did?"

"Then she was smart to use a knife and not her police-issued Glock."

"That's not funny," she said softly. "I don't think this is the right line of work for you."

Depleted and frustrated, Carter told her honestly. "I don't think you're the right wife for me."

He could feel her staring at him, but he didn't open his eyes.

He'd had enough.

A very long moment passed, as a wall of tension rose and finally subsided between them.

Then she surprised him.

She didn't complain. She climbed into bed, and they made love.

CARTER WOKE WITH the hot sun on his face, as his cell phone vibrated on the nightstand.

Kathy was fast asleep behind him. He rolled over, hoping like hell it would be Tommy O'Toole returning his call.

It wasn't.

"Lieutenant?" he said, answering the phone.

Franco sighed through the line. Not a good sign. "How quickly can you get in?"

"Give me twenty," he said, as he rolled out of bed and got his bearings. "How bad is it?"

"It's bad."

"Broad strokes?"

Again, Franco sighed, and Carter could almost see the lieutenant raking his rough hand through his thick, black hair and pacing his office with a glass of whiskey sloshing around in his hand, insomnia and hairbrained determination having kept him burning the midnight oil until dawn.

"Ellsworth turned Jimmy and all the Campopianos loose."

"Are you kidding me?" Carter blurted.

"The filthy judge *expunged* the arrests, and worse, Ellsworth denied Danny's bail."

"Surprise, surprise, the judge who's paid to protect the Campopianos decides to keep the cop who's investigating the Campopianos in jail," Carter summarized, shaking his head and debating whether to make coffee or grab his first cup at the station.

"The blood soaked shirt that Jill found," Franco began, and it already didn't sound good.

"What about it?"

"It wasn't a match for Bobby."

"It's probably a match for Paul Decker," Carter reasoned, as he started the coffeemaker in the kitchen then doubled back to throw on some clothes in the bedroom upstairs.

Franco grumbled, "We can't proceed as though Jimmy killed a man who might not be dead. This is exactly the type of sloppy police work that Ellsworth can use to the Campopianos' advantage, goddamnit!"

"Look, I'll be there in twenty," he promised Franco, as he jogged down the stairs again. "How's Danny doing?"

"She's a zombie."

His tie was crooked, and he hadn't bothered grabbing his suit jacket. It was too hot out there already. He ended the call in the entryway and pulled on his shoulder holster, his Glock already fixed inside.

He found the keys to the Crown Vic, locked the door on the way out, and neared the parked sedan just as the morning sun poked in-between a set of apartment buildings. Harsh sunlight stung Carter's eyes, as he threw the driver's side door open and fought the urge to punch the window.

That's why Ellsworth had signed the search warrant, he thought, as he climbed in behind the wheel. It wasn't strictly a 'controlled opposition' tactic, as D.A. Sarah Hovey had suggested. The dirty judge was being used. The Campopianos had *wanted* Ellsworth to sign the warrant. They had even wanted to get arrested, all for *this moment*. So that Ellsworth could set them free and expunge the arrests.

The Campopianos were rubbing it in Carter's face that they *owned* Kensington.

Carter had barely fit the key into the ignition when from out of nowhere, a rope lassoed him from behind, cut into his throat, and pulled him hard against the headrest.

He choked and clawed at the rope around his neck, desperate to press his fingers under the slick cord.

Whoever was in the backseat strangling him was taking their sweet time.

Suddenly, the passenger side door popped open and Jimmy Campopiano sat down, closed the door, and studied Carter, as Carter felt the air drain from his lungs.

Jimmy was calm, cool, and collected, as he addressed Carter. "There's been an interesting turn of events, Detective."

Carter was beyond light-headed from lack of oxygen. His vision was darkening, and he could barely make Jimmy out from the corner of his eye, as the mobster removed the Glock from Carter's shoulder holster.

With Carter's gun in his possession, Jimmy told the Campopiano who was strangling Carter with a rope from the back seat, "Give a rest, Nico."

"Sure thing," said the man, good-naturedly.

The rope around Carter's neck went slack, but Nico didn't let go. He kept the detective tethered and restricted to the driver's seat.

"This is where we're at, Detective Dobbs," Jimmy went on, as he admired the sheen of Carter's gun.

Carter thought about Kathy and the kids, and silently prayed that they wouldn't come outside.

"Your investigation has crossed a line," Jimmy explained. "I don't appreciate being arrested, as you might have noticed. But at least now you know how things work. But see, *before* you and your partner were investigating freely. However, *now* your partner is in a very bad position."

"Danny's 'bad position' has nothing to do with our investigation of Bobby's murder," Carter wheezed out from the driver's seat. The rope cord around his neck was still taut across his vocal chords. "You're dirty, Jimmy, and I'm going to nail your ass to the wall."

Jimmy chuckled and told Nico, "This guy has balls."

"He's got balls," Nico agreed.

Jimmy pressed Carter's gun against the detective's temple and yelled, "If you know I'm a killer, why are you pushing me now? Eh?!"

It took a moment, but the mobster lowered the gun and composed himself, then he told Nico, "I came here to be a nice guy."

"You've always been a reasonable man, Jimmy," said Nico from the back seat.

"Thank you." Jimmy turned his attention to Carter. "I'm here to make a deal with you, Dobbs. You've seen what my judge can do. Your partner is looking at Murder One and you know it. If you back off and do what I tell you to do in terms of Bobby's murder investigation, I'll make Danielle Foster's problem go away, just like that."

Jimmy snapped his fingers.

"She'll walk out of the precinct in a *day*, two days *tops*. I can do that. I'm a powerful man. My Pop and I are still kicking around some ideas, but we're thinking maybe Bobby's case goes cold or maybe Decker takes the fall for it—"

Carter hissed through clenched teeth, "Did you kill Bobby?"

"Did I kill Bobby?" Jimmy turned to Nico and pointed out, "He wants to know if I killed Bobby."

Nico chuckled, and Jimmy bonked Carter on the head with the butt of his own gun.

"Pay attention!" he yelled, and Carter flinched. "I need an answer from you, Big Man. You want to cut a deal? I guarantee Foster will not go down for that murder. All you have to do is back off and work with me."

"How do I know you'll do what you say you'll do for Danny?" Carter hissed between clenched teeth.

"I stand by my word."

"What if Ellsworth won't go for it?"

"Dobbs," Jimmy countered, "what if I let all the chips fall where they may, and Danny goes to prison, and I get arrested again, and Ellsworth lets me off, because I own his ass. What then?" Jimmy asked Nico, "Do you see what a nice guy I am?"

"Jimmy, you're a saint," Nico praised.

"You hear that, Detective? I'm a saint."

"You're a dog," Carter wheezed. "You killed your brother because he was gay."

"Look, my Pop has had enough. I'll win a pissing match with you any day of the week, but for my dad's sake, we need to get this settled. You think I can't make good on my word? You think I don't *speak for* Harlan Ellsworth? You want to have tea with the guy?"

Carter glanced at the mobster sideways. Jimmy wasn't kidding.

"You want to talk about dogs? Eh?" Jimmy asked. "I got a trained one. He'll shake your hand and roll over and everything."

"When and where?" asked Carter.

Chapter Fifteen

IT WAS WAY TOO humid for leg warmers, but that hadn't stopped Eva Campopiano from pulling on a pair of black leg warmers before leaving the mansion for St. Christopher's Catholic School that morning.

Father Silva had given her a pass to stay home and mourn Bobby's death for another week, but she didn't trust the priest. There might have been a hidden loophole. What if she took the days off and then, by some administrative policy, wouldn't be allowed to graduate with her class in a couple weeks?

She felt odd and out of place traipsing onto the Catholic school grounds, but at least she was here. Nothing was going to prevent her from graduating high school and getting the hell out of her father's house.

Under her school uniform, she wore ballet tights and a black leotard, which meant that using the bathroom would be a pain, but that was a hassle she was willing to deal with. It felt like she hadn't been to ballet class in ages.

Immediately after school, she planned to head to the Brooklyn Ballet Studios. Her hair was already swept up into a bun. She had her cyanide capsule in a small, antique container in her leather knapsack. Jimmy had scared the crap out of her the other night, but she was starting to feel confident that they were out of the woods.

Bobby had used his, evidently. Eva hadn't even known that her brother had kept his capsule. For some reason, when Bobby had left their father's house, Eva had imagined he had also been freed from the brainwashing they had all endured.

But Bobby hadn't. If he had taken the suicide pill with him, then he had never really escaped anything, had he?

"Sorry for your loss, Eva."

That was one of the school boys. He held the large wooden door open for her, and she entered the schoolhouse. Fresh, spring air breezed through the Catholic school. All of the windows had been opened. St. Christopher's had never spared expenses, but it was too early in the year to blast the air conditioners.

As Eva trailed through the hallways, students offered her their condolences left and right. The majority of teachers at the school were nuns, and there were also a few priests who taught. They, too, conveyed their sympathy for her loss, stopping her in the corridors and reminding her that there are better places to be than this cruel world.

She honestly couldn't pinpoint how she felt about that, or how she felt about receiving sympathy and condolences from classmates she hardly knew. She felt numb and yet furious, which wouldn't have made sense to her, except that she was experiencing these contradicting emotions.

Eva couldn't deny that Bobby's murder had shocked her. But at the very same time, it hadn't surprised her.

She swung into her homeroom class, found her assigned desk, and sat down, as other students dressed in their Catholic school uniforms filtered in and got settled.

Being here was better than being at home, and

she was already looking forward to ballet class.

When she had left the house that morning, Jimmy still hadn't gotten home, but her mom had promised her that everyone who had been arrested would be let go. Maria had hugged her and had told her not to worry.

But Eva hadn't been worried. She never worried about Jimmy. Her brother was too strong. A formidable presence. Jimmy was never *in* danger. He *was* the danger, and sometimes Eva wondered if it was her *father's* thumb that she was desperate to get out from under, or her *brother's*.

The school bell rang. Homeroom started. Eva said, "Here!" when her name was called.

As the class unfolded and the day wore on, Eva struggled to stay present. She kept slipping into heavy thoughts.

She had seen her brother Bobby the morning of his murder. She had acted naturally. She hadn't treated him like an outcast or pariah. She had congratulated him on being cast in Romeo & Juliet.

That morning, she had been glad to run into Bobby at the coffee shop across the street from the ballet studios. The fact of the matter was that they practiced ballet at the same studio, but rarely ran into one another. Her plan that morning had been to sneak off to the Brooklyn Ballet Studios before school, dance in one of the studios, and skip homeroom, which at St. Christopher's was also first period.

There had been something about running into Bobby that morning, though. It had felt wrong and off, even though she had been happy to catch up with him. She hadn't ended up practicing that morning, either. She had rushed off to school instead.

What would've happened if Eva had gone up into the ballet studios that morning? Would she also be dead? Or would Bobby still be alive today?

The memory flashed through her mind. Bobby had slipped through the glass entrance door that day just as Catherine had knocked into Eva, having rushed up behind her.

Catherine had caught the door in her hand and had shouted, "Bobby, we need to talk!"

"Excuse you," Eva had grumbled. Her sister-in-law hadn't even offered a quick *'I'm sorry'* for having bumped into her.

But that was Catherine, wasn't it? She had always been like that.

Eva floated through the afternoon in a fog of confused reasoning.

No one would ever understand her and Jimmy.

Why had he married Catherine?

Why was she even thinking about any of this?

She wondered why her pop even cared that Bobby had been killed. Jimmy hardly gave the loss a second thought outside of implementing the damage control strategy that, as far as Eva could tell, wasn't exactly working.

"Ms. Eva?" said Father Silva from behind.

Eva had pushed through the wooden exit door of the Catholic school with a cluster of other high schoolers.

She cleared the fray then turned and found the priest approaching with an empathetic frown on his face.

"I have to go to ballet class, Father," she told

him, as she squinted through the bright sunlight.

It was a beautiful day out. Blue skies and warm winds, the scent of freshly cut grass filled the air.

"How are you holding up?"

"Fine," she said flatly.

"You didn't have to come in," he reminded her.

"I couldn't stay home," she said honestly. "The cops tore the house apart."

That seemed to surprise him.

"Pop, Jimmy, and all the men in the family got arrested except for Lorenzo, but it didn't stick," she explained.

"Arrested for Bobby's murder?" Father breathed, as his mouth curled with a slight grin.

She nodded.

"That's preposterous."

"Yeah, that's why they got released earlier today."

He considered the magnitude of the police's failures, then remembered why he had stopped her.

"I believe there's something you may have forgotten to do prior to Bobby's Requiem Mass," he mentioned, as if it was a serious matter. It wasn't, but to him, it was, obviously. "Didn't your father ask you to go to Confession?"

"I went to Confession," she lied.

"No, you didn't."

"You're not the only confessor, Father."

"You haven't gone to Confession in quite a while."

"I only have to go to Confession if I sin," she pointed out.

His black eyebrows shot up to his wispy, white hairline. He narrowed his eyes on her.

"I think we both know you haven't been living a sinless lifestyle," he said in a low tone of voice.

"Excuse me, Father, I have to get to ballet class," she said coolly.

She turned on her heel and started walking briskly along the cobblestone path that cut through the church grounds. Father Silva followed after her and kept at Eva's heels.

"I think you know what happened, Eva," he hissed, pressuring her.

She could hear the desperation in his voice.

"That falsified *suicide note* is going to hurt me, Eva, if you don't come out with the truth."

"If I come out with the truth in Confession, you can't do a damn thing with it," she reminded him without slowing her brisk stride.

"You *do* know who killed Bobby, don't you!"

When she ignored him, coming to the hot city block where St. Christopher's ended and Church Avenue began, its sidewalk bustling with New Yorkers, she turned to face him and sternly warned:

"I just want to get out of here! That's all I want. That's why I didn't stop Catherine that morning. She hates me, but she and I have only ever wanted the same thing… for me to go far, far away. You have to let me go, Father. You have to!"

A strange glimmer of understanding mixed with marked confusion crossed his angry face.

Yes, she wanted to get to ballet class. But they both knew right then and there that Eva wanted to be free.

When she started on her way again, Father Silva didn't stop her. He didn't say a word. And she didn't look back.

Ballet class at the Brooklyn Ballet Studios was challenging, hot, and crowded. The class was full of high school age ballet dancers, mostly girls. They all wore black leotards, pale pink tights, and ballet slippers, some canvas, others leather. Everyone looked neat, tidy, and uniform with their hair slicked up in tight buns, while the ballet instructor, a retired Russian ballerina who walked with a cane, chain smoked in front of an open window and yelled at them. She shouted in tempo with the crackling vinyl record player that was blaring classical piano music:

"Dégagé, la cinquième, et dégagé, la cinquième, et dégagé, la cinquième!"

Barre work was taxing. Eva's leg muscles burned. When the class came to the center of the room, the Russian instructor yanked Eva by the wrist, positioning her in the very center of the front row of the class. Some jealous girls behind Eva glared at her, but soon the only emotion any of them was capable of feeling was a kind of personal satisfaction that they were surviving this elegant torture, otherwise known as *'ballet.'*

Three hours later, Eva and the rest of the ballet dancers were throwing their street clothes on in the anteroom. There was no point trying to use the changing rooms. They were packed with other girls for the next class.

"Do you have tickets to Romeo and Juliet?" one of the ballet dancers asked Eva, as she pulled a loose tee shirt over her sweaty leotard and spritzed perfume under her armpits.

"Opening night," Eva told the girl. "I'm going with my brother. What about you?"

"Dress rehearsal," said the girl with a sulk.

All of the Brooklyn Ballet Studios students were welcome to attend the dress rehearsals for free, but it was an inferior experience to seeing the ballet opening night.

Eva pointed out the silver lining. "You'll get to see the show before anyone else does."

"I guess," she said before she made her way through the crowded anteroom to leave.

Eva checked her cell phone. There was a text message from Jimmy. She felt a smile come over her. Jimmy had texted an address and told her not to go home first.

She composed a fast reply, saying she would meet him there. She was about to leave ballet class on foot.

"Why are you going with your *brother*?" another high school ballerina asked Eva.

The girl had overheard, and finally had her shorts and sneakers on. Her dance bag was slung over her shoulder.

"Because I'm not allowed to date," she told the girl honestly.

"So you're dating your *brother*?"

Eva glared at her but held her tongue. She already had to deal with Catherine's snide attitude at home. She refused to engage with the same nastiness after ballet class.

Ignoring the rude girl, and trying not to feel the violent need to lash out at some dumb girl who happened to be sort of right, Eva pulled her leather knapsack onto both shoulders and padded out of the anteroom, down the narrow staircase, and out of the building.

On the sidewalk, she headed west towards

Ocean Parkway where she crossed the busy intersection and started walking south along Ocean towards Caton Avenue.

There shouldn't be more than five or six blocks to go, she realized, recalling this side of Kensington that she rarely ventured into.

She kept her pace up. A fresh layer of sweat beaded up on her forehead and across her chest. Good thing her hair was still in a high bun, keeping her long, brown hair off her shoulders.

After a bit, she caught sight of the wooden sign gleaming in the sunlight.

O'Toole's Irish Pub sat on the corner of Ocean Parkway and Caton Avenue, just where Jimmy said it would be in his text message.

Maybe her brother would buy her a drink, she hoped, as she crossed the congested intersection and came to the bar.

She pulled the door open and found the barroom was lively. There were two bartenders behind the long wooden bar, and almost all the tables were occupied with patrons enjoying themselves.

Eva glanced at her cell phone and considered composing a text to Jimmy to tell him she had just gotten there, but she felt eyes on her, glanced up, and saw her brother on the other side of the room.

He had just slipped in from a back room, it looked like.

She made her way to him, and he took her by the shoulders, gave her the once over, and asked, "Did you go to school today?"

"And ballet class," she said. "You okay?"

"I'm always okay," he told her with an easy smile.

As he pulled her through the swinging door that led into the back where offices, storage rooms, and closets were located, he hooked his arm around her shoulder and spoke quietly into her ear, "Listen, I don't want you by yourself very often or for very long."

"There's tons of kids at school and ballet class," she assured him, as he walked her down the hallway towards an office, its door open.

"That's not what I mean, and you know it," he whispered. "I don't want you at home with her.'"

She glanced up at her brother with huge, upset eyes.

"I just want to move out, Jimmy."

"Don't talk like that, eh? Everything's going to be fine. I simply don't want you home alone with her until I get *everything* back under control."

She knew he wasn't going to bring her into the office until she promised.

"Where am I supposed to go?" she asked.

"That's why you're here with me right now," he explained. "Otherwise, I think we can get you working at Rocco's, that'll keep you out of the house and safe until late at night when I'm home again."

She knew better than to argue, not that she wanted to work at Rocco's.

He pulled her in and kissed her temple then ushered her into the office where a troubled-looking middle aged man was slumped behind the cluttered desk on the far side of the room. He was a rugged, muscular type. He wore a tee shirt. A classic Irish guy with salt-and-pepper hair and leathery skin, a handsome face.

It was obvious Jimmy had been making the man

miserable.

The guy looked like he hadn't slept in days, yet his gray-blue eyes were sharp. He locked his attention onto Eva. It was obvious he wasn't happy about the new character at his establishment, assuming this was his bar.

"This is my baby sister, Eva," Jimmy told the man. "Eva, this is Tommy." He pulled out a chair for Eva, giving her a front row seat at the bar proprietor's desk, even though he said to Tommy, "Don't mind her. Consider her a fly on the wall."

Tommy looked at Jimmy dead-pan for a long moment then asked, "She's a fly on the wall?"

"Don't pay her no mind. She's like a fly."

"I'm a fly on the wall," she agreed without a shred of irony. "Can I have a beer?"

Tommy stared at Eva then returned his attention to Jimmy, and the mobster gave him a little figurative nudge. "Why don't you give her a beer, eh?"

There was a mini fridge behind the desk. Tommy turned, grabbed a cold one out of the door, and cracked it open for Eva, all the while he appeared to be a man trapped in a surreal version of what had formerly been a normal life.

He set the opened, longneck bottle of beer on the desk in front of Eva, looked at Jimmy who had sat down on the chair next to his sister, and asked, "When will Danny be released?"

"Soon," he promised, as Eva sipped the cold, bitter beer. Jimmy's smooth talking and slick wit told Eva that her brother was already twelve steps ahead of this dude. A humble smile came over Jimmy. "You know, Tommy, if you had taken me up on my offer to help you out in the first place, your girlfriend wouldn't have wound up in jail."

Tommy seemed to slip into worried thoughts, yet he seemed surrendered to whatever solution Jimmy had cooked up. Eva knew when her brother had brought another man to his knees. She had seen him in action many times before.

"Lucky for me," her brother went on, "if I help her out, I help myself out. But that's the commitment that I need from the other detective, and I'm going to need that commitment from Danny, too."

Tommy nodded. "Yeah, I'll get her to agree to that," he promised.

"Good," said Jimmy. "And there can't be any betrayals, you understand? If Carter comes wearing a wire or anyone gets smart and tries to get the police involved, all hell is going to break loose."

"Yeah, I got it," he said.

"I really mean it, Tommy."

The fear behind Tommy's eyes was replaced with rage. "I got it," he repeated.

"I hope you do," Jimmy pushed. "Because if you had told me what was going on in the first place, I could've solved your problem *without* your girlfriend facing murder charges. I didn't know who your girlfriend was, Tommy." Jimmy began chuckling. "I mean, it's a *very* small world."

Tommy didn't find it very funny.

Eva asked her brother, "What are you talking about?"

"That female detective who's been on us."

"What about her?"

"That's his girlfriend," he said. "I'll tell you about

it later."

Eva took another long pull of beer.

Jimmy sobered from chuckling and sternly reiterated, "If your girlfriend or her partner take advantage of my kind nature, and try to turn this into a sting operation to entrap me and my family, Tommy, I promise you, I'll make sure no one regrets it more than you."

"That's not going to happen, I swear."

"I've been a friend to you," he warned.

Numb, Tommy agreed. "You've been a friend to me."

Jimmy checked the time on his expensive watch. "He should be here soon."

Eva wondered, "Who?"

"Detective Carter Dobbs," he told her. "We're going to talk to our favorite judge, and then the police are going to stop bothering us for good."

Eva didn't even try to understand what that meant. She gulped down more beer, glanced at her brother, and asked, "Do I have to come? Or can I stay here?"

Tommy told Jimmy, "She can't stay here."

Jimmy disagreed.

Chapter Sixteen

THE BROOKLYN Navy Yard dominated the waterfront between Navy Street to the south and Kent Avenue to the north. Formerly an authentic shipyard, the Brooklyn Navy Yard had since developed with a variety of manufacturing businesses occupying the old brick buildings.

The Yard was gated. Employees had IDs with magnetic strips, which triggered the gates to open.

Carter's only option was to enter the Navy Yard at Vanderbilt Avenue where there was a guard station.

He squeezed the brakes of his wife's boxy minivan, making the turn onto Vanderbilt that fed directly into the security booth entrance, as dusk gathered across the sky and the humidity thickened.

The Brooklyn Navy Yard had excellent surveillance coverage. There was a camera at every entrance and the wide expanse of brick buildings had cameras and check-in points. He had known this would be the case, which was why he had left the Crown Vic at home and taken Kathy's old, burgundy minivan. The thing had a strip of wood paneling on the side and no hubcaps.

He rolled to a stop at the security guard booth where a man in a blue collared uniform took his ID and asked him which building he was going to.

Carter was hardly comfortable providing the information, but Jimmy had told him not to be intimidated.

Carter told the guard he wasn't going to one of the buildings, but rather to Dock 72.

"It's not an active dock anymore, you know that?" the guard mentioned as he jotted the details down on his clipboard.

"I know," he said, keeping himself tucked deep in the minivan so that the security camera that was fixed over the security booth and angled down wouldn't capture more than his arm.

Within the booth, a portable printer spat out a sheet of paper. The guard handed the sheet to Carter and said, "Put this on your dashboard if you leave your vehicle, otherwise Security will call to have your minivan towed."

"It's my wife's minivan," said Carter, not that it mattered.

"That won't make a difference to the tow guy."

The guard's humor was lost on Carter.

"Drive straight through. Dock 72 is straight ahead, but veer right after this row of brick buildings."

When the electronic barrier-gate arm lifted, Carter released the brakes and rolled through.

As he kept an eye out for a sign for Dock 72 Way, he hoped like hell he was doing the right thing. He hadn't looped Franco in. He couldn't risk it. Not when Danny's freedom was on the line. If he had told Franco that Jimmy had approached him to cut a dirty deal, Franco would have leapt at the chance to wire Carter and catch Jimmy and the judge in one fell swoop.

But Jimmy had specifically told Carter not to try anything. He wasn't even armed. He had left his police-issued Glock in his locker at the 66th. And he had to figure that Jimmy would check Carter for a wire first and foremost.

Carter was not about to cross the line that the mobster had drawn in the sand. His throat still ached where Nico had held the rope cord around his neck. If Carter's skin tone hadn't been so dark, the bruising would probably look horrendous. That being said, he doubted Jimmy was as smart as he let on. Carter had one trick up his sleeve...

All he had to do was get through this. Get Danny out. Figure out what the hell happened to Nora. Damn, if the bodies weren't stacking up. Carter wondered when and where Paul Decker's murdered corpse would surface.

He found Dock 72 Way, a little blue road sign marked the spot. The actual dock behind it was a cement slab that jutted out into the East River. The security guard had been correct, however. The dock wasn't active. No ships were docked. Other than a few seagulls, there were no signs of life in the immediate area.

There were also no security cameras, Carter realized, as he glanced around for other vehicles. He was the first to arrive. Across the East River, Manhattan began twinkling, as dusk turned to night.

He killed the engine and turned off the headlights, but left the key in the ignition.

Matty's spy pen was tucked into the breast pocket of his button down.

He was ready.

A moment passed.

Then bright headlights cut between the brick buildings, and the vehicle they belonged to drove at a crawl straight towards Carter.

As the luxury sedan purred its way past the minivan, Carter noted the vehicle was sleek and black. Its windows were tinted, and he couldn't see the driver, who was now angling the sedan around, parking parallel to Carter, but a good distance away.

He really didn't like all the cloak and dagger tactics, so when Jimmy Campopiano stepped out of the black sedan, Carter climbed out of his wife's minivan, and they met each other halfway.

The warm winds breezed through, blowing Jimmy's suit jacket and causing his black, slicked hair to come loose and fall into his eyes.

"Dobbs," he said with such confidence that it rattled Carter's resolve.

Carter tried not to show it, though. He nodded at the mobster, and greeted him. "Campopiano."

"How's the neck?"

"Feels worse than it looks," he told him honestly.

"You know I have to see if you're wearing a wire," Jimmy mentioned as he began patting Carter down.

Carter wasn't wearing his suit jacket. It was too warm for that. His button down shirt was already stained with sweat, the white tee shirt underneath was damp. The spy pen was clipped to his pocket and recording.

"What's this?" the mobster asked, referring to the spy pen.

"That's a spy pen."

"What's a spy pen?"

"It's a toy. It's my son's. I grabbed it by mistake when I needed a pen," Carter said, mixing lies with the truth, as he held his breath.

Jimmy pinched the butt of the spy pen and pulled it out of Carter's pocket. Carter's heart leapt up his throat, as the mobster eyed the plastic recording device.

"A spy pen, eh?"

"My son wants to be a private eye," he said, trying not to let his terror show.

Jimmy narrowed his suspicious gaze on Carter, rolled the toy between his thumb and forefinger, and then slid the thing back into Carter's pocket, unconcerned.

He proceeded to work his way around Carter, checking for a wire by patting his chest, stomach, and then his shoulders and rib cage in the back. He was pleased to confirm that the detective wasn't wearing a wire.

"Where's Ellsworth?" Carter asked, as the mobster came to face him again.

"He'll be here."

Carter needed to know, "You were locked up, so how did you find out about Danny?"

"Didn't Danny's case come across Ellsworth's desk?" Jimmy pointed out.

Something wasn't right. The chain of events had been too fast. Carter questioned, "Ellsworth didn't know Homicide had arrested Danny, not at that moment. He denied her bail this morning, true."

"Ellsworth is a smart guy," Jimmy offered, but the explanation was thin.

Carter didn't know Harlan Ellsworth personally, but he had a hard time imagining that the judge saw Danny in court that morning and immediately connected that she was the detective investigating Bobby Compopiano's murder. On the one hand, fine, it was *possible*, Ellsworth could've connected all the dots in the blink of an eye, first thing in the morning, but Carter had his doubts.

Night pressed in. The shipyard lights illuminated the building entrances throughout the Navy Yard, but the majority of the place was cloaked in darkness. Shadows covered Jimmy's face, and then they were blinded by a vehicle that had just turned onto Dock 72 Way, having emerged from between two brick buildings.

It had to be Ellsworth.

The vehicle—a large, polished, black SUV—pulled up in the space between Jimmy's luxury sedan and Carter's minivan.

Carter and Jimmy stepped out of the way, coming to the edge of the cement slab where only a low, metal railing separated the parked cars from the East River.

Heat rolled off the SUV's engine. The headlights cut out, and the dirty judge that Lieutenant Martin Franco had been tracking for years eased out from behind the wheel, shut the driver's side door, and joined Jimmy and Carter, as little waves smacked against the cement dock.

Ellsworth was bald and had the melted appearance of an old man in his 70s. He had probably once been a member of the *'good boys' club'* before he had tested his footing on the slippery slope of 'looking the other way' in exchange for easy cash. Decades later, this was what had become of the man.

He had the dead eyes of someone who had grown so accustomed to compromising his own soul that his conscience had prematurely died in his skull.

Dressed in a dark suit and wearing a trench coat despite the humidity, Ellsworth greeted Carter with a cool mix of acknowledgment and apathy.

"I don't think I've ever seen you in my courtroom," the judge mentioned as if this was a casual meeting on the courthouse steps during broad daylight. "Have you been with the 66th Precinct long?"

"Not long, no," he replied, holding his tongue from addressing the judge as 'Sir.' "I worked in Vice before, purely undercover, and even when I had made a case, my lieutenant kept me away from testifying so that I could maintain my cover."

"I see," said Ellsworth, bored with the pleasantries already. "Well, Jimmy here has explained the situation to me. The Campopiano case isn't going to be the hard part. I'm sure you'll agree that it's impossible to discover who took Bobby's life. I trust you can navigate the necessary leads versus dead ends so that after what seems to be a natural yet thorough investigation, the case goes cold."

Carter glanced at Jimmy, and Jimmy mentioned, "Framing Decker would be a risk. He could push for a trial, and he could get his lawyer to try to play the 'discrimination card,' which could cause a trial to go high-profile. Too loud and messy. It's best if the case goes cold."

Carter was convinced that Jimmy had murdered Paul Decker, so yeah, pinning a murder on a dead man was generally a bad idea.

"I'll let the case go cold," Carter agreed in a hollow tone, while his gut twisted and his conscience screamed at him. Even though he knew he was lying through his teeth to these dirtbags, he still couldn't stand the sound of his own agreement. "Under the condition that Danny walks. Homicide has to totally drop it."

Ellsworth had no problem agreeing, but Jimmy looked nervous.

Ellsworth told Carter, "I'll reinstate her opportunity to bail—"

"I want her to walk," Carter pushed.

The judge explained, "Things have to look organic and logical. Step by step. I'm not going to wave a magic wand and erase the charges. That'll draw attention."

This was making Carter nervous.

"She'll have a bail hearing," Ellsworth continued. "I'll grant her bail, and she'll be released. Then Homicide is going to have the D.A. file subpoenas, depositions, etcetera, etcetera, and their goal will be to pressure Danny into cutting a plea bargain, but they'll have a feeling that Danny will want a trial. They'll be committed to getting their ducks in a row."

Carter had to grit his teeth together to keep himself composed. This was *not* the picture that Jimmy had painted. He didn't want Danny to have to go through any of that.

Ellsworth promised him, "None of that is going to happen. Every motion they file, every move they try to make, I'll simply deny their request or I'll stall or I'll slow them down."

Carter told Jimmy, "I don't want this thing dragging on like that."

Ellsworth told him, "The only way this thing doesn't drag on is if your partner *didn't* kill her mother, and Homicide catches who did."

The judge let that hang for a moment then pushed, "I thought we were all functioning under the assumption that Danielle Foster stabbed her mother to death?"

A very dark look came over Jimmy, as he said, "To my knowledge, no one else did."

Carter couldn't tear his attention away from the mobster. Jimmy looked ill. It occurred to Carter that Jimmy might need the Nora Foster murder to 'go away' just as badly as he needed the Bobby Campopiano murder to go cold.

"Dobbs?" Ellsworth asked Carter.

Was Carter going to stand there and agree that Danny had taken Nora's life? He suddenly felt off balance. He didn't want to let himself analyze the possibilities, he really didn't. He had been actively denying that Danny had done it, but she hadn't denied *attempting* to kill Nora.

"Yeah," he said in a small voice, the lump that had formed in his throat had muffled his reply. "Yes," he repeated. "All these cases need to disappear."

"Then the only promise we need," concluded Jimmy, "is that Danny will drop my brother's murder investigation."

If Danny hadn't killed Nora, then Danny would also have to drop Nora's murder investigation, and so would Detectives Crouse and Toliver.

But Carter knew his partner. The second she was back in her right mind, she was going to want to know who took her mom's life, who keyed into her apartment and left that creepy note, and who went to Nora's afterwards and stabbed the old woman to death.

"Do we have an agreement?" Jimmy pushed when Carter had fallen into deep, wandering thoughts.

Carter nodded and found the right response. "Yes."

Ellsworth said, "Good," as he pulled his cell phone from the front pocket of his trench coat. "One phone call, and I can put this in motion."

He stepped aside, sent the call through, and meandered away from Jimmy and Carter, as he spoke to whoever had the power to initiate Danny's release process.

"You look nervous, Dobbs."

"Funny, I was going to say the same thing about you," he shot back.

"This is all going to work out," he promised, and for a moment Carter hoped the mobster was right. "Smooth sailing."

"Danny is going to have questions."

"You'll handle her," he said with the utmost confidence in Carter. "And that boyfriend of hers will handle her, too."

Mention of Tommy gave Carter pause. "What do you know about Danny's boyfriend?"

"Tommy?" Jimmy said with a wry smile. "Oh, Tommy and I go *way* back. I've been keeping an eye on O'Toole's for years."

Carter stiffened, as his blood ran cold in his veins.

Did Jimmy have Tommy under his thumb, too?

If this had been a game of chess, Jimmy had just suggested that he was the queen, zooming across the board and taking out whatever piece he wanted. Hell, he *owned* the game board, and Danny, Carter, and Tommy were the pawns.

Chapter Seventeen

DANNY HAD BEEN sitting in the precinct jail for over 24 hours. Her mother's blood had long since dried on her skin. She had been given meals, permitted bathroom trips, and had even changed into a pair of mint condition sweatpants and a sweatshirt, courtesy of the Kensington Police Department. The sweats had the P.D.'s logo on the back with "66" printed on the upper left side of the hoodie's chest.

She hadn't been given the chance to shower. She felt like hell, and it was safe to assume she looked just as bad.

Having been denied bail, Danny had wrestled with fears all day and deep into the evening. Someone had killed Nora, and Danny had a very dark feeling that she was going to take the fall for this.

Whoever had taken her mother's life had easily entered Danny's apartment. They had left a strange, emotion-filled apology note, opened the window, and had failed to shut and lock the apartment door on their way out.

Nora had let her killer in, that was the worst part. That was the glaring fact that had been making Danny's head spin. Nora had not only opened the door, but had allowed the murderer to come all the way into her apartment.

Over the years, Danny had seen enough crime scenes and enough stabbings to know that Nora hadn't been attacked at the apartment door. The entirety of the attack had taken place in the kitchen.

There had only been the faintest smear of blood on the door frame, which the killer had left on his way out.

That meant that, again, Nora knew the person.

It caused her physical pangs of anguish, remorse, and dread, but she couldn't deny that deep down she suspected Tommy was responsible.

Tommy had been caught up in the middle. Danny had sucked him in, and though she hadn't intended it, Tommy had been trapped in the dark, poisonous tangle of Danny and Nora's unhealthy, codependent relationship.

Danny hadn't complained about Nora to anyone but Tommy. And Nora hadn't tried to keep anyone away from Danny except Tommy. As far as motives were concerned, Tommy had a solid one. The only other person more likely to have killed Nora than Tommy was Danny, and Danny hadn't done it.

Lying on the hard bench inside her jail cell, she had one arm draped over her eyes and both knees were up. They had given her a thin pad so that she wouldn't have to lie on the cold, steel bench, but this was hardly comfortable.

The lights were bright. Her head was pounding from stress and grief.

Had she gotten what she had wanted?

That summed up the darkest feeling of all…

Someone had killed Nora, because Danny hadn't had the strength to go through with it herself.

Hard emotions had waged a war inside of her. There was a warm glow of relief in her heart because her mom was dead, but the guilt it stirred up in her soul was insufferable. If she beat herself senseless and threw herself against the jail cell bars, screaming and vomiting out every last painful emotion, it still wouldn't be enough to expel the soul-murdering self-hatred that was taking deep root in her psyche.

What if she went to prison for the rest of her life?

Would she care?

"Foster!" the police officer standing guard shouted, as he stomped down the aisle with a jangling ring of jail keys in his hand. "You're being released."

She popped up, squinted through the blinding lights, and was on her feet in a second.

"Released? I was denied bail," she questioned, confused.

"That was an administrative error," said the guard with a shrug, as he unlocked her cell and pulled the clanking door aside. As she padded out, he told her, "Lieutenant Franco is down the way."

Danny glanced past the uniformed guard and saw Franco standing in the corridor. He must have pulled all kinds of strings. Her eyes filled with tears. She walked briskly and met him in the corridor where another police officer was posted, but sitting on a chair.

The compassion behind Franco's black eyes made Danny's heart swell in her chest.

He clapped his big hand on her shoulder and used a discrete tone to ask, "I know it's been a long one, but we have to talk in my office."

She nodded, delirious from stress and the overwhelming relief that was crashing over her in hard, mind-reeling waves.

Franco said, "I'm glad you're out, Danny," as he

walked with her down the narrow corridor and through the metal detectors at another guard station, exiting onto the landing where they came to the stairs that led them up to the first floor of the precinct.

The way Franco had remarked that she was 'out' sounded trustworthy. *Was* she 'out'?

"Who paid the bail?" she asked, as they made their way through the S.V.U. bullpen.

The lights were dim and no one was there, considering the very late hour.

"I did, but through a relative's name," he told her as they came to his office.

The door was open, and as soon as Danny padded into the room, her baggy sweatshirt sleeves pushed up and her cheeks feeling suddenly hot, she saw Carter leaning against a bookshelf with his arms folded.

His eyes brightened when she walked into the room. He unfolded his arms, and she could tell he had the instinct to hug her, but instead he grinned and shook her hand enthusiastically.

"We're going to get the bastard," he told her.

Franco filled her in. "Ellsworth."

"We're going to get him," Carter repeated.

Franco invited them to have a seat, and once he rounded to the business side of his desk and sat, he got Danny up to speed.

"Ellsworth was the judge who denied your bail, and at the same time, he let the Campopianos walk," Franco began. "Then, Ellsworth was the one who pushed your bail through."

"Why the 180°?" she asked.

"To put it simply, Jimmy approached Carter to

make a deal after you were arrested. The second Jimmy got released this morning, he ambushed Carter and proposed that if the 66th drops the Campopiano case, letting the investigation go cold, then he'll have Ellsworth release you immediately."

Carter added, "I didn't buy it until I met with Ellsworth."

Danny was following, but her heart sank. This had nothing to do with her mother. The excitement behind Franco's eyes had everything to do with his decades-long investigation of the dirty judge and nothing to do with getting real justice for Bobby Campopiano or for her mother.

"So, Ellsworth released me, and now Carter and I are going to turn our backs on Bobby's case?" she questioned Franco.

"Not at all, but we're all going to focus on getting Ellsworth," he informed her.

She didn't like the sound of that. "Who killed my mother? Who's going to get to the bottom of that? *Homicide?* You think Crouse and Toliver aren't going to try to get me some other way?"

Danny knew why she was getting emotional, yet she also knew that Tommy was the most likely to have killed her mother, so she had to wonder what in the hell she was pushing for. Lack of sleep and lack of hope had rendered her priorities so confused that she couldn't even think straight.

"How?" she asked, looking at Franco and waiting for him to explain an actionable plan.

"We're going to do this by the book," he told her, first and foremost.

There was a plastic evidence bag on his desk, which Danny only now noticed because Franco picked it up to show her the pen inside. The pen resembled a fancy, expensive Montblanc rollerball pen, the kind that came packaged in a velvet box. And yet, this pen appeared to be made of plastic and didn't look quite right.

"What's that?" she asked.

"This is our hurdle," Franco told her.

Carter clarified. "It's a spy pen."

"What's a spy pen?"

"It's my son's. It's a toy. For 'spies.' It looks like a pen and it writes like a pen, but it's really an audio recorder."

She touched eyes with Carter and then took the evidence bag and examined the spy pen.

"I couldn't go to meet with Ellsworth wired up with a standard microphone. Jimmy would have shot me in the back of the head. So I put Matty's spy pen in the front pocket of my shirt."

Franco was too excited, he had to interject, "Carter recorded the entire conversation with Ellsworth. Jimmy, too."

Carter clarified, "We didn't get a confession in terms of Bobby's murder. But the entire conversation was recorded, clear as a bell."

"The difficulty will be the fact that this is audio and not video," Franco went on.

In New York State, it was actually illegal to record audio of anyone without their expressed consent, which wasn't the case for videos, interestingly.

Danny pointed out, "The audio won't be admissible in court."

Carter objected, "When Jimmy asked me what it was, I told him it was a spy pen."

Franco replied as if this wasn't the first time he'd had to argue with Carter. "You didn't tell Jimmy you were recording him."

"It was implied," Carter maintained.

Franco shook his head. "Sarah already vetoed it."

"Semantics," he said brightly, his eyes full of victory.

"It won't be admissible as evidence," Franco barked. "However, it has *convinced* Sarah Hovey to move ahead. Like I said, we're doing this by the book. We're going to get the proper warrants, establish hard evidence, and that's all thanks to you, Danny. If you hadn't been arrested, Jimmy wouldn't have gotten bold. He *really* tipped his hand. They're all going to go down for this."

Mentally putting the pieces together, she concluded out loud, "Right now, Jimmy thinks he successfully used his power to guarantee the entire Campopiano murder investigation will go cold, because he got one of the lead investigators out of trouble, and now she owes him?"

Franco allowed, "I'm not saying you're in a *great* position, but it's temporary."

"He thinks I'm in debt to him."

"He thinks you're paying off that debt by letting Bobby's murder go cold," Franco corrected her. "There's nothing else you'll have to do."

"What's Homicide going to do?" she wanted to know since Crouse and Toliver had never struck her as the types to give up.

"It doesn't matter what they do," Carter assured her, "because Ellsworth is going to be the brick wall that they meet every time they try to take a run at you."

"What about Sarah? How much does she really know?"

"Everything," Franco said. "But this has to stay quiet, and stay between us."

Danny didn't like it.

But as Franco had pointed out, it would be temporary.

Franco suggested, "We can reconvene about this first thing tomorrow morning. Go home, get some rest, and let's meet here a little later than usual. Let's say tomorrow at 10am."

Danny and Carter stood and crossed the office, but as Carter opened the door, she turned on her heel, locked eyes with Franco, and realized, "Taking down Ellsworth means taking down the entire Campopiano crime family."

Tension rose in the air. Franco said, "When you pull out a weed, you have to get it by the roots, otherwise the thing will grow back."

Ellsworth was the symptom, not the disease.

As Danny left Franco's office, she knew she would be far safer in the precinct jails than she would be anywhere free in Kensington.

"Are you going to be okay?" Carter asked her, as they crossed the warm bullpen, exited the Special Victims Unit department, and crossed the dimly lit lobby.

"Yeah, I'll be fine."

"You need a ride home?"

She was about to take him up on it, but when they stepped outside into the humid night air, Danny saw Tommy waiting across the street.

Their eyes locked.

"Did you get a hold of Tommy?" she asked Carter.

"No," he said, turning to see who had stolen her attention.

"He knew I got released. He's here."

She lifted her hand to wave at him, and he started for the crosswalk to meet her.

Carter asked her, "Are you sure you're going to be okay?"

She looked up at her partner. "I'll find a way to be fine, but, no, I'm not okay."

He seemed to accept her honesty, or at least he couldn't argue with it.

Tommy cautiously approached, having crossed the street.

Where had he been? Had he killed Nora? What did he think he was doing here?

Danny didn't know, but she didn't have to ask. Carter was already demanding answers.

"Do you have any idea how many times I called the bar, stopped by, and ran around looking for you?" he asked Tommy, who already looked like he had been beaten up emotionally several times throughout the past few days.

Regardless, Tommy wasn't about to get pushed around. "I'm sorry, do I owe you something?"

"Guys, please," Danny said, getting in-between them when they came nose to nose.

"Are you my keeper?" Tommy snapped at Carter. "I didn't know I was expected to keep you informed about everything I do!"

"Guys!"

"Did you have something to do with Danny getting locked up?" Carter demanded to know, but

Danny wedged herself between them and shoved them apart.

"Carter! Please!" When she pushed them apart, she ran her fingers through her hair and felt disgusting. "It's late. I need a shower. Please."

Carter had it in him to walk away. "I'll see you tomorrow, Foster."

"See ya," she breathed.

Once Carter had walked up the street, climbed into a minivan, and driven off, the tension subsided and a different uneasiness rose between Danny and Tommy.

"Where have you been?" she asked him softly.

"Come on," he suggested, indicating that his truck was parked up the street. "Why don't you come back to my place tonight."

"Are you going to answer me?" she said.

She stopped walking and folded her arms.

"Are you?" she pushed.

He neared her. "No."

She stared at him for a very long moment. She searched his eyes, and even though her gut told her that he'd had something to do with what had happened to Nora, she realized right then and there that for tonight maybe she didn't want to know the truth.

"Come on," he gently coaxed. "You're going to have to come right back here tomorrow morning, right? Let's get some sleep."

He held his hand out for her to take, and she did, sliding her hand into his.

They walked down the sidewalk, and when there was a gap in the flow of traffic, they crossed the street and came to his parked truck. He unlocked the vehicle and opened the passenger side door for her. As she climbed in, he rounded the hood, opened the driver's door and settled in behind the wheel.

His bar wasn't far. He lived in the apartment above O'Toole's. The entrance was in the back and there was another entrance inside the rear of the bar, which also connected to the narrow staircase that led up to the second floor.

Tommy parked around the back. O'Toole's was fast approaching closing time.

The patrons inside weren't loud, but Danny could hear their muffled voices and quiet rock music coming through the walls, as she followed Tommy into the building and up the stairs.

When they reached the landing, Tommy keyed into the small apartment and flipped on the lights. The familiar scent of his home comforted her.

"I need to shower," she said, suddenly exhausted.

He pulled her in and held her close. "I'm so sorry."

She knew he was sorry, but she wondered what exactly he was sorry for.

Had his apology sounded like an admission of guilt?

"I know," she breathed.

"I'm so sorry, Danny," he repeated, holding her so tightly that she couldn't move.

The crib.

The note.

'I'm sorry about Gregory.'

Danny pushed the memory from her mind, urged Tommy back, and told him, "I really have to get washed up. Then I need to crash."

He let her go, and while she slipped into the small bathroom, turned the water on, and took a good, hard look at herself in the mirror, Tommy collected some clothes for her to sleep in. One of his dresser drawers had been hers.

As she stepped into the hot shower, having stripped down, Tommy eased the door open and set the clean, freshly folded garments on the closed toilet lid.

"Thanks!" she said, and he left her to shower in privacy.

Five minutes later, she emerged from the steamy bathroom feeling warm and relaxed, and wearing the cotton tee shirt and sweatpants he had supplied. Her hair was damp and helped cool her down as soon as she entered his bedroom where the air conditioner was blasting.

Tommy was already lying in bed, nearly dead to the world, himself.

She crawled into bed next to him and curled into his arms.

Her eyes drifted shut, and somewhere between a waking and dreaming state, she murmured, "Whoever killed my mom went to my apartment first. They left me a note that said 'I'm sorry about Gregory'."

"Shhh," he whispered, as he stroked the back of her head, running his hand over her wet hair.

"I didn't kill her, Tommy."

"I know."

"I—"

"Shhh," he breathed, barely whispering. She nearly dozed off, slipping into sleep, but he roused her when he whispered, "You have to drop it, Danny. Just be glad you're home. Nothing bad is going to happen to you. But you have to drop it. Nora's gone now. You have to let her go."

❄

THE NEXT MORNING, Danny slept in. She woke with the sun on her face, and just as she opened her eyes, she felt the incredible freedom of having forgotten all that had happened.

A split second later, reality came rushing back.

The murder, the blood, holding her mother's dead body, warm and slippery with blood, and everything that had transpired slammed into the forefront of her mind.

She told herself to focus on the Campopiano murder investigation. If she could throw herself into that case, she had a decent chance of suspending the waking nightmare that had become her life.

But then she remembered the 'deal,' and Franco's orders.

Ugh, she groaned.

Did she have a single reason to get out of bed?

She rolled over onto her side. Tommy wasn't there. She drank in the peace and quiet for a moment, then climbed out of bed and found him in front of the kitchenette, cooking eggs. There was a pot of brewed coffee, so she helped herself.

"Want me to drive you in?" he offered, as he flipped the three eggs that were sizzling in the pan.

"I'm thinking about walking," she said. She tasted a sip of her coffee then sat in an armchair in front of the sunny window.

He glanced over his shoulder at her. "Let me drive you."

Something was up with him.

"It's no problem," he insisted.

"Alright," she said. "But I need to get dressed properly at my place."

"I'll bring you," he offered without a moment's thought. "I'll drive you over after we eat."

Skeptical, and though she was suspicious, she agreed.

They ate breakfast, Danny threw on some sweats that she could actually leave the apartment in, and they drove a few doors north along Ocean Parkway. Tommy had to park illegally in front of her building since there were no spots, but he didn't wait in the truck.

He would rather risk getting a ticket than leave Danny to go into her apartment by herself, which wasn't Tommy's typical attitude towards a situation like that. But then again, nothing about their current situation was typical.

At her place, she found a pressed pair of slacks, a thick cotton tee shirt that was black, tight-fitting, and professional. In her bedroom, she threw those on, and found a secondary blazer that she could wear since her other one had been water-logged with the East River and then stained with Nora's blood. Right now, that entire outfit was sitting in the Evidence Room of the 66th, and she had no hope of ever getting those garments back again.

When she was changed and ready to go, she found Tommy in the baby's room, staring at the crib. The note was gone, probably in Evidence, as well, not that Crouse and Toliver would need it unless it would help them to build their case *against* Danny.

A strange, sad mood came over Tommy, as he stared almost unseeingly at the crib, like he was a million miles away, locked in some regret-filled corner of his own mind that he couldn't get out of.

When he spoke next, she couldn't tell if he was speaking to himself or to her.

"I really am sorry, Danny."

She closed her eyes for a moment and then forced herself to ask, "Sorry for what?"

Whatever he wanted to admit wouldn't come out.

"I should get to the station," she told him.

He pulled himself together, and they left. Danny locked up, and soon, after a short drive, Tommy pulled up along the curb in front of the precinct, and she gave him a kiss.

"Don't disappear again, alright?" she said in an attempt to be lighthearted.

"I'll stick around," he promised.

With that, she climbed out of the truck, crossed the sunny sidewalk, and found Carter at his desk inside.

"You came in earlier than 10," she pointed out, as she pulled her rolling chair out and got settled.

"The bloody dress shirt from the Campopianos' mansion is driving me nuts."

"I thought Franco told us to stop investigating."

"He's obsessed with getting Ellsworth," he said, which was true enough. "Right now, that's all he cares about, and I think he'll be happy as long as Ellsworth goes down. Even if Jimmy walks."

Carter wasn't exactly painting Franco in a flattering light this morning.

Danny suggested, "Don't you think that once Ellsworth faces the music, he'll roll on Jimmy and all the Campopianos?"

"Maybe, maybe not," he frankly replied. "How many inmates does Jimmy control on the inside of any of these New York prisons? Ellsworth might not talk at all. He might resign himself to the fact that he *is* going to prison. He would probably rather be alive in prison than dead the second he sets foot on the compound yard."

Once again, Carter's intelligent, fast-working mind had catapulted him way ahead. He was doing more than jumping to conclusions. He was downright fictionalizing them.

"Whose blood was on that shirt?" he ruminated to himself, puzzled. "It wasn't Bobby's. It wasn't Paul's. I had Jill run some tests based on what we discovered at Paul's boat. The bloody dress shirt is the hardest piece of evidence we have that *someone* got murdered. But who?"

The door to Franco's office flung open, and the lieutenant filled the doorway.

"Foster, Dobbs," he barked as he crossed through with the district attorney, Sarah Hovey, at his heels. "Let's meet in the conference room."

Danny and Carter followed them through the bullpen and into the warm conference room where no one had bothered to turn on the air conditioner. The room was hot with sunshine and dusty.

Franco opened a window to get some air, while Danny flipped the AC on. Sarah closed the door and soon they were seated around the conference table.

Sarah opened her briefcase and placed a stack of manila filing folders on the table in front of her. She was an organized woman with a sharp mind and very little patience.

"I'm going to cut to the chase," she said. "We have an uphill battle ahead of us. I can't use the spy pen to establish probable cause to go after Ellsworth in any capacity. But I have *you*, Carter, as a witness to all that was said. *That* I can use, and later down the road when you're questioned, *you* can refer to the spy pen, if that makes sense. Essentially, I can't present this as though you were a cop going in with the intention to record the audio. But I can present *you* as an off-duty cop who was ambushed, pressured, and then witnessed the corruption first hand."

Franco clarified the angle for Carter, even though the detective was no idiot. "We're going to need you to make a formal statement."

"How is that covert?"

"We have to do this by the book, Dobbs," Franco insisted.

"Then plan a sting operation," he countered.

Sarah told him, "We're past that."

"I literally pulled off a one-man undercover op," Carter said, nearly laughing at them.

"But we can't use what you have, because none of it was by the book," Sarah reminded him. "You should've come to us."

Getting angered, Carter raised his voice. "If I had come to you, you would've put a wire on me and followed behind me, driving in a giant, conspicuous *van*, and I would be dead by now."

"Not necessarily," Sarah replied, but she wasn't

convincing.

Carter snorted and shook his head. He asked Franco, "You're the one leading this charge. What do you want to do?"

Sarah reiterated, "We want you to make an official statement for the police record."

Carter didn't even look at her. He addressed the lieutenant. "What do *you* want me to do?"

Franco turned to Sarah and asked, "Is there any way to move forward with a sting operation, and essentially recreate the meeting that Carter already had, this time doing everything by the book and getting a recording that we can use?"

"With my son's spy pen?" Carter interjected. "I'm not going in there wearing a wire."

The D.A. told Franco, "You asked me to lead you through this so that there would be zero chance of Ellsworth getting off due to some minor, investigative technicality, and that's what I'm doing. The only way to do that is, step one, Carter has to make a statement."

"Jimmy and the Campopianos ambushed me in my car in broad daylight!" Carter said. "And that was for the purposes of being 'nice' and 'making a deal' with me! The second they find out I made an official statement, they're going to have me and my entire family killed!"

Danny volunteered herself. "I'll go in, wired."

Everyone stopped arguing and looked at her.

"I have a reason to approach Jimmy now that I'm out. I have a reason to approach Ellsworth, too."

Carter objected, "Danny, it's too dangerous."

She locked eyes with him. "They can't kill my

family. Everyone's already dead."

Chapter Eighteen

"YOU'RE NOT thinking straight," Carter told Danny when they returned to their desks, having spoken with Franco and Sarah Hovey. He pulled out his chair, sat, and kept his tone quiet. "Talking to the Campopianos while wearing a wire amounts to a suicide mission, you know that."

"I'm not going to talk to the Campopianos while wearing a wire," she reminded him, as she rolled her chair close to her desk and booted her computer. "I'm going to talk to Ellsworth."

Carter had been to the puppet show. He had seen all the strings.

"Jimmy's not going to let you or anyone talk to Ellsworth directly."

She leveled him with a firm stare. "I'll find Ellsworth at the courthouse. Jimmy won't be there. If you haven't noticed, we just got yanked off our murder investigation. Our only chance of actually *solving* Bobby's case will be if we catch Ellsworth. It's all tied together."

Carter shook his head. She had no idea the grave danger she would be putting herself in if she went through with whatever 'by-the-book' sting operation Franco was cooking up with the district attorney.

But Carter couldn't jump on the grenade to save Danny. If he made a formal statement, he would be as good as dead. From where he was sitting, he didn't want Danny to jump on the grenade, either. But were there any other options?

"I don't like it," he grumbled. "I worked in Vice for years. I know how to go into a dangerous situation and catch a criminal, and it doesn't involve doing something stupid like wearing a wire."

"It involves a young boy's spy pen," she suggested, and a wicked little smirk cracked the corner of her asymmetrical mouth.

Her grin was contagious, and he chuckled, shaking his head. He was glad she had a sense of humor after everything that had happened to her.

"Hey, Matty's spy pen proved to be better technology than anything the 66th has to offer."

"Ain't that the truth," she agreed. "When Franco and Sarah have a plan, trust me, we'll all discuss it before anyone sends me into the lion's den. I don't have the feeling that we'll be asked to move on this immediately."

"Maybe I should've looped Franco in before I met with Jimmy and Ellsworth," he thought, second guessing himself.

"I think you made the right move, Carter. If you had looped Franco in, he would've either put a wire on you, or he would've forbidden you to go. At least now, we have Sarah convinced and on our team, and we have you as a witness. Your testimony will always outweigh the evidence in a court of law, especially at a jury trial."

He knew she was right. Yet once again, the 66th Precinct was asking Carter Dobbs to sit on his hands and exercise the kind of patience that didn't come naturally to him.

"Jimmy and the Campopianos know where I live," he stated, as his mind filled with dangerous scenarios he prayed would never play out. "I don't like that Jimmy has Tommy under his dirty thumb."

Danny froze, staring at Carter, as sunlight cut through the windows, casting the other side of her face in dark shadows. Her brow furrowed with confusion.

"What are you talking about?"

He was genuinely confused that she was confused.

"You didn't know that?" he asked. He had assumed that the Jimmy - Tommy connection was an aspect of the nested secrets that Danny had been keeping from him. "According to how Jimmy framed it, he and Tommy 'go way back.' I got the impression that their relationship is a classic mafia protection racket."

"A protection racket?" she questioned, shaking her head. Then she realized something. "I saw Jimmy at the bar once, but it looked like he was having a beer."

"At an Irish pub?" Carter pointed out. "The more I investigate the Campopianos, the more real estate I discover they control. They practically own all of Kensington."

As Danny slipped into deep thought about Jimmy Campopiano having gotten his controlling hands on the most important man in her life, Carter's desk phone blared.

He picked up on the first ring when he saw the internal, three-digit number.

"Dobbs," he said.

"This is Cruz up in Missing Persons," said the police officer on the other end of the line.

Carter and Officer Cruz hadn't exactly gotten along throughout the weeks since Carter had joined the Special Victims Unit.

Curtly and to the point, Carter asked, "What have you got for me?"

"Paul Decker isn't missing."

As Officer Cruz conveyed the facts, Carter covered the mouthpiece of his phone and told Danny, "Decker isn't missing."

"A coworker came in again to formally report Decker missing," Cruz went on. "I looked him up, called the numbers, and he picked up when I tried his cell phone."

"Where is he?" Carter asked, as he jumped to his feet.

Danny was already on her feet. They had thought the lover had been murdered. He was alive?

Officer Cruz said, "At the Brooklyn Marina, Slip 112."

"Thanks, man," Carter told the cop, as he stood, letting bygones be bygones.

"No problem."

He hung up and threw on his suit jacket. "Decker's back on his boat."

Danny shot him a sideways look as they walked briskly through the bullpen and into the small dingy lobby of the station house.

"Good thing you didn't push for that warrant," she teased him.

"Good thing I never jump to conclusions," he played along, as he shoved the glass door open for her and followed Danny out into the humid light of day.

"How do you want to spin this to Franco?" she asked, coming to the passenger side of the parked Crown Vic.

"I don't," he told her honestly.

They climbed into the sedan, buckled up, and Carter eased into the street, squeezing in-between a delivery truck and a flashy convertible that was full of designer dogs and the trophy wives that spoiled them.

"Let's chalk this up to following up with a Missing Person claim," he suggested, "and only write up a report *if* Franco asks us to account for how we spent our lunch hour."

"What are the chances that the Campopianos will be keeping an eye on Decker?" she wondered.

Carter knew where the question was coming from. On the one hand, Franco had told them not to investigate for the time being. But Franco wouldn't kill them if they did. Jimmy Campopiano, on the other hand, would not be pleased to discover the cop he had just pulled strings to free from jail was already breaching the unwritten contract between them.

"I wish I knew," he replied darkly.

"Are you surprised Paul isn't dead?"

He glanced at her then returned his attention to the tight grid of traffic that had congested their route to the Belt Parkway.

"As a matter of fact, I am," he told her honestly. He turned onto a one-way cross street, getting off the main road that wasn't moving. "When Jill found the men's dress shirt, soaked in blood, in the laundry room of the Campopianos' mansion, the first victim that came to mind was Paul. Bobby crossed my mind too, but too many days had gone by. If it had been Bobby's blood, it would've been dried, maybe even hard as a rock."

"But it wasn't Decker's blood," she added, having gained that detail from Carter earlier.

"It wasn't Decker's," he confirmed. "It wasn't

Bobby's. Jimmy had showered and the house smelled like bleach."

Danny looked at him, puzzled. "Whose blood was it?"

He touched eyes with her then, as he concentrated, merging onto the Belt Parkway where traffic was flying at fifty miles per hour, he admitted, "I don't have a damn clue. But once we find out, the case against Jimmy will build itself."

"To what end? So that Ellsworth can throw the whole thing out?"

"If we can bring Ellsworth down *now*, then every murder charge against Jimmy and the Campopianos will stick."

"Timing is everything," she agreed, as they flew north on the parkway.

To the west sat New Jersey across the blue, sparkling waters of Upper Bay. Soon the Statue of Liberty came into view and the East River separated Brooklyn from Manhattan. Sailboats with huge, white sails eased lazily through those sparkling, brackish waters. There wasn't a cloud in the sky.

Carter exited the parkway and after a tight clover leaf off-ramp, he turned onto Furman Street and they drove directly under the cool shadow of the Brooklyn-Queens Expressway, which was suspended high above them and humming with traffic.

Moments later, they came to Pier Zero at the Brooklyn Marina. Carter squeezed the brakes and they rolled along the one-way that was lined with parked vehicles on either side.

Carter remarked, "It's Hail Mary time."

Though he was correct, and usually a miracle was required in order to find a vacant parking spot in this nook of Brooklyn, Danny pointed up ahead and shouted:

"There! That's a freaking spot!"

Must have been their lucky day, and it was about damn time that the tides had turned in their favor.

Carter came up beside the vacant spot and maneuvered the Crown Vic, parallel-parking perfectly by sliding the sedan with a few, smooth angles.

They climbed out into the warm sunshine. Cool winds breezed in from the water and the air smelled of seaweed and salt.

Carter glanced up and down the street. It was quiet. This wasn't a well traveled road. They hadn't been followed.

As they made their way over to the piers where the wooden docks were jutting out into the East River, Danny pushed a pair of aviator sunglasses onto her face.

"How do you want to play this?" she asked him, as their heels struck the wooden docks.

"Paul's going to think we're working for Jimmy and not the precinct," he agreed. "Let me lead with the bloody shirt and the cyanide capsule that we found in Lorenzo Campopiano's bedroom. That ought to give Paul some hope."

"You got it, but Carter?" she asked as they came to Slip 112.

"Yeah?"

"If you let me fall in the river again, I'm not going to be your friend no more."

He chuckled and promised, "I won't let you take a *running leap* into the East River."

"I fell in through no fault of my own," she

joked.

"Could've been worse," he teased.

"How?"

He shot her a glance and smiled. "At least you floated back up."

They came to Paul's 40-footer. The sails were open and it looked like Paul was planning on heading out into open waters.

"Hey, yo' Paul Decker!" Carter shouted, assuming Paul was beneath the deck, in the cabin of the sailboat. "It's Detectives Dobbs and Foster here to speak with you! Paul?"

The sailboat tipped and dipped, even though no wakes were rolling in. Paul climbing the stairs to come up from the cabin caused the boat to rock.

When he emerged at the front of the cockpit, he was wearing a bright orange polo shirt and crisp white boating shorts, and his platinum-white hair was pulled back into a dainty ponytail.

"Paul Decker, hello!" Carter greeted the older man.

The look of intense displeasure on Decker's face said it all.

"What the hell do you want?"

Danny told him, "We thought something had happened to you. We were worried."

"Somehow, I doubt that," said Paul, as he turned the engine, preparing to putter out beyond the buoys and set sail where the winds were strong.

Carter pushed, "We would really like to speak with you. Can we come aboard?"

Paul sauntered over to the side of the sailboat, planted both fists on his hips, and lifted his head high.

"It took *days* for me to recover from the *emotional trauma* I suffered at my *lover's* funeral! I'm not going to let you retraumatize me!"

Danny promised, "We don't want to retraumatize you, Paul. We really just want to talk."

Carter added, "There have been significant developments in the case. We would like to share them with you and see if they help you remember anything that we can use."

When it looked like Paul was softening, Danny told him, "Bobby's killer is still out there."

"Fine," said Paul.

He returned to the cockpit and killed the engine then came to the stern of the sailboat. There he picked up a rope that loosely connected the boat to the dock and pulled it taut. The rear of the boat floated over the water until its polished side pressed into one of the buoys meant to cushion the boat from the wooden pillar of the pier.

Carter stepped onto the stern of the boat first and then helped Danny up after him. He had a firm hold on her hand and upper arm so that even if she lost her balance, she wouldn't fall. He had her.

"Have a seat," said Paul, inviting them to sit in the sunshine on the deck.

There was a long bench that flanked the starboard side of the sailboat. Carter and Danny sat down on the thick, blue padded bench. The view of Manhattan across the water was breathtaking. Too bad the scenery was lost on Carter. All he cared about was getting to the truth and beating Jimmy Campopiano at his own game.

Paul sat down, crossed his legs, and gazed up at the flawless blue sky.

Carter asked him, "Where did you go?"

"I'm not going to tell you that, Detective," Paul informed him, confidently setting his own boundaries. "I was in fear for my life, though. You saw what Jimmy and the Campopianos did to me. I thought they might come after me."

"We thought they *did* come after you," Carter told him frankly.

"I was bleeding from the nose badly. I left quite a mess here, but no, they didn't come after me."

"Do they know that you live here?" Danny asked.

Paul looked at her like she had just fallen off the turnip truck. "Do they *know* I live *here*?" he mocked. "They know everything. You're investigating them, you can bet they know where *you* live, too."

It gave Danny pause and she fell silent, considering what Paul had said, while Carter pressed ahead.

"My partner and I obtained a search warrant, and when we searched the Campopianos' house, we found considerable evidence. One piece of evidence was a men's dress shirt that was covered in blood."

Carter let that hang, and after a moment, Paul asked, "Who's blood?"

"We don't know," he said honestly. "But it wasn't Bobby's."

"The Campopianos kill people like they're playing a game of dodgeball, did you know that?"

"Do you have any idea who might have been killed?" Carter asked. "Is there anyone you know who Jimmy might have 'taken out'? Anyone who disappeared?"

Paul racked his brain then shook his head. "No

one comes to mind."

"We found cyanide capsules in one of the kids' rooms at the house," Carter went on. "Bobby had cyanide in his system, and we probably shouldn't be telling you this, but it was cyanide that killed Bobby."

Paul's eyes widened. As the information sank in, he gasped and slapped his hand over his mouth.

Carter asked, "Do you know something about that?"

Malformed anger filled his tone, and he insisted, "Bobby didn't kill himself!"

Danny assured Paul, "We don't think Bobby would've cracked the cyanide capsule in his mouth except under duress. He didn't want to be tortured to death. We are, of course, proceeding as though this was a homicide."

Carter asked, "Did you know that Bobby had a cyanide capsule?"

Paul drew in a deep breath, filling his lungs with air, closed his eyes, and took a moment to compose himself. He said, "Yes." When he opened his eyes, they were glassy with tears. "But Bobby didn't kill himself."

"We don't think he did," Carter assured him, reiterating Danny's promise.

"He had a dark side," Paul began to explain. "I knew about the capsule. It's made out of a kind of plastic. It won't melt in your mouth. You have to crack it open with your teeth for the liquid cyanide to kill you."

It wasn't clear to Carter why Paul would mention that specific detail until Paul went on to confide a strange, dark habit that Bobby used to have.

"He sometimes kept it in his mouth."

Carter felt his eyebrows shoot up.

Danny was momentarily speechless, but soon asked, "Bobby sometimes kept the *cyanide capsule* in his *mouth*?"

"I hated when he did that," Paul said with a defeated sigh. "It scared me, but yes. Sometimes he would put the capsule in his mouth and rattle it against his teeth. It made me *very* nervous, but he promised me that the capsule was made of a hard plastic, and he explained to me that it wouldn't melt."

Carter asked, "Why would he keep it in his mouth?"

"Bobby once told me that it made him feel alive. He said that when he had it in his mouth, it reminded him that he was living by choice, not by obligation."

Chapter Nineteen

DANNY AND CARTER had barely returned to the police station when Franco called them into his office.

Danny's stomach tightened with nerves, but she knew what she would say if he confronted them about sneaking off to speak with Paul Decker.

But Franco wasn't aware that they had, which became obvious once Danny and Carter entered the lieutenant's warm office and shut the door.

"We can move on this fast. Today," Franco told them, as he rounded to the business side of his desk with a steaming mug of coffee in his hand. He had caught them on his return trip from the break room. "Sarah pushed, and we were granted a probable cause warrant to wire Danny and record Ellsworth."

"That *was* fast," she remarked, as they all sat down.

He gulped his coffee then set the mug down in favor of referencing the game plan he had typed on his computer.

"If you can get Ellsworth to say *anything* about accepting bribes, we can use it to get a warrant to search his finances. We need the 'what,' the 'when,' and the 'why' of any single deal he's made with the Campopianos. Considering that you, Danny, embody all three, Sarah and I believe you can go in there to thank Harlan Ellsworth, period. That's your 'in' and that's what you can lead with and use to provoke him into confirming *anything*."

The only true professional undercover investigator in the room was Detective Carter Dobbs, and he looked scared as hell for Danny.

Franco noticed and said, "She's going to meet Ellsworth in his chambers at the courthouse. She isn't going to be in danger there."

"No," Carter agreed. "She's not going to be in danger at the courthouse. The second she leaves and word gets out, however... *that's* a different story."

"Which is why, Danny, you *are* going to get him to admit *something*. Do not leave until Ellsworth has at least said, 'you're welcome,' okay? As long as you get us something, Sarah and I can move very quickly. We'll pull the Campopianos off the street. We'll arrest Ellsworth, so that the Campopianos can't walk again—"

"Franco, this is bigger than the Campopianos," Carter interrupted with a punch of skepticism. "How many other mobsters and crime families have been paying Ellsworth off? You think *they're* going to turn a blind eye? There's a lot of muscle out there that's keeping Ellsworth on the bench."

"You think I don't know that?" Franco challenged. He was calm, though. Too calm. He lifted his hand and said, "You know what, Dobbs, you're excused."

"What!"

"Danny is our forerunner. We're covered. You can return to your desk."

Carter kept his mouth shut, following the order. He struggled to keep a lid on his strong opinions, however, and though he was itching to point out all the flaws in Franco's plan, he knew better than to argue with the lieutenant.

He left them and closed the door on his way out.

It wasn't until Carter was excluded that Danny

fully realized her partner's anger had been a form of protection. As Franco went on to explain the ins and outs of his plan, providing her with specific angles she could use when speaking with Ellsworth, Danny knew that Franco wasn't concerned with her welfare or the danger she would be placed in. His focus was purely on getting the corrupt judge. If Danny became collateral damage in his effort to secure the arrest, that was a risk that Franco was willing to take.

"Let's get you wired up," said the lieutenant. "Ellsworth will be out of court in about twenty. You'll show up to speak with him in his chambers. And remember, Danny, Sarah can use just about *anything*. Please, don't leave until he admits something."

If she left that courthouse without some kind of admission from Ellsworth, she would be as good as dead.

DANNY HAD NEVER worn a wire before. The thing was bulky, and the way the techies had taped the microphone, wire, and battery box around her torso made her feel three times her natural size. Her skin was slick with sweat, and she couldn't tell if that was due to the warmth of the sunny afternoon or the fact that she was growing nervous with each step she took.

Walking towards the courthouse, she glanced at the unmarked van where Franco, two police officers, and one techie were listening from inside. The van stuck out like a sore thumb. She felt conspicuous.

She hoped she wasn't making a colossal mistake. Carter's warnings weighed heavily on her mind, but she was already in the thick of it and couldn't turn back now.

Justice Harlan Ellsworth presided over the Eastern District of New York's U.S. District Court in Cadman Plaza of Downtown Brooklyn. Unlike most courthouses throughout the country that were built of granite, supported by Roman columns, and had a classic architectural design, the Brooklyn courthouse was a modern building with a massive glass-encased foyer that more closely resembled a luxury high-rise condominium.

The foyer was cool and sleek with polished marble floors and tons of sunlight. The place had a corporate yet ominous energy. Cut-throat attorneys rushed through, and criminals wearing expensive suits darkly hoped for the best as they located their courtrooms.

Danny checked the directory, a large digital sign. There were 84 courtrooms within the building. Ellsworth's courtroom, as well as his office, were on the 13th floor.

The tremendous lobby had four bays of elevators. The latter bays went straight up to floors 15 through 30, so Danny came into the first bay where clusters of well-dressed people were waiting for the next elevator. When an elevator came, people poured out of it and then Danny and a handful of others piled in.

At least she was living by choice, not by obligation, she thought, remembering what Paul had said about Bobby. This sting operation was the closest thing to Russian roulette that Danny had ever volunteered to play, but at least she had chosen it.

The elevator doors dinged open and whooshed shut at just about every floor. When the elevator dinged at the 13th floor, Danny squeezed between two sets of attorneys who had been whispering to their clients, and started down the marble corridor.

Ellsworth's judicial suite was on the west side of the building. The glass door was clearly marked, and when Danny let herself in, she was met with a sizable anteroom where a secretary was seated behind a desk. All of Ellsworth's staff had desks and offices within the suite, including Ellsworth's office.

She hadn't called ahead. This visit was completely unannounced. She hoped like hell that despite the fact that the surveillance van was thirteen stories below and on the other side of the building, Franco would be able to hear and record her. She did not want to imagine what would happen if this mission failed due to technical difficulties.

"I'm Detective Danielle Foster, here to see Justice Ellsworth," she told the secretary, a cozy-looking young woman who probably had no idea that Ellsworth had been a puppet for the mafia for longer than she had been alive. "I'm just stopping by."

The young secretary was kind and accommodating. As she called Ellsworth, Danny got the impression that unexpected visitors didn't come by regularly. There was virtually no red tape other than waiting for about three minutes in one of the leather chairs in the anteroom.

Danny quietly spoke into her shoulder as she

pretended to look for something in her purse. "If you guys can still hear me, send me a text, I need to know we're all good."

Not even a second later, her cell phone vibrated. She swiped the screen, and found a text message from Franco—*We good.*

"Detective? The judge will see you now," said the secretary, as she indicated that Danny could walk straight back.

Danny stood, peered down the carpeted hallway, and after the young woman had reiterated that Ellsworth's office was straight ahead, she ventured in that direction.

'Justice Harlan Ellsworth' was engraved on the wooden door. Danny knocked and heard the judge within the office invite her to come in.

She eased the door open and cautiously entered the room.

Ellsworth was seated behind a grand, mahogany desk. His black robe hung on a wooden rack nearby. Bookshelves packed with leather-bound law books lined the walls.

Harlan Ellsworth appeared relaxed yet curious about Danny's unexpected visit.

It wasn't until Danny had closed the door behind her and turned that she realized Guido Campopiano was seated on one of the chairs in front of Ellsworth.

Holding his black fedora hat in his hands, he looked just as surprised to see the detective as the detective was to see him.

Danny froze and a cold sweat broke out across her chest, dampening the layer of grease that had already formed.

"Detective," said Ellsworth. "I trust you've met Mr. Campopiano."

"Of course," she squeaked. She had to swallow the lump in her throat before trying again. "Mr. Campopiano, how are you?"

Panic surged through her mind. She didn't know what to do, or whether she should abort the mission. Her gut told her that she was already dead, she might as well go down swinging.

Her cell phone began vibrating in her purse. She didn't have to answer it to know that it was Franco. She ignored the call and its incessant buzzing.

"Your Honor, I was hoping to speak with you privately," she said as calmly as she could.

Maintaining her objective was her prime concern now that she had officially signed her own death warrant.

Guido glared at her, but there was no confrontation as the older Italian-American man stood and shook Ellsworth's hand.

Carter had arrested Jimmy and all the Campopianos, and though Guido and the rest had since been turned loose, Danny doubted that Guido would ever forgive and forget.

On his way out, Guido said, "You've got some nerve coming here."

It sounded like a threat. He excused himself from the office and shut the door behind him on the way out.

Ellsworth was the first to speak. Danny hadn't even sat down.

"Considering my signature is on your bail disposition, I think we both know you shouldn't be here."

"Jimmy never told me not to thank you," she said boldly.

He narrowed his eyes. "You should've been granted an opportunity for bail in the first place. There's no need to thank me for having caught an administrative error."

"Do you think I did it?"

Ellsworth stiffened. He didn't answer her. He knew she was up to something.

"Do you?" she pushed.

"My focus is strictly dedicated to making sure *juries* arrive at a reasonable verdict. Unless someone is standing trial in my courtroom, I don't trouble myself to try to determine whether or not they *did it.*"

"All the evidence suggests I'm guilty."

"What is it that you want, Foster?"

Her cell phone began buzzing again like crazy inside her purse. She was too much of a rookie to pull this off, and she knew it. Desperate, she racked her brain for a clever conversational strategy, but nothing came to mind.

"Why are you protecting the Campopianos? They're guilty, but even if they weren't, you've crossed a major line. Do you have any idea how transparent you look?"

"Do you have any idea how much danger you're putting yourself in?" he countered.

"Are you threatening me?"

"No, I'm asking you to slow down and think about what you're doing. You shouldn't be here. You're compromising your own case, and you know it. If your case is assigned to a different judge, you'll be finished, Danielle, do you understand that?"

"Guido Campopiano knows I'm here speaking with you. I'm finished already."

Genuine concern for her welfare shined through the judge's response. "No, you aren't. Let it go, and everything will be alright."

For the third time, her cell phone started buzzing in her purse. She didn't say another word to Ellsworth. She turned on her heel and let herself out. As she passed the secretary's desk, walking through the carpeted anteroom, she answered Franco's call.

"Get the hell down here!"

"Guido saw me," she whispered.

"Why do you think I called you the first time? I know that!"

She wasn't looking forward to this. She made her way to the elevator, rode it down to the lobby, and crossed the marble foyer, as the orange light of the setting sun cut through the glass walls.

Outside, she squinted and made her careful way down the granite steps. The surveillance van was parked in the same spot, but when she rounded towards the street, heading that way, Tommy caught her by total surprise.

"Danny, we need to talk," he said, stepping in front of her.

"What are you doing here?"

A glint of terror darkened his eyes. "I have to talk to you about something serious."

"How did you know I was here?"

"I've been following you. Keeping an eye on you—"

"Why?"

"Please, can we go somewhere?"

Technically, no one was supposed to know that she was wearing a wire and in the midst of a sting operation even though it had gone badly and was over.

"I have to handle something, can I meet you at your place?"

"No, I don't want to let you out of my sight."

"Tommy, I'm an armed police officer. I can protect myself. The only thing you've ever fought was a fire."

She immediately regretted having said that, but Tommy wasn't insulted. He was purely determined to talk to her about something important as soon as possible.

"It's going to have to wait," she told him. "Right now, I'm in the middle of something."

She walked around him, but wasn't sure that climbing into an unmarked van would be the smartest thing to do.

Once she crossed the street, however, she realized she didn't need to make that choice. Franco was already out of the van and standing on the sidewalk.

She glanced over her shoulder. Tommy was planted on the sidewalk with his hands on his hips and staring at her.

"I know that didn't go well," she admitted.

"We need to regroup."

To say the least.

'REGROUPING' AT the 66th had more to do with

Franco assigning just about every on-duty police officer to a protection detail for Danny.

Franco hadn't ripped her a new one, even though she feared he would. No one could've foreseen that Guido Campopiano was meeting with Ellsworth the exact moment that Danny had gone in wired. That had been a stroke of exceptionally bad luck, but technically no one was to blame.

When Danny left the precinct, two police officers were with her. Franco had ordered them to drive her home and sit in their parked cruiser outside of her apartment building all night. It was hardly necessary, but she hadn't argued with Franco.

One of the officer's opened the rear door of the police cruiser for her.

Tommy shouted, "Danny! Hey!"

She turned, as Tommy caught up to her. His truck was parked way down the block. He had been waiting for her.

She told the cop, "It's okay. He's my boyfriend. Give me a minute."

"You're done for the day?"

"The lieutenant assigned a protection detail to stay with me," she said, offhandedly explaining why she was with the cops. "They're going to watch the apartment."

"I'll take you home," he offered.

"It might not be safe for us to—"

"Danny, this can't wait."

Sensing the gravity of the situation, she agreed, informed the cops that she would ride with Tommy, and then climbed into Tommy's truck, which was parked down the block.

Tension rose between them, as he started the

engine and pulled out into the street. The cruiser followed behind them. Tommy didn't say a word. He seemed to be using the time to mentally work something out in his mind.

It wasn't until they were upstairs, safely locked inside her apartment with the police keeping watch in the cruiser outside that Tommy dared to explain what had been on his mind.

"I didn't want to believe it," he said when they were sitting on the couch. The soft lighting of the apartment washed across his worried face. It sounded like he was apologizing. "I think I went into denial until you were arrested…"

Danny felt her stomach bottom out with dread.

Jimmy said he and Tommy go way back…

"What?" she breathed. "Tell me."

"Jimmy did it," he said with bitter remorse.

"What are you talking about?"

"He killed Nora."

The revelation slammed into her like a sandbag.

She asked, "How did Jimmy get his hooks in you?"

Tommy skirted over the mafia protection racket and the financial burden it had caused, and he went straight to blaming himself for having opened up to Jimmy about Gregory, though Tommy had tried not to at first.

As Tommy explained to her, he had confronted Nora in person the day she was killed. He hadn't known that the Campopianos had followed him. He had almost lost control with the old woman, but Tommy had come to his senses.

That's when Jimmy had appeared, walking right into Nora's apartment through the open doorway.

He had shoved Tommy out, and the rest Danny knew.

When Tommy finally finished explaining every last horrible detail, he looked pale and empty.

"I don't know who left the note," he said in a flat tone. "But it wasn't Nora, and it wasn't me."

Danny recalled the faint smear of blood she had seen on Nora's doorway when she had come home that afternoon soaked and desperate to change her clothes.

"I never thought Jimmy would follow me," he promised her, practically pleading. He couldn't look her in the eye. "I never meant for him to do that to your mom, or for you to get arrested for it. Danny, you have to believe me."

"I do," she said in a small voice.

The bloody shirt that had been driving Carter nuts came to mind—the white men's dress shirt.

Jill had discovered the bloody shirt in the Campopianos' laundry room the same day Nora had been killed.

The timeline fit.

Danny had just been arrested. The shirt that Jill had found in the basement of the Campopianos' mansion had been *wet* with blood.

She found her cell phone and quickly dialed Jill Andover.

"Who are you calling?" Tommy asked.

"I can get Jimmy for this," she told him. "I'm calling forensics." A beat later, she greeted Jill with absolutely no preamble. "How soon can you run a DNA test?"

"How soon can you give me the item you want tested?" Jill asked.

Danny was on her feet, as Tommy looked on from the couch.

"You already have one of the items. The bloody dress shirt from the Campopianos'. I think it's my mom's blood."

There was hesitation on the other end of the line and then Jill blurted out, "You think the Campopianos killed your *mother*?"

Danny and Tommy locked eyes, and she told Jill. "That's exactly what I think."

Once Jill got over the shock, she said, "If I get started right now, I can have results in 24 hours, *maybe* 12 hours, but that's pushing it."

"You can test the murder weapon," Danny said. "The knife is in Evidence. I'll make a phone call and get it over to you immediately."

"That'll work," said Jill.

Danny thanked her, ended the call, and got busy.

"Danny?" Tommy asked from the couch.

"You just made my case. It's almost over," she said, excited, as she called the Evidence Room of the 66th, making the necessary arrangements.

She held off on calling Franco, and decided she would loop Carter in after Jill returned the DNA results. But Danny was already smiling on the inside. They had Jimmy Campopiano. They *had* him… And if they could nail Ellsworth then the charges against Jimmy, once pressed, would stick.

Chapter Twenty

HOME HADN'T FELT like home since the cops had combed through every inch of the Campopianos' mansion. Even Eva's bedroom looked altered. It had been days since the police had used their search warrant to turn the place upside down, but her room still didn't feel right.

Eva was practicing ballet in her bedroom. There was a portable barre and sprung ballet floor set up in front of her window. With her ankle on the barre, she stretched the length of her leg then lifted her pointed foot off the barre a few times to test her strength.

The bedroom door was closed behind her. The twinkling street lights beyond her window made the neighborhood outside seem peaceful.

In order to keep sane, Eva had trained her mind to think only of her upcoming graduation. Somehow and some way, once she graduated, she would be out of here. She would miss Jimmy, of course. But whenever the anticipated sadness came to mind, she focused on looking forward to Romeo & Juliet. Jimmy had promised to take her to the opening night of the ballet. He already had the tickets.

She lowered her leg from the barre and lifted the other one. She slid her pointed foot up her calf and when her toes reached her knee, she lifted her leg, extending her pointed foot, and gracefully rested her perfectly straight leg onto the barre.

As she stretched, she listened through the floorboards to the sounds of her father having after-dinner drinks with Father Silva and the rest of the family downstairs.

Catherine and baby Rosa were tucked in their bedroom. Eva could hear Rosa cooing and giggling through the walls. She had been avoiding Catherine. Whenever she was home, she stayed in her bedroom. She never lingered after the family meals. She was doing everything Jimmy had told her to do, and yet with each passing day, Eva felt less safe.

Having stretched properly, she turned to face the full-length mirror that filled the far wall, and with one hand on the barre, she began pointing and retracting her foot, performing tendus to warm up her ankles. She slid her pointed toe in rhythm with the classical piano music that played softly through a set of speakers.

She loved Romeo & Juliet, the tragedy and the ballet. One day, she would perform Juliet's role on stage. She knew she would. She would escape the family like Bobby had, and she would make her dreams come true, even if Catherine came after her. She would rather die trying and live life to the fullest for a few months than stay here and let her family slowly kill her spirit.

Jimmy was the only one giving her hope and keeping her alive, but he was no longer a good enough reason to stay in Kensington, or Brooklyn, or in this house for that matter.

She recognized the sounds of her brother's footfall coming up the stairs. He crossed the hallway. When the sound of gentle knocking came at her door, she knew it was Jimmy.

"Come in!"

The door opened, and Jimmy slipped into her bedroom.

"Father Silva is gone, and Pop wants to speak with us," he told her, as he drifted across the room and came to the edge of her portable ballet floor.

She didn't stop her ballet warm-up. She looked at only herself in the mirror, while Jimmy studied her figure for a moment. The black leotard and pale pink tights she wore left virtually nothing to the imagination.

His hands were in his pockets, and a few locks of black hair had fallen into his eyes.

"Come on, Eva."

"I thought you said everything was over. What's there to talk about?"

"We'll find out when we go downstairs," he said.

"You don't know?" She found that hard to believe. "Am I in trouble?"

"No." He locked eyes with her in the mirror. She wouldn't budge. "What do you want? You want me to run away with you?"

That was exactly what she wanted, but she didn't feel like being mocked because of it.

"Let's go, Eva."

He took her by the upper arm. She didn't fight him, but when they crossed the room, she grabbed her pink sweatpants that were draped over the foot of her bed. She took a moment to pull them on, and it meant wriggling one foot then the next out of her leather ballet slippers.

"Are you ready?" he asked.

"Almost."

She slipped on a pair of bunny rabbit slippers, pulled a pink hoodie on, and when her brother chuckled to himself and shook his head, she knew she looked perfect.

"And you want to live all on your own someplace," he teased. "You're just a baby."

Jimmy opened the bedroom door for her, and when they crossed the hallway, Catherine peered out of the bedroom she shared with Jimmy. Eva caught sight of Catherine's spying eye, then Catherine clicked her door shut.

After descending the stairs, Jimmy and Eva crossed the marble foyer, passing the statue of the Blessed Virgin Mary, walked down the carpeted hallway, and came to their father's study where Guido was already seated in one of the leather armchairs and smoking a cigar.

There was a glass tumbler of scotch on the low, mahogany table in front of him. The ashtray next to it was clean.

Eva slowed her step when she saw that Uncle Tony, Cousin Nico, Gran-Pop Pasquale, and even little Lorenzo were there, seated around the study.

She wished her dad would stop treating her like one of the boys. Why couldn't she stay in her room like Catherine, or be left in peace like her mother?

Jimmy's hand was on the small of her back. He nudged her forward and steered her towards a leather loveseat that was directly across from Guido.

When they sat down, Eva crossed her legs and arms, giving her brother as much room as possible. Jimmy opened his arms, draped one across the back of the loveseat behind Eva's shoulders and the other he placed on the long, leather arm.

Guido frowned at them, and Tony and Nico knew not to stare at the unusual closeness that Jimmy and Eva shared.

Guido puffed his cigar, blew smoke through his

weathered mouth, and told the men, "One of the detectives went to see Ellsworth. I want her dead!"

Eva flinched, jumpy in response to her father's sudden outburst.

Guido took a breath and added, "I want both of them dead. Danielle Foster and Carter Dobbs."

Jimmy nodded.

Guido asked him, "You cut a deal with Dobbs?"

"I did."

"And this is how he repays you?"

"It's not right," Tony agreed.

"Son, I have to ask you," said their Pop. "Have you lost control?"

"No," said Jimmy.

"Are you sure you haven't lost control?"

"No, Pop," he insisted, but Eva could hear the fear in her brother's voice.

Nico attempted to vouch for Jimmy. "I was there when Jimmy talked with Dobbs. He was in control. We have Dobbs."

"We don't have Dobbs!" Guido exploded, slamming his fist against the leather arm of his chair. "We don't have that woman detective, and we don't have that police precinct! Jimmy, how the hell do we not have the Kensington Police Department under our thumbs? How?! After all these years, what the hell have you been doing out there? Eh? The 66th should have been the first organization to take control of!"

Tony rubbed his hands together and asked Guido, "How do you want us to do this? Taking out two detectives at the same time, and immediately, is a tall order."

As the men discussed their options, Jimmy

moved his hand from the back of the leather loveseat to Eva's shoulders. He shifted his weight, nearing her. She knew that he was trying to tell her that it would be okay, but she didn't believe him.

The men talked, planned, and conspired.

According to the plan that their Pop was cooking up with Uncle Tony and Cousin Nico, Eva would have to do more than simply keep her mouth shut.

Lorenzo was dozing off. Seated between his dad, Nico, and Tony, Lorenzo started faintly snoring.

Nico asked Guido, "Can Eva take him up?"

Guido asked her, "You understand what you have to do?"

"Yes," she said.

"You were paying attention?"

"Yes, Pop."

"You don't need us to explain it to you again?"

"No, Pop, I got it. I know what to do," she promised.

"Fine, take Lorenzo."

"Thanks, Pop," she breathed.

As she slid off the loveseat, Jimmy whispered to her, "I'll be up shortly."

She eased around the wooden coffee table and scooped Lorenzo up. He felt like a heavy sack of potatoes, but she heaved him into her arms. He flopped against her, his head resting on her shoulder, and she carefully carried him out of the study, closing the door behind her on the way out.

Soon, she climbed the stairs, rounded the landing, and gently deposited Lorenzo onto his bed. She flipped on the nightstand lamp and caught her breath. She couldn't put him in bed. He was wearing a button down, slacks, and a belt, dressed like a little mobster.

Eva began selecting a tee shirt and pajama bottoms from the dresser drawer when Lorenzo's mother, Bianca, entered the bedroom with Eva's mother, Maria, Tony's wife, Alice, and Catherine. The baby wasn't with Catherine, likely Rosa was asleep in her crib.

"I can get him changed, Eva, thank you," said Bianca, speaking in a soft tone of voice.

Maria closed the door behind her and the women tensely approached Eva.

Maria asked her daughter, "Should we be worried?"

"I don't know, Ma," she said honestly.

"The search warrant, those arrests," Maria recalled. "What will the police do next?"

Catherine demanded, "More to the point, what is Jimmy going to do next? Why are they keeping us in the dark?"

Bianca told Catherine, "Stop yelling at her."

"I *will* yell at her," Catherine maintained.

Eva hotly defended herself, "You think I *want* to be included in those meetings?"

"I don't care what you want," Catherine snapped. "What are they planning to do? Tell us!"

Eva hated the position she was in. She hadn't asked for this. But she knew her place, and it wasn't beneath Catherine.

"Tell us," Catherine hissed again.

"No," she stated before crossing the room for the door.

Catherine caught her by the arm and jerked her.

"He's *my* husband," she warned.

"Then he'll tell you, won't he?" she replied, spitting each word through clenched teeth.

Catherine growled under her breath, "You *know* what I'm talking about."

Jerking her arm free, Eva barked, "Get your hands off me."

She flew out of the room, charged down the hallway, and spilled into her bedroom where she slammed the door behind her.

A wall of tears immediately filled her eyes. She surrendered to her emotions, letting the tears fall and her sobs out as quietly as possible.

What her father expected her to do…

How would she live with herself after doing something like that?

The doorknob turned behind her, and as she stepped away from the door, Jimmy slipped in.

He read the anguish on her pretty face, but promised, "It's all you have to do, Eva. Then it will be over."

"It will *never* be over," she cried in a strained whisper, "and you *know* it."

He pulled her close, his strong arms wrapping around her damp, tired body, and Jimmy kissed her, smashing his warm lips against her mouth.

"It's going to be okay," he promised between kisses.

She melted with intoxicating lust, as he began pushing her sweatpants down, pulling her hoodie off, and yanking her leotard down.

Catherine pounded on the door. "Jimmy! I know you're in there!"

Jimmy and Eva bit into each other, gasping and tumbling towards the bed.

Catherine rattled the doorknob and pushed, but the door was locked.

"Jimmy, come out now!" she demanded, pounding harder and harder against the door.

In the next room, the baby started shrieking.

Maria, Bianca, and soon the men were in the hallway, yelling at Catherine to calm down. She screamed at them and they screamed back, but Eva could barely hear them. She was with her brother, and her brother was inside of her, and she didn't care who knew.

Chapter Twenty-One

DANNY WALKED briskly through the corridor, having arrived at the Kings County Hospital. She already felt grimy with sweat and the two to-go cups of coffee in her hands weren't helping.

Morning sunlight cut through the windows until she turned the corner, coming to the Medical Examiner's office where Carter had been waiting outside of the closed double-doors with Officer Sean Quinlan.

"Quinlan, I would've brought you one if I had known you would be here," she told the police officer, as she handed Carter one of the coffees.

Carter thanked her and peeled the plastic lid back.

"I've already had more caffeine than I can handle," Quinlan told her with an easy smile.

"Jill *does* like to start her day with a big pot," Danny agreed, having read between the lines. "She hasn't been too snappish towards your dedicated police work?"

"I think she's finally warmed up to me," he mentioned, as he opened the door for them. "You can go in. Jill is expecting you."

Entering the morgue, Danny noticed the stainless steel tables were bare this morning, and the place didn't stink of dead flesh and abrasive disinfectants.

Quinlan didn't follow in after them. He remained in the corridor as the door clicked shut behind the detectives.

"Morning!" said Jill, chipper from where she sat

behind her desk where several monitors were lined in a row.

"I wasn't expecting to hear from you until this afternoon at the earliest," Danny commented, as she padded over slick linoleum floors with her partner close behind.

"I got a jump on things the second you called last night," she explained. "I couldn't stay cooped up at my apartment with Sean."

A wry smile formed on Jill's face, but she suppressed it.

Danny and Carter touched eyes, knowing that *something* romantic had developed between Jill and Sean, even if the M.E. was still trying to actively avoid her growing feelings.

"You came here last night?" Carter asked.

"There's more room to breathe here."

"But Quinlan came with you," he pointed out.

She narrowed her eyes at him and refused to address the implication.

On the table next to her desk was a plastic evidence bag with the bloody, white, men's dress shirt inside. There was another evidence bag with the knife that had been used to stab Nora Foster to death.

Jill clicked her computer mouse, and the large images of the DNA test results filled the monitors. To Danny's untrained eye, the results looked like blurry boxes stacked in a long row.

Pointing to the image on the left, Jill explained, "This is the DNA from the shirt, and the other image here is from the knife."

Jill let that hang for a moment as if it would mean something.

Carter played ball. "They're the same?"

Jill swiveled on her chair and looked at Danny with the round, sympathetic eyes of a friend who had both good and bad news.

"They *are* the same."

"Goddamnit!" Danny blurted, the reaction flying out of her without her permission. She paced away and plowed all ten fingers through her short mop of brown hair.

Carter and Jill fell silent. They knew better than to try to calm her down.

She kept moving, circling the stainless steel tables, to gain some space and perspective, but the walls were closing in. Planting her fists on her hips, she shook her head, knowing that this was all her fault. It had to be. Because if it wasn't Danny's fault, then it was Tommy's.

She couldn't live with that.

She tried to get a grip on herself. She had expected this. She knew that Jimmy had taken her mother's life. Tommy had told her as much last night. But last night, she hadn't let herself *go there*. She had kept a lid on it. She had remained stoic, determined to remain a cop and not react like a daughter.

The DNA test results had just shattered the distinction.

Turning on her heel, she demanded, "Was it *Jimmy*?"

Jill replied, "According to the DNA on the shirt, and the *hair* on the shirt that we discovered, yes. Jimmy Campopiano was wearing this white dress shirt. Were others involved in Nora's murder? That I can't say."

"He killed her?" she asked Carter, yelling so hard and loud that it sounded like a statement.

Cautiously optimistic, he dared to suggest, "Jimmy won't get away with this."

"He won't?" she challenged, locking eyes with her partner who should know better by now. "What the hell *hasn't* he gotten away with, Carter?"

Carter approached her and spoke in a low, warning tone, "You have to get ahold of yourself. You know as well as I do that this changes everything. Franco will have to remove you from the case if you show any signs of going off the rails."

Furious, she shot back, "We're arresting Campopiano, right now!"

"Yes, we are," he agreed. "But if you try to lead the charge on this, you're going to get yanked, and you know it."

Breathing heavily, she pressed her mouth into a hard line, clenched her teeth, and paced away again.

Carter pulled his cell phone from his slacks, as he returned to Jill and asked her, "Can you email those results to Franco?"

"I'm on it," she said, and she dove into doing just that.

Carter sent the call through and got the lieutenant up to speed, but Danny was a million miles away. Desperate to put the pieces together, her mind raced. At what point had Jimmy learned about Nora? Why had he killed her? Had it been for no other reason than to get Danny locked up so he could demonstrate his power and get her under his control? Or had it been to avenge the infanticide of Tommy's son?

Hell, if it even mattered! She raked her fingers

through her hair again, coming undone.

Jimmy had done what Danny hadn't been able to.

So, who did she hate right now?

She couldn't see straight. Thinking straight was far beyond the realm of possibility, but when Carter neared her, she pulled it together enough to hide the fact that rageful darkness had become her.

"Franco will meet us at the Campopianos with an arrest warrant," he told her. "Hey, Danny?"

She tried and failed to lift out of the mile-long stare that had come over her.

"Danny?"

Jill looked on, worried for her friend.

Then, like flipping an internal switch, Danny turned her back on the part of herself that was heartbroken, enraged, and overwhelmed with complicated emotions.

Effectively letting that part of her—her humanity perhaps—die, a state of numb, calm, emptiness filled her.

"Let's go," she said.

When she charged out of the morgue, pushing the double-doors open and rounding into the corridor past Officer Quinlan, she couldn't feel her own body. She was detached from the world and from herself, yet she retained one clear objective in her mind.

She would destroy every last one of them, or die trying.

Carter jogged up beside her, and they cleared the lobby, spilled out into the hot, bright day, and walked briskly to the Crown Vic that was parked illegally in a No Parking Zone.

As they climbed in, buckled up, and took off, Carter told her from behind the steering wheel, "If we don't find out who killed Bobby Campopiano by the end of this, I'm going to drive my fist through a wall."

"I'll do far worse than that," she admitted darkly.

Traffic was cranky, so as they drove, Carter slapped the cherry siren on top of the sedan. The vehicles in front of them pulled aside, honking at each other as if using their horns to complain would get them back on the avenue faster.

Once they hit Flatbush, it was a straight shot to Church Avenue where they sailed west until Argyle Road.

Danny heard the distinct wail of police sirens moments before they drove farther south and cop cars came into view. Franco had angled his SUV onto the Campopianos' lawn and the cruisers hadn't done a better job of parking.

The second Carter squeezed the Crown Vic between the SUV and a cruiser, Franco climbed out with the arrest warrant in hand.

"Jill deserves a medal," the lieutenant remarked, as his detectives joined him on the lawn.

Danny agreed, but Franco was distracted by her unemotional attitude.

"Whoa, Foster, you can hang back here with me." Franco slapped the warrant into Carter's hand and the detective proceeded up the stone steps of the mansion.

"Are you kidding me?" she fired back, hotly.

"You're not going to be the arresting officer this time, Danny. You're too close to this thing."

She had half a mind to shove him off of her and

follow Carter inside, but that half of her mind had been paralyzed in the irreversible psyche-death that had occurred back at the morgue.

She still had her pride, though, so she paced off across the lawn to get a better view of her partner pounding on the front door.

"Hey, yo', Jimmy!" he shouted at the second floor windows, having taken a step back. He held the warrant up in the air. "You ready for Round Two?"

Jimmy peered down through the gauzy curtains.

"Let's see how long it takes Ellsworth to transfer your bribe money to an offshore account this time, EH?" Carter shouted.

Franco cursed and ran his big hand down his face.

Danny grinned and shook her head.

At least she wasn't the only one who would have a big, fat target on her back.

The front door flung open, but it wasn't Jimmy Campopiano who flew out of the house.

Eva stormed across the landing, slapped her two palms against the firm wall of Carter's chest, and shoved the detective with all her might.

"Leave him alone!"

Carter barely took a step back, but Eva got a good slap in, striking his face, before he captured her and gently tossed her towards one of the police officers.

The officer caught her, wrangled her flying fists, and as Carter entered the house, Danny jogged up the steps to Eva and grabbed her by the shoulders.

"You want to get arrested, too?"

"Jimmy didn't kill Bobby!"

"That's not why we're here," she yelled back.

Taking the girl by the upper arm, she pulled her down the steps and across the lawn, while additional police officers entered the mansion, having heard an altercation between Jimmy and Carter within the house.

Eva wouldn't listen to reason or shut her mouth.

"He didn't kill Bobby, alright! I'll tell you everything, just don't do this! He didn't kill Bobby, I'm telling you!"

Danny shook her. "He killed my mother, and you earned yourself a trip to jail, too, for hitting Detective Dobbs—"

"You don't understand! He can't go to prison!"

"What do you know about it?" she demanded. "You want to talk? Talk! Who killed Bobby?"

The answer that tumbled out of Eva was hardly English, and then the girl broke free when Carter pushed, shoved, and dragged Jimmy Campopiano out of the mansion, having handcuffed the mobster after roughing him up inside.

Eva wriggled past a line of police officers, threw herself onto her brother, and clung to him in a desperate panic that instantly boggled Danny's already shattered mind.

Eva kissed her brother on the mouth. "Don't go! Don't leave me here!"

Catherine spilled out of the house and demanded to know what was happening. The woman was barely dressed, and when she saw Eva kissing and clinging to her husband, she flew into a rage, clawing at the girl and screaming:

"Get away from him, you little pervert! He's *my* husband!"

Catherine clobbered Eva, taking a handful of the girl's hair and scratching her face, while three police officers got in the mix to pry the women apart.

Carter pushed Jimmy forward with two police officers in assistance. One opened the rear door of the nearest police cruiser, and the other helped Carter to fit Jimmy in the back seat.

When the police officers had succeeded at separating Catherine and Eva, the women were bloody and disheveled.

Danny pulled Eva aside once again and asked, "You know who killed Bobby?"

"Yeah, I do," she said like some kind of mastermind genius who thought she had all the power.

"Tell me!"

"I will. But under my conditions."

Chapter Twenty-Two

FEELING SHARP AND high from the adrenaline rush of making a solid arrest, Carter grinned at Jimmy Campopiano. The mobster was behind bars in the basement of the 66th Precinct, jailed and riddled with guilt.

Something told Carter that the look of white-faced guilt on the man's face had little to do with the killings he had committed.

"Your sister must really love you."

"Shut your ugly mouth," Jimmy hissed, glaring at the detective through his eyebrows from where he sat on the jail cell bench.

"How does your wife feel about that?"

"How does *your* wife feel knowing she's married to a dead man?" Jimmy countered, but he had shown too much emotion. He was rattled. Scared. They both knew he wasn't going to skate his way out of this one so easily.

"Are you threatening me?"

"Would it make my situation worse if I was?" he shot back dangerously.

Carter studied him. Jimmy knew where he lived. But Jimmy hadn't seen his own arrest coming. The mobster had thought the Kensington cops would be too stupid to figure out that the blood on that shirt had belonged to Nora Foster.

He had thought wrong.

Carter turned from the bars, but Jimmy wasn't done with him.

"You'll never get all of us."

Carter paused, slowing his step, but he didn't turn around.

"That's what you want, isn't it?" Jimmy pushed. "To take my family out? You have no idea who you're messing with."

He could've taken the bait, returned to the bars, and promised Jimmy that the Campopianos were finished in Kensington, in Brooklyn, and in all of New York City, period.

But he was better than that. Giving Jimmy the satisfaction of yanking him back into an argument that wouldn't make a damn difference in the long run was not a victory that Carter was willing to give the guy.

He started walking again, and it wasn't until he turned the corner, exited the jails, and made his way up the stairs that a sinking feeling hit him in the gut.

The last thing Carter wanted to do was indulge fear, but he needed to make sure that his wife would be safe, the kids, too.

In the small lobby outside of the S.V.U. and Homicide departments on the first floor, he pulled his cell phone out of the front pocket of his slacks and placed a call to Kathy's cell phone.

His wife picked up on the third ring.

When he heard her voice come through the line, calm yet classically disgruntled, his racketing heart rate subsided in his chest.

"Kathy," he replied, trying to sound calm himself. "I need you to get the kids and go to your mom's."

There was silence for a beat then she complained, "Are you kidding me?"

At least she was alive.

"Just do it!" he barked.

"Your line of work is no problem, darling," she

sang sarcastically. "Of course, we'll drop everything. I'll yank the kids out of school. We'll drive three hours north. Would you like us to change our names, too? Join Witness Protection?"

He was in no mood. "If that was an option," he allowed.

"Unbelievable. You know what, Carter? No, I'm not going to take the kids up north. You seem to think your police work is fine. And you know what? I'm going to *choose* to believe you!"

The line went quiet.

"Kathy?"

She had hung up.

"Kathy!"

He charged into the bullpen and told the first cop he saw, "I need you to go to my house."

Whether or not Carter had the authority to order two police officers to check on his wife and stay with her until he was certain there would be no retaliation for having arrested Jimmy, was anyone's guess. But the cops didn't question him.

"Unbelievable is right," he grumbled under his breath, as he crossed the room and found Danny standing with Franco near the conjoined desks that belonged to him and his partner.

Franco wasted no time briefing his detectives.

"With Jimmy arrested, we can expect that Ellsworth is going to get him out, get him off, or accomplish both in one fell swoop. Sarah's running through the options, now, in terms of what we can do to catch Ellsworth, or at least track him."

"Eva Campopiano knows who killed Bobby," Danny interjected.

She suddenly had Franco and Carter's full

attention.

"She wouldn't tell me, but said to meet her at Decker's boat," she added.

"Decker knows who killed Bobby?" Carter questioned, skeptical.

"That I don't know," she admitted. "And I don't know what Eva's up to, but you saw the look on her face when you arrested her brother."

"I saw the look on *both* their faces when they *kissed*," he allowed, as he touched eyes with Franco and clarified for the lieutenant's benefit, "there's more going on between them than natural *sibling* love."

Danny added, "The wife, Catherine, accused Eva of being a 'pervert' and yelled at the girl that Jimmy is *her* husband."

"It was dark," said Carter.

A look of veiled disgust screwed Franco's face up.

"That family has one hell of a secret," Danny surmised.

"What if it spells murder?" Carter proposed.

Franco didn't like the mess. "Jimmy and Eva have an incestuous relationship that Catherine and the family know about, and *Bobby* gets murdered?"

"Reality is stranger than fiction," Carter pointed out.

"Christ," the lieutenant muttered under his breath. "How the hell Paul and his boat connect to this is worth checking out."

"Let's head over," Danny suggested, and they started off.

Franco called out after them, "Keep your phones close. The second I hear from Sarah, we'll have to move!"

As the detectives crossed the sunny sidewalk and flanked both sides of the Crown Vic, Carter asked her, "You think Jimmy will drag Tommy into this to get to you?"

She locked eyes with him over the top of the sedan, "If he does..."

She didn't finish her point, but her expression said it all.

They threw the car doors open, climbed in, and started off for the Brooklyn Marina with all four windows down. The humid air of Kensington, ripe with the scents of dogwood and steaming trash, hardly took the edge off.

They reached the seaport after a tense, silent ride, both detectives brooding over Eva's insistence that her brother hadn't killed Bobby and her convenient timing of offering to tell all.

Carter parked at an awkward angle, blocking the marina's pedestrian entrance and stirring up a flock of seagulls. They climbed out, walked south through the hovering gulls along the dock, and glanced around, looking for the Catholic ballerina who had probably been having sex with her own brother for years.

When had it started? Who had known? And why had the family done nothing?

Most importantly, was the dark, family secret even connected to the murder?

Or was it a labyrinth of smoke and mirrors that would only lead them further away from discovering the truth?

The maw of brackish waters where the East River flowed into Upper Bay offered picturesque sights of sailboats breezing by, a perfect day for boating. But the yachters' paradise was lost on Carter.

Kathy weighed heavily on his mind. He couldn't trust his wife to do what she was told. But at least the cops he had sent over were obedient. He didn't even *want* to have authority *over* his wife. He just wanted her to take him seriously and be supportive. He was sick of the power struggles. He was sick of plowing through good therapists and watching his stubborn wife replace them as soon as they smartly exposed her controlling nature.

He couldn't afford to be sick of his marriage.

But he couldn't afford *this,* either—the distractions.

They rounded onto Slip 112 and were halfway down the dock, Paul's sailboat bobbing against the padded pier ahead, when a man shouted from a distance behind them.

"Detectives?"

It was Paul Decker.

He wasn't on his boat.

Carter did a double-take, glancing at the boat to make sure the girl wasn't onboard.

"Paul!" Danny called out, as the older man walked briskly down the wooden dock, his white hair blowing in the warm winds. "Hi! Eva Campopiano asked us to come. Is she here yet?"

"Eva?" he asked, confused, as if he didn't even recognize the name. "Bobby's sister?"

"She didn't talk to you?" Danny asked, suddenly thrown, as well.

"I don't have a relationship with her," he said.

There was nothing clever or conniving about his

reaction.

"I've been gone for a day," Paul went on. "I just returned to town."

Intuition slammed into Carter's gut.

Paul shook his head, adding, "Why would Eva tell you to meet me here? I don't really know her. She doesn't even have my number."

"Run!" Carter yelled, as he tore off, running across the dock, away from Paul's sailboat.

He hooked Danny with his arm, and pulled her, sprinting fast and tearing into Paul, who he grabbed.

BOOM.

The impact of the explosion hit Carter like an invisible tsunami. Shielding Danny and Paul, he became airborne, as the sailboat went up in flames. Shrapnel rocketed from the boat in all directions as black smoke rose in the warm air.

Carter, Danny, and Paul crashed against the wooden dock. Chunks of fire rained down over them. Carter crawled over Danny, protecting her, while Paul held his hands over the back of his head.

Eva Campopiano had set them up.

But the bomb had detonated too soon.

Carter lifted his head, eased off Danny, and stared at the sailboat that was being devoured by flames on the water.

Boaters rushed over and panicked at what in the hell that had been. A crowd formed. People placed calls to 911 while others used their cell phones to take photos and videos.

"You okay?" he asked Danny.

"Yeah."

Carter crawled over to Paul, who was unscathed, but shrieking at the loss of his most prized possession.

"You hurt?"

Paul cried, "You can't beat them! Don't you get that? My whole life was on that boat! They've taken Bobby from me, and now my home! If Bobby had left me a cyanide capsule, I would eat it right now!"

Carter caught his breath and locked eyes with Danny.

She wasn't about to give up, no matter what...

...and neither was he.

Chapter Twenty-Three

THE NIGHT was warm. The air smelled of dogwood, a sweet fragrance that filled Eva Campopiano's heart with bittersweet hope, as she walked arm-in-arm with Jimmy towards the Brooklyn Center for the Performing Arts.

Her red, velvet high-heels clicked with each step. She wore a slinky, black evening gown. Her brother was dressed in a tuxedo, his hair slicked back, his face neatly shaven.

The travertine glass entrance of the performing arts center sparkled with white and blue lights, as patrons of the Brooklyn Ballet streamed inside, wearing formal wear—ball gowns and tuxedos—and smiles on their faces.

It was a beautiful evening to attend the opening night performance of Romeo & Juliet.

Eva still felt traumatized, having helplessly witnessed Jimmy's arrest. But his booking had been processed quickly. Ellsworth had forced a bail hearing, and Jimmy had been released and placed under house arrest.

Under the pant leg of Jimmy's crisp tuxedo, the ankle monitor beeped, but only softly. Jimmy had used electrical tape to cover the two-way microphone on the device. The second he had left the house with Eva, the siblings all dolled up, his ankle monitor had gone off.

But they had time. They would have this night. And both had promised not to spoil the evening by listening to the device or looking over their shoulders.

At least the incessant beeping was muffled. The

monitoring police officer's voice had also come through the device, ordering Jimmy to call and explain his reason for leaving the house, or suffer the consequences.

Jimmy Campopiano had no intention of doing either. He had delivered Eva the hard news. The evidence against him for having murdered Nora Foster was staggering. He had told his sister that they would always have the ballet, but when the curtains closed, it would be over, forever.

Eva held her brother's arm tightly, as they entered the theater. The performance stage was lit beautifully, and the orchestra was already playing classical music, as the house filled and patrons of the ballet found their seats.

Jimmy showed an usher their ticket stubs. The usher directed them straight down the aisle, pointing towards the left side of the house where Section A was located.

As they continued down the red, carpeted aisle, moving slowly with the crowd, Eva reminded herself not to be afraid. There would be consequences as a result of having lured those detectives to the sailboat. The bomb had been a disaster, and their situation would only be much worse because of it. But none of that really mattered.

When Jimmy found their row, he urged her to go first, gently guiding her with his hand on the small of her back. She came to the middle of the row, found their seats, and they sat down. The seats were perfect, nearly in front of center stage, which offered the best views of the performance.

Jimmy took her hand in his, leaned in, and kissed her cheek.

"You're gorgeous," he whispered before kissing her again.

An older couple behind them complimented Jimmy, "Isn't she lovely? How long have you two been together?"

Eva smiled at her brother, and Jimmy searched her eyes, as he replied to them, "Practically my whole life."

They chuckled and remarked about their own long, happy marriage, then the lights dimmed and the orchestra began to play, the string instruments striking attention-grabbing chords.

The ballet performance would start momentarily.

Jimmy wrapped his arm around Eva, kissed her cheek again, and whispered:

"They never stopped us, and they never will."

Tears filled her eyes.

"Don't cry," he said softly.

She tried not to, and agreed, "It'll all be over soon."

On stage, the company of ballerinas glided out from behind the curtained wings. Eva squeezed her brother's hand. She loved him, and no one had ever been able to take that away from her. She knew that the world would never accept their special love, but the world was wrong, and that was why they were planning on leaving it...

...tonight.

CARTER PUNCHED his clenched fist into the palm of his hand and yelled, "What do you mean, we can't connect the explosion to the Campopianos?!"

Franco fired back, "The forensic experts we would need to properly investigate the boat bomb is far beyond this precinct's budget right now! Listen, Dobbs, I didn't say it's never going to happen. I said, it isn't going to happen in the immediate future!"

"It's *causal*, Lieutenant! Eva Campopiano told us to meet us there, *then* the sailboat blew up. Cause and effect! Causal!"

"Circumstantial!" he hotly corrected him. "You think I'm happy about this?"

Carter took an angry lap around Franco's office, while Danny looked on with folded arms. The bullpen beyond the office was dark and empty. She felt spent and ready to drop, yet her deeply determined energy was driving her. She wanted to get these bastards.

Franco reminded them, "We have enough circumstantial evidence to choke a damn pig, but even a judge that's still wet behind the ears is going to dismiss all of it. A corrupt judge like Ellsworth isn't going to look corrupt if he throws all of our circumstantial evidence out. Hell, the fact that he released Campopiano with an ankle monitor and a court date next week is technically by the damn book!"

"Can't Sarah do anything?" Danny asked.

"Is she a fundraiser?" Franco questioned, looking at her as if Danny had suddenly sprung a second head. "We've put in for the funding, and we've put in for the right forensics team. There's nothing more I can do!"

"While all the evidence washes away or sinks to the bottom of the East River," Carter complained.

Franco pointed out, "If any of the Campopianos, or if their trigger man, had been *watching* at a distance from Decker's sailboat, you two wouldn't be alive. That's good and bad. You're not dead, congratulations, but whoever pulled the trigger to detonate the bomb wasn't in the vicinity, which means—"

"We'll have a harder time finding out how they pulled it off," Danny supplied.

She fell into deep thought. Eva was having sex with her brother. The wife knew about it, possibly the entire family knew. But Bobby got murdered. Something wasn't adding up. Why Bobby?

It was almost as though the family was either protecting Jimmy and Eva, or turning a blind eye. Bobby was the only one who had left the family, in a sense choosing to be an outsider...

"Foster, what are you thinking?" Carter wanted to know.

"Eva was in on it, to some capacity," she said, sharing her thoughts but badly. "Eva saw Bobby that morning. Bobby made himself an outsider. He separated himself from the family. Did he rock the boat on his way out? I don't know. But Catherine might have been rocking the boat."

"Acting like an outsider, yet in the family?" Carter suggested, spitballing with his partner. "She couldn't have been happy to discover her husband was banging his own sister."

"How do Catherine and Bobby connect, if at all?"

Carter shook his head, stumped.

Danny went on, "Killing you and me, that makes sense. But why take Decker out, too?"

"Erase the family shame of having a homosexual for a son?" Carter guessed.

She didn't like it. She shook her head. "Decker must know something."

"He knew about the cyanide capsules," Franco pointed out, though his attention remained on a stack of color photographs that were spread across his desk.

The photos depicted the sailboat on fire, smoking, and also the aftermath, its wreckage and destruction. Many of the images had been sent into the precinct from witnesses that had recorded the event on their cell phones.

"He did," she allowed, as she racked her brain even harder. "Bobby used to keep his capsule in his mouth at times… to remind himself that he was living by choice, not by obligation…"

Carter pointed out, "Bobby had to have known about Jimmy and Eva."

Danny agreed. "But he didn't wage a war. He didn't expose them. He left."

"Maybe that was the problem," Franco proposed. "If he left the family, he's not easy to control."

"There's a time delay, though," said Danny. "If Bobby being on his own opened the family secret up to being exposed, why would the Campopianos wait five months to take Bobby out?"

"Let's think about this," Carter said, backing everyone up. "Who would've been the most hurt to discover Jimmy and Eva were *involved?*"

"Catherine Campopiano," said Danny.

And Carter added, "The woman who had just had Jimmy's baby."

The pieces were there, but they didn't fit neatly together, thought Danny. Franco was right. The circumstantial evidence had piled up a mile high, but it didn't do them a damn bit of good.

What they needed was a confession. Screw the evidence and forget *building* a case. They needed one of the Campopianos to come clean and tell them what the hell had happened to Bobby that morning.

Franco's desk phone blared, ringing loudly.

He answered, "Lieutenant Franco's office."

When Franco fell silent and locked eyes with Danny, she knew something wasn't right.

Still on the call, the lieutenant relayed the information to his detectives.

"Jimmy's monitor went off. He left the mansion. He's at the Brooklyn Performing Arts Center."

Carter screwed his face up. "Why?"

"The ballet," Danny blurted out. She was already turning for the door. "It's opening night."

Carter was hot on her heels, as he asked, "Why would he risk it and go to the ballet?"

"It's Romeo and Juliet," she reminded him.

Carter cursed under his breath, and they broke out into a jog, getting to the Crown Vic as fast as they could.

The ballet story was about two star-crossed lovers that killed themselves because they couldn't be together.

Danny hoped like hell that she wouldn't discover the same thing seated in the audience.

❄

PERFORMING ON stage, Tracy Jones swooned and glided, playing the Nurse opposite the principal male ballet dancer's Romeo. Eva could almost hear the Nurse's lines, as Tracy danced to the classical orchestral arrangement.

Juliet is grief-stricken that she can't be with you!

This was the part of the story when Romeo would determine that suicide was a better option than going on living without his Juliet. But Romeo would not die alone.

Eva smiled sadly, watching the emotional performers on stage, as tears streamed down her face.

Romeo rushed off. The full company of ballerinas swirled and twirled across the stage, as the scenery changed. Then Romeo leapt up the lattice and spilled into Juliet's bedroom.

It was time.

He had the solution.

The most famous scene in the story was about to unfold.

Jimmy turned to Eva, leaned into her, and kissed her wet cheek.

"Don't be scared," he breathed against her cheek.

In her hands, she clutched the little pill box where she had been keeping her cyanide capsule, the one that Jimmy had told her to keep with her at all times, the one that would end the torture of being hated in her own home; the solution that would end the agony of knowing she would never be allowed to go free.

Jimmy rolled his own cyanide capsule between

his thumb and his forefinger.

"I'm not going to go to prison, Eva, and neither are you," he told her as if it was good news.

"I know," she agreed.

He took hold of her chin, angled her face to his, and pressed his warm lips against hers.

Just as Romeo on stage promised Juliet, the performers dancing and twirling, Jimmy told Eva, "I intend to spend eternity with you."

He helped her to place her capsule on her tongue. It felt cool and slick. She fit it between her back teeth, as Jimmy slipped his own capsule into his mouth and did the same.

Juliet was dead on stage, and Romeo danced his last, as Eric MacDermott, playing Friar Lawrence, bounded through, arriving too late to stop the tragedy.

Eva stared deeply into Jimmy's eyes.

They bit down hard, cracking their cyanide capsules.

At the front of the house, near the orchestra pit, Detectives Danielle Foster and Carter Dobbs crept across the aisle with flashlights in their hands.

But just like Friar Lawrence in the story, the detectives were too late.

Eva felt her throat constrict and lock up. Air didn't reach her lungs. The light from the cops' flashlights stung her eyes.

"Campopiano! No!"

As Eva's world went black, she found her brother's face and kissed him, ready to start their eternity together.

Chapter Twenty-Four

THE STONE STATUE of Saint Christopher seemed to both snarl and smile in the hot sunshine on the church grounds.

Whether the saint was a dog, a wolf, or a monster, Danny couldn't decide. Chiseled from gray, granite stone, the statue reflected a deep, secret truth that lurked inside of Danny. Maybe it lurked inside of everyone.

There was a monster within her, within all of us, and it had the power to rear its ugly head…

…unless you controlled it.

She had seen the world through the eyes of her animal self, and yet there was hope.

Somehow, this monster named Christopher had become a saint.

She was no saint, though, and she wasn't interested in trying to become one. But she had tamed the darkness within her. She had learned how to turn to stone; how to accept the dog within that had reared its ugly head, filling her mind. There was an animal inside of her, but she had learned how to carry on. She was doing the best she could.

Carter joined her in front of the statue, and they stared at it for a moment.

Then he told her quietly, "Catherine is finishing up with Father Silva. She should be out in a minute."

Catherine Campopiano, horrified by her husband's suicide at the Brooklyn Ballet, had requested to speak with the detectives. She wanted to confess, but not before she gave her real confession, which she was doing now inside a confessional booth in the Holy Cross Chapel at St. Christopher's Catholic Church.

"What do you think of that?" she asked her partner, referring to the stone statue of the monster man.

He shrugged, "At least it's honest."

"That's what I was thinking."

Behind them, Father Silva emerged from the Holy Cross Chapel with Catherine. She wore all black, but pulled the black lace veil from her face, as she walked with the priest.

When they reached the detectives, Father Silva said, "Catherine would like me to remain with her."

"That's fine,' said Danny.

They didn't sit. Catherine kneaded her hands together.

"I probably should've come to you sooner," she admitted.

Father Silva was quick to point out, "You were married, Catherine, and obeying the marriage sacrament. No one will fault you."

Danny wasn't so sure about that, but she was willing to hear the widow out.

"It was an accident," she said, quietly finding the strength to finally tell the truth. "I didn't even know I had killed him until he was dead."

"Bobby?" Carter pushed her to clarify.

"That's right," she said, as she glanced at Father Silva for reassurance.

"Go on, my dear," he gently told her.

She sucked in a deep, fortifying breath, steadied her nerves, and began explaining the hell she had been living in.

"You both know about Jimmy and Eva. You

found out. I didn't find out until I was pregnant with the baby. At the time, Bobby was still at the house. When I found out, it was like, my eyes were opened. Not only could I *see* the attraction between Jimmy and Eva that had always been there, but it was *obvious*. Every glance they shared, every touch..."

She trailed off, shaking her head.

"But that wasn't all I saw. I realized that the family knew; that Jimmy marrying me gave them hope that he would stop sleeping with his own sister. It was like I had been duped. Like I was being made a fool. Jimmy would even go into Eva's bedroom for hours, and everyone knew what they were doing in there!"

Emotions tumbled out of her, anger and horror and grief, but she went on.

"Some nights, Jimmy would stay in Eva's room! All night!"

She belted out a sob, buried her face in her hands, and as Father Silva comforted her, she shook her head.

"Please," Danny said. "Go on."

Sobering up from the hard emotions, Catherine shook her hair out of her eyes and explained, "When Bobby left the family, he left for so many reasons, I'm sure you know that. But a big reason was that his sexual orientation was completely rejected by his family, and yet they all accepted, enabled, my God, they may have even *condoned* the sexual relationship between Jimmy and Eva. Bobby couldn't take it, which was how I *knew* he was on my side..."

She took a deep breath, preparing herself to

come out with it.

"I got fixated on him, on Bobby. I'm ashamed to admit, I became obsessed. I convinced myself that he could help me. All I wanted was for Eva to be sent away. I wasn't asking for too much. I wasn't even asking Jimmy to leave the house with me so that we could have a proper marriage. That morning, the morning of Bobby's death, I went to beg him I went to the Brooklyn Ballet Studios. I was determined to *beg him* to help me…

"But when we got upstairs to talk… He criticized me! He wouldn't help me convince the family to send Eva away! He pointed out my own flaws and asked me what was wrong with me! He told me to get a divorce! He…he…he… If only he had agreed to help me!"

When Catherine fell apart again, Danny and Carter gave her a moment.

But then Carter had to push a little. "Catherine, what happened?"

Sobbing out the truth that had been eating away at her soul, she cried, "I slapped him across the face!"

As she fell into a crying fit, falling into Father Silva's arms, Danny and Carter glanced at one another. Danny knew what had happened. The murder *had* been unintentional.

Danny surmised, "Bobby had that cyanide capsule in his mouth."

Catherine shrieked, "I didn't know! I couldn't control myself! When I slapped him with all my might across the face, I didn't know!"

"The impact cracked the capsule in his mouth," Carter supplied. "And he died."

"Yes! But I didn't understand why he had dropped to the floor," she said, begging the detectives to believe her. "I didn't know. I was so confused. And he was dead! I couldn't comprehend it! He had no heartbeat, no pulse! He was lifeless, and all I had done was hit him!"

"What happened next?" Danny asked solemnly.

"I called Jimmy. He came. He rushed me out just as Tony and Nico arrived. On my way out, Eva was still on the sidewalk. Her job, I suppose, was to stop any ballet dancers from going up to the studios, but I don't know if any dancers came before the men were finished hanging Bobby. I went home."

Danny and Carter touched eyes, then Danny explained to her the good and bad news.

"You didn't kill Bobby, and in my professional experience, you aren't even guilty of manslaughter. But Catherine, we're going to need you to make a formal statement at the police station, and you're going to have to name names. I can talk to the D.A. to get you out of any lesser charges—"

"Charges?" Father Silva asked, alarmed. "She's innocent."

"She isn't innocent," Carter told him. "She's been an accessory to the indecent disposal of a body, if you can even call it that, and other offenses. But again, like Detective Foster said, if you make a statement, testify, and work with us, your involvement will not be held against you."

Father Silva nodded. He could see it was not only a reasonable offer, but a generous one.

"Okay," Catherine breathed. "I'll do it."

"There's a light at the end of the tunnel, Catherine," Danny told her kindly. "Now you're free to live the life ycu deserve."

She stuttered, inhaling a sharp breath and steadying her shaky hands, and said, "I hope so."

Epilogue

CATHERINE CAMPOPIANO bounced her daughter, Rosa, on her hip, as she rode the elevators up to the 13th floor of the U.S. District courthouse in downtown Brooklyn.

She had spoken with the cops, kept herself clear of suspicion, and had survived days of panic and unbridled mourning at the Campopiano mansion. A house full of frantic, husbandless women was Catherine's new definition of hell.

She had to get out of there.

The elevator doors dinged open. Her baby mimicked the sound and giggled, as Catherine stepped into the corridor and found Justice Harlan Ellsworth's judicial chambers.

Rosa had balled her pudgy fist around a lock of Catherine's hair. Getting her daughter to release her would prove more challenging than removing a wad of gum, so she tolerated Rosa's yanking, as she neared the secretary.

"I would like to speak with Judge Ellsworth, if possible," she told the woman who was seated at the desk.

As the secretary scanned her computer monitor, presumably looking for the visitor's appointment, Catherine mentioned, "I didn't call ahead. Catherine Campopiano."

The surname rang a bell in the woman's mind, and she wasted no time pressing her desk phone to her ear.

"Sir, Mrs. Campopiano is here to see you. *Catherine.*" As she returned the phone to its cradle, she told the widow, "Harlan will see you now. You can go ahead."

"Thank you," she said, feeling suddenly nervous.

She rubbed Rosa's mushy back, giving her daughter a few pats to prevent her from getting fussy, and made her way down a hallway that led to Ellsworth's office. There were other offices and an open area where assistants and interns were keeping the judge's affairs organized this bright, sunny Monday morning.

Catherine paid them no mind. She knocked softly, and when she heard Ellsworth invite her in, she eased the door open.

The judge stood up behind his desk to greet her. He welcomed her with a gentlemanly smile, complimented her baby, and asked her to have a seat.

That's when her nerves started ratcheting, twisting her stomach into knots and chilling her spine.

She must be crazy to be here, she thought, as she crossed the stately room and eased onto one of the chairs in front of his desk.

Once she sat down, Ellsworth followed suit.

"To what do I owe the pleasure, Catherine?"

Rosa was glancing all around with huge, blue eyes, and cooing at her surroundings. She was so wiggly that Catherine had to place her on her lap, but it wasn't much better.

"When will Guido and the others be released?" she asked frankly.

An awkward smile came over him, as if he wasn't accustomed to delivering bad news to fair ladies.

"Catherine," he began, but needed a moment to form an answer. He clasped his hands together and leaned forward. "It was your statement to the police that got them arrested."

"Was that a mistake?" Her heart lurched up her throat. "I thought it would look suspicious if I didn't speak with them. And I was nervous. I really *was* responsible for Bobby's death. I shouldn't have hit him. If I had controlled myself that morning, Jimmy and the others wouldn't have had to stage the scene, you know."

"My dear—"

"Money is no object, as I'm sure you know," she interrupted, sounding suddenly desperate. "Please, your Honor. I'm stuck in a house full of crazy women!"

Calming her emotions was a Herculean task, but she managed and tried again.

"Jimmy left me nothing, did you know that?" she stated, holding her head high as if she might retain a shred of dignity despite the humiliation she had suffered. "His will is worthless, as far as I'm concerned. He never had his own house. His assets weren't his own, everything is the joint property of the family. Do you think I want to stay there?"

"I'll be straight with you, Catherine. Right now, communicating with Guido isn't easy for me. However, we're working on transferring a substantial portion of his cash to an offshore account, an LLC that I have access to. Once I retrieve funds from there, I can disperse them. You have not been abandoned or forgotten, I promise you."

She drew in a deep breath, but wasn't pleased

that she would have to exercise patience.

Like a gentleman, Ellsworth yearned to comfort her. She could see that.

But it wasn't enough.

"Why can't you have them released on bail immediately?" she pushed. "Haven't we kept you happy over the years? Haven't we paid you enough?"

"Catherine," he warned.

"You're being very 'businessy' about this. Must we always pay you perfectly beforehand? Can't you do us this favor and take action before you get your hands on our money?"

"Now, Catherine," he warned again, but she wasn't finished.

"What about me? What about my baby?" she demanded.

Gentleman or not, Ellsworth's temper pierced through his otherwise comforting attitude.

"Listen to me, I have bent the law to the point of breaking it to keep your husband out of prison, and this I have done at my own risk *after* Jimmy has *killed people*. And he's not the only one I've done this for. My God, I've made a greater career out of working for Guido Campopiano than I have after thirty years on the bench. I will not allow you to come into my office and regard me as if I'm some kind of cold, calculating businessman. What haven't I done for the Campopianos?"

She didn't have an answer, but she knew he had said as much as she needed him to...

Suppressing the grin that was threatening to appear on her pretty face, she glanced at Rosa to compose herself.

"What's next?" she asked the judge. "Tell me the

light at the end of the tunnel that Maria, Bianca, Alice and I should look out for, please."

He sighed, but just as he was about to answer, the office door behind Catherine slammed open, and Detectives Danielle Foster and Carter Dobbs barrelled in with their guns drawn.

"What is this?" Ellsworth exclaimed, jumping to his feet, as uniformed police officers charged into the room and fanned out.

Danny had the pleasure of enlightening the dirty judge, "Harlan Ellsworth, you're under arrest—"

Ellsworth locked his furious eyes on Catherine. "*You*—"

Lieutenant Franco entered the office, stepped forward, and informed Ellsworth, "We have you on bribery, you have a right to remain silent—"

"You think I don't know my rights?!"

The police officers apprehended Ellsworth, handcuffing him and dragging him out from behind his desk, as Rosa shrieked at the commotion, confused but sensing her mother's anxiety.

Catherine was only excited. She stood, and Danny neared her.

"You did great," said the detective before she smiled at Rosa and gave the baby a pat. "And so did you!"

Catherine told her, "I was worried she would spit up on the microphone or pull it off."

As Franco, Carter, and the cops dealt with escorting Ellsworth out of the building, Danny helped Catherine set Rosa on the judge's desk, lift the baby's shirt, and carefully remove the wire they had taped to her.

Catherine noticed Danny's eyes were glassy with

a wall of tears.

She placed a warm hand on the detective's arm and said, "I'm so sorry for your loss."

For a moment, Danny looked surprised that the woman knew she had lost her infant son.

"Do you think you'll have another?" she asked the detective.

Danny seemed unsure.

"Catherine, we can connect you with an advocacy agency and a great attorney to help you file for assets. You shouldn't be left penniless."

Catherine scooped Rosa up into her arms. "I just want a home of my own and to live a normal life."

"Don't we all..."

O'TOOLE'S IRISH Pub was hopping with cops. Bartenders couldn't pour pints and mix cocktails fast enough. Franco had bought out the bar tonight. All drinks were on him, and no one was expected to show up on time tomorrow.

He had succeeded after years of quietly tracking the corrupt judge. Ellsworth was locked up, and Franco had already gotten word that the man who had been accepting bribes for decades was now filing a guilty plea.

Given Ellsworth's career, the judge wouldn't end up in a maximum security prison with the criminals he had locked up. Instead, he would be incarcerated at a minimum security prison where white collar criminals spent their days writing memoirs and playing racket ball, but Franco hardly minded. Justice was being served, and most importantly,

Ellsworth's dirty name was in the paper and on the news.

Everyone in Brooklyn would know exactly what he had done. And they would all know that Lieutenant Martin Franco had been the cop that had put him behind bars.

The celebration was in full swing.

Danny raised her frothy pint of I.P.A. in the air, grinned from ear to ear, and congratulated Franco. She clinked glasses with the lieutenant and then Carter. They had formed a tight circle in the middle of the crowded bar.

"It was one hell of an investigation," Carter said before gulping his beer. "Didn't I say the crime scene looked like the mob had staged a suicide?"

"You did," she allowed, patting him on the back.

Franco was more reserved with his compliments, but he, too, had to admit that his newest S.V.U. detective had excellent instincts and the right brand of passion to keep their department's clearance rate higher than any other precinct in Brooklyn.

Danny glanced at Tommy. He was lending a helping hand behind the busy bar, but the grin on his face said it all. He had been freed from the mafia's protection racket. Now every cent he earned would stay in his own pocket.

"Foster?"

When Danny glanced over her shoulder, she found Detectives Crouse and Toliver.

Toliver looked forlorn with remorse, and though Crouse just looked stubborn, she knew both cops intended to bury the hatchet.

"I think we owe you an apology," said Crouse.

"You were only doing your job," she assured them, but Crouse had more to say.

"I went off the rails," the older detective admitted, shaking his head at himself. "I questioned your ethics based on personal assumptions I had formed."

Danny realized his apology meant more to him than to her, so she let him continue.

"You're a good detective, Foster. I shouldn't have led with a presumption of guilt, and I shouldn't have attacked your integrity as a cop. I got caught up in an investigation strategy and obviously, it bit me in the ass."

Toliver agreed with the position they had both put themselves in. "If you think we aren't eating crow…"

"It's water under the bridge," she promised them, as she held Crouse's gaze until she was sure he believed her. "My mom's killer is dead. My son's killer is dead. It's not the ending I would've liked, but I lost my head too, and now that all has been said and done, I can't deny that justice has been served."

"I'll drink to that," said Crouse.

He lifted his glass, and they all drank.

Franco and Carter turned, opened the circle, and they all flowed into conversation, as Jill Andover pressed into the bar with Police Officer Sean Quinlan. The cop was dressed in plain clothes, and even more surprisingly, he was holding Jill's hand.

Carter elbowed Danny, "Let's hope Jill can keep this one around."

"Something tells me she won't be able to run Sean out of her life so easily."

Tommy found his way out from behind the bar and joined Danny. Even Carter's wife, Kathy, made it to the party. Relaxed and smiling, she hooked her arm with her husband's, and Danny let herself enjoy the moment.

Free from guilt.

Free from remorse.

Free from the heartbreak of having lost her son and her mother and her sanity.

Just for a moment…

…she let herself feel free.

When she locked eyes with Tommy, she knew that he was giving himself a moment to feel happy, too.

Just one moment, but it was all they needed.

THE END

If you enjoyed this novel, please leave a positive review!

ALSO BY MIRA GIBSON

Thomas from the Sea

Who Killed Leeanne?

The Kensington Killers
Lunatic (The Kensington Killers, Book One)
Crank (The Kensington Killers, Book Two)
Maniac (The Kensington Killers, Book Three)
Cold Dark Fear (Prequel to The Kensington Killers)

The New Hampshire Mysteries
Daddy Soda (A New Hampshire Mystery, Book One)
Rock Spider (A New Hampshire Mystery, Book Two)
Tar Heart (A New Hampshire Mystery, Book Three)

ABOUT THE AUTHOR

I write mystery novels, detective novels, sleuth mysteries, and dark psychological thrillers! You can find me most days working on my computer in the sunshine of beautiful Long Beach, NY, where I dream up characters and write dark mysteries.

Find me on Facebook! **/MiraGibsonAuthor**

Visit MysteryRoyalty.com to learn more.

Copyright © 2024
Published by: Mira Gibson

All Rights Reserved. This book or any portion thereof may not be reproduced or used in any manner whatsoever without the express written permission of the publisher except for the use of brief quotations in a book review. All characters appearing in this work are fictitious. Any resemblance to real persons, living or dead, is purely coincidental.

For questions and comments about this book, please contact www.mysteryroyalty.com

www.ingramcontent.com/pod-product-compliance
Lightning Source LLC
Chambersburg PA
CBHW031154010826
48971CB00012B/289